O.J. LOVAZ

SILENT PRETTY THINGS

A NOVEL

ISBN: 978-1-7374113-1-4

For my awesome wife, Sandra

And my amazing daughter, Gabriela

PROLOGUE

Strange, very strange, thought Officer Gary Mitchell. *A murder in these parts. In Blake County, of all places. Heck, this might be the most peaceful area in all of Pennsylvania. Bountiful nature, cute little towns and villages, cobblestone streets, coffee shops, bakeries, ice cream parlors, antiques, dainty useless specialty stores…and murder?*

He lit a cigarette. *Blustery tonight, not cold, but cooler than the last few nights. End of summer; end of life. Every day is the end of the world for someone out there.*

Death always put him in a weird, contemplative mood.

Snap out of it, man. Let's make that call.

Oh, he's going to love it! Almost 1:00 a.m.—why these things always happen right smack in the middle of the night?

Anyhow, let's see what Wozniak makes of this one.

CHAPTER I

A thunderous bang shocked Michael Donovan from his light doze. Heart thudding in his chest, he scanned the area and spotted a large brown tome, open face up on the floor. The darn thing must have been sloppily placed on its shelf. He picked it up—nineteenth-century courthouses, many of them still in use. He was fond of sharing such tidbits of information with anyone interested. Not many were these days.

The library of the Blake County Historical Society was otherwise utterly silent. There had been no visitors that day, or the day before, or the day before that. The small museum on the lower level occasionally still received visitors, but scarcely anyone ever made it up to the archives and library department.

Michael glanced at the clock on the wall: twenty minutes before closing time—finally! On his timeworn desk, a book he had been reading to pass the time, something about the unsung heroes of World War II, lobbied for his attention. He put it in the top drawer. In another instant, he would have turned off the lights, but he heard the distinctive sound of the door chime announcing that someone had come in.

He turned around to see a blond woman in her mid-twenties, very attractive, with green, catlike eyes, and a captivating aura of sophistication and grace.

The woman stood by the door with the weightless poise of a magical creature whose feet barely touched the ground. She wore a faint and apologetic smile. "I'm sorry to come in at such a late hour. I can see that you're about to close for the day. I could come back tomorrow." Her voice was soft and velvety, yet also rich and powerful.

Thrown into a daze, Michael barely recovered before it got awkward. "Oh no, it's fine. It's great to finally have a guest here today. I'm Michael Donovan, director of the archives and library." He immediately hated the way he dropped his absurd, inflated title on her like that. "How may I be of assistance?" he added with a slight nod.

"You're very kind, Michael. My name is Anna Goddard. My grandfather was Charles Goddard. He passed away about three years ago. You may have known him, as he was prominent in our town as a businessman and philanthropist."

Name dropping within two minutes—must be a new record! Michael sounded the spoiled-rich-girl alert. "Charles Goddard, yes, I met him once at one of our galas years ago, though only briefly. I'm sorry to hear that he's no longer with us. Your grandfather was a generous contributor to this institution." He could vomit right now. How he had despised that conceited old man!

"Yes, thank you for your…thoughtful words. He did care a great deal about protecting our heritage. Actually, that is what brings me here. You see, I believe my grandfather donated a small collection of family photographs, deeming them of interest to local historians. I understand a few were from the inauguration ceremony of the St. Mary's School in the 1960s and some from the school's basketball championship in 1984."

Anna stepped closer to him. "My father played on that championship team, and he has never stopped talking about it." She smiled roguishly. "So, anyway, I would very much like to see some of those pictures, if you really have the time to help me find them. It's just a matter of curiosity, really," she added graciously, as if she felt the need to explain herself. Her charm was undeniable.

"It will be my pleasure. If you don't mind my asking, is your father Rick Goddard, the football coach?" Michael had never really met the guy but had heard he was an arrogant jerk. Like father, like son.

"Actually, that's my uncle. He doesn't coach anymore, though. Haven't seen him in a long while, not since he remarried and moved to California. My father is Victor Goddard. I can't imagine that you'd know him."

She paused briefly and seemed to inspect her new acquaintance, in the subtlest manner, as if collecting her thoughts. "He's in the real estate business, just as my grandfather was, but he's not as well known, gregarious, or interested in cultural and philanthropic endeavors." Her tone held a slight hint of contempt for her father.

"I see. Well, why don't we go ahead and look up those photos for you?"

"If it won't take too long, of course. I don't want to keep you hostage here—you probably have plans, somewhere you have to get to."

"Nowhere I must get to in a hurry," Michael said. "So time is on our side."

"Is it ever?" She flashed a cute little smirk.

"What, time? No, I guess it never is. You're right about that." He couldn't agree more.

He sat in front of a tarnished, clunky desktop computer, probably over ten years old, and started typing search queries. "A lot of these pictures have been digitized and kept in our online repository. Some of the older ones we haven't got to yet, and we keep them in hard-copy collections or even in boxes in the backroom."

Anna scanned her surroundings inquisitively. "So you're the boss here then?"

"Boss? Well, I'd say I'm more like the sheriff of a ghost town. There's nobody to order around here, not that I would want that anyway. Here, I found something." He beckoned to her to come over and take a look.

Anna came around and stood behind him. Her movements were smooth and delicate. Was she being deliberately provocative? Nah, it was probably all in his head.

The computer slowed to a crawl, but Michael was in no hurry. "These pictures are from St. Mary's inauguration ceremony in 1963. It says right here that they were donated by your grandfather. I take it that you went to St. Mary's?"

4

"Yes, I did. There wasn't much of a choice, with my grandfather being one of the school's original board members. My father went there; so did my brother. If I didn't want my kids to go to St. Mary's, I'd probably have to get away from here."

"Oh, you have kids?" Michael blurted out, feeling embarrassed before the words had even come out. He turned slowly toward Anna and faced her.

Her face took on a curious expression, like she was studying him. "No, no, I mean in the future, if and when I have kids of my own." She paused, the corners of her mouth beginning to curve slightly up. "I don't even have a boyfriend."

"Right, right…I'm sorry." Michael promptly ended his intrusion trying hard not to blush, his heart racing in his chest, warm all over.

"It's quite all right."

Moving back to the task at hand, he sensed her close proximity behind him, leaning down over his shoulder so that he could see her delicate face and long neck out of the corner of his eye. A few golden strands of hair brushed on his shoulder and neck, and he could smell her perfume, with sweet notes of jasmine and vanilla—his mind drifted for a moment, intoxicated, feeling an irrepressible pull toward her.

"Here, could you open this one?" she asked, pointing to a thumbnail on the computer screen, rushing Michael back to his body.

He opened the low-quality picture. Five men and two women were standing in front of the St. Mary's school building, with its original façade. Two of the people, Michael could recognize—Father Patrick Thompson, a young priest at the time, who had retired a few years back; and Robert Mason, the town's mayor back then, who went on to become a representative in Congress.

Anna pointed to a tall, heavy built man in the middle of the lineup. He was wearing a gray suit and tie with a matching hat. "This here is my grandfather."

Michael would have never recognized Charles Goddard in that photograph. He had met him as an old man, and time had certainly not been kind to him.

"I'm probably older now than your grandfather was in this picture." He faced Anna and got lost in those stunning eyes of hers only inches away.

"Well, let's see." She sat up on the corner of his desk. "This was 1963, so he must have been, um,"—she thought about it for a moment, making a cute thinking face while she did the math—"about thirty years old. Yes, that's about right. And how old are you?" She casually blurted out the question, then laughed, rolling her eyes. "That's so inappropriate. You don't have to answer that."

"Oh, I don't mind. I just turned thirty-three last week, actually." Certainly not something he felt like celebrating. An empty, dimly lit station in transit to the next depressing milestone; sprinting to middle age while not having accomplished one damn thing he really cared about. Time only marches forward, his mother used to say—a precious gem meant as encouragement to seize the day that now seemed brutal and merciless.

"Well, happy birthday, then. You look younger. Like twenty-nine, I'd say. The thirties are the new twenties anyway, right?"

"Wouldn't that make you a teenager?" Michael joked.

"But, Mr. Donovan, I haven't even told you my age," Anna teased.

"And I'm not going to ask, but you look young."

"That's kind of you, and so very gracious. But I'm not too young."

"Too young for what?" Michael's pulse revved with excitement.

"I just mean that I have lived, that I am not some naive, immature girl."

"Fair enough." He chuckled to mask his jitters. "I'm still not going to ask your age."

"Well, I won't tell you then. I'll keep it a mystery for a little longer."

"I love a good mystery." Michael could high-five himself right now.

Anna squinted her eyes slightly and fixed them on him with a mischievous spark, then jumped off the desk, and turned her attention back to the computer screen. "It's getting late. Let's see if there's anything else worth looking at here."

Rushing things with women had not worked well for Michael before. No sense in risking coming on too strong.

He opened up a few more pictures from the school's inauguration ceremony—they all showed the same people. None elicited a reaction from Anna.

What was she really after? Was this trip down memory lane solely curiosity as she said? She didn't seem very curious anymore. Perhaps, these were not the pictures she had hoped to find. They were, admittedly, rather boring.

"Would you like to see more recent ones?" Michael asked. "Earlier, you mentioned St. Mary's basketball championship in 1984; you know, the one your father won't stop talking about? I bet those would be more interesting. Should we search for them?"

"Sounds like a good idea." Anna glanced at the clock on the wall and stepped back around the desk. "But it's already twenty minutes past closing time. I should go."

"Oh, don't worry about the time. It's really no trouble."

"Well, the thing is, I'm free tomorrow." She ran a finger through the back edge of his desk. "So, how about I come back around eleven in the morning and we look at them then, if you're not too busy?"

Ah, his luck hadn't run out just yet. *Au contraire, my dear comrade!* The prospect of seeing her again was an unexpected treat.

Michael rose to his feet. "Yes, that will be perfect. I could look up those pictures before you come. With a bit of luck, we'll find your dad doing a slam dunk or something."

"Yes, wouldn't that be something?"

"It would sure make a great gift for him."

"Yes. Well, it's a date, then. It's been a pleasure meeting you."

A date, she said. Michael struggled to restrain the wayward little muscles in his face which desperately wanted to broadcast his elation. "The pleasure has been all mine. Until tomorrow then."

As Anna stepped out, she peeked back at Michael before she went downstairs toward the exit. Michael stayed a few minutes longer, daydreaming about tomorrow.

When he left the building, the sun was setting, and the clouds over the horizon were alight with hues of red, orange, and yellow, a spectacular sight that he might have ignored many times before, as one does when staring at the ground; but on this day, he had come out gazing up at the sky. Michael opened up his car's convertible top, put on some classic rock, and drove away under a perfect summer night.

CHAPTER II

Anna Goddard headed to the wooden deck in the back with her cup of espresso and a blueberry muffin. No buildings obstructed her view to the east, so on clear mornings such as this she liked to sit there sipping her coffee, watch the sunrise, listen to the birds, spy on busy squirrels and chipmunks, breathe some fresh air and, on the best days, ponder essential questions.

She owed this Friday morning delight to some neighbor's dog that had decided to bark as stridently as possible at six in the morning, the loathsome noise piercing through the shallow walls of her townhouse.

She loved her charming little home—it was cozy, modern, and kept her close to Misty Pines' town center, restaurants, and shops. Location, location, location! Certainly not the mansion expected of Charles Goddard's granddaughter, but it was hers, free and clear of her father. She grinned into the sun, comforted by that fact.

Unwelcome memories from last Sunday at her parents' house intruded in her mind: the ominous text message that flashed on her father's phone and her bizarre exchange with her mother afterward.

It all triggered in her such horrid suspicions—Anna chased the thoughts out of her head. She conjured up Michael's image to keep her company.

She had enjoyed the little glances between them, the zesty little remarks, and, yes, brushing up against him just a little, just enough to raise his temperature.

Since she wouldn't be meeting with him until 11:00 a.m., she had plenty of time on her hands to do some research. She went to get her tablet and came back outside.

One of the neighbors—a lady in her late forties, Anna reckoned—had come out to her own deck. She lit up a cigarette and stood by the railing, enjoying the view. She acknowledged Anna with a courteous smile, "Good morning."

Anna responded in kind, then sat down and located the web address of the Blake County Historical Society. Now to find the staff directory.

The lady with the cigarette, however, seemed to be in the mood for a little small talk with her young neighbor. "I've always enjoyed this view. It's so nice, don't you think?"

Anna glanced at her, "Yes, it really is." The sun was rising majestically above a long band of mature trees, mostly red maples and oaks.

"I've seen you around, but I don't think we've formally met. I'm Michelle"

"I'm Anna. Pleased to meet you."

"The pleasure is all mine." She took a big puff from her cigarette, observing Anna, and then exhaled the smoke in a perfectly steady flow. "One should always know their neighbors. Nowadays, we all seem to live in little bubbles, you know. Everyone is immersed in their own tiny worlds. People don't even know whether the person next door is a Nobel Peace Prize winner or a hardened criminal." She raised the cigarette back to her mouth but paused to ask, "How long have you lived here?"

"A little shy of a year. How about you?"

"Scott and I have lived here for over fifteen years. We raised our daughter here. Ashley is off to college now, all grown up." A slight note of melancholy deepened her voice as she mentioned her daughter.

"Must be tough for the two of you." Anna approached the rail and stood alongside Michelle.

"Even harder than I thought it would be, but I don't show her that. Don't want to rain on her parade. She's so excited about college, and I'm mighty proud of her." She took another big puff, suddenly pensive; then as she addressed Anna again, she exhaled the smoke through the right corner of her lips, pointing away from her. "She wants to be a doctor, and by God, she will do it. She has the best of me and her dad, and much more," she said fondly.

"I like how you just lit up talking about her, with such pride, and love..." Anna choked up, but she couldn't understand why, which mortified her.

Michelle seemed touched by her words. "You're very sweet. I'm happy I met you this morning. I will have to come back out here more often. Maybe we can chat some more."

"I'd like that."

Her neighbor had finished smoking her cigarette; she put it out on a ceramic ashtray she had on a small round table and waved Anna good-bye.

Anna stayed out there another minute before retreating into the living room, where she threw herself on a big white sofa, with her back resting on a large fluffy beige pillow. There she picked up where she had left off with her research and, in a matter of seconds, found what she was looking for—Michael's bio.

"Michael Donovan joined our institution in 2007..." She skipped a few lines. "Michael's passion for preserving and promoting our local history is evident in the various articles he has published..." She skipped again. "Under Michael's leadership, the library and archives department has become a key enabler..." She stopped there. Flattering but too institutional.

They had a nice picture of him, though—black suit with a white shirt and a red tie. His dark hair was shorter and nicely styled, though too formal for her taste.

Yesterday, his attire had been more casual—black pants, an aquamarine dress shirt, and no tie. His hair slightly ruffled, as if he had been caught in a gust of wind, and he must have not shaven his beard for at least three days. It all gave him a sort of scruffy charm and an air of spontaneity.

Anna leisurely checked out content posted online by her friends, including a remarkable travel video about the Russian city of St. Petersburg. Time slipped away from her, and now, she'd have to hurry. Almost invariably, time resolves to accelerate as soon as one presumes to have lots of it. This reminded her of the words she had exchanged with Michael the evening before. "Time is never on our side," he'd said, or had she said that?

When Anna arrived at the historical society, she found only four other vehicles in the lot. She parked her white Volvo sedan next to a red convertible Mustang. Might be Michael's—he'd look great in it.

She went inside feeling either excited or jittery, maybe both, and reminded herself she was there first and foremost to unearth the past.

Anna went upstairs and saw Michael speaking to a girl and a boy, at first glance both under ten years of age and not one year apart. A man stood beside them, presumably their father. She cracked the glass door open and slipped in as quietly as she could, but the door chime revealed her presence.

Michael glanced at her and continued with his commentary; the kids completely absorbed in the story. "So, you see, this is not just the stuff of movies. Possibly as many as a thousand women disguised themselves as men to fight in the Civil War, in both armies."

"How come they didn't get caught?" asked the girl.

"Well, sometimes, they did get caught and were expelled or even sent to prison. But lots of them never got caught. You see, a young woman could easily pass for a boy by just getting a short haircut and putting on men's clothes. And soldiers never took their clothes off; they didn't take baths or anything. When they had to, you know, go to the bathroom, they just went in the woods where no one could see them."

"Ugh, that's icky!" blurted the boy.

Michael laughed. "Yes, you're right about that."

"Thank you, that was very interesting," the father interjected.

The kids thanked Michael with genuine smiles on their cute little faces. In another moment, they were heading out, asking their father to please take them to the gift store.

Anna was now alone with Michael.

"Hey there," he said casually as she approached.

"I see you're a natural teacher."

Michael stuck his hands in his pockets as if cold. "It's easy with kids. They still have that natural curiosity."

He was clean-shaven with his hair brushed back, but a few strands were already beginning to defy orders, falling over his temples. She imagined him under a full moon with the wind blowing his hair and felt tempted to get her hands in there and mess it up.

Michael sat down and pointed at the computer screen. "I have your pictures right here, the ones from St. Mary's basketball championship in 1984."

"Oh, great. Let's take a look."

"That was the first and last time they won the tournament. They haven't made it to the finals again since, so it was kind of a big deal. And your dad was part of that team—that's something!"

Anna couldn't care less. "Yeah, it's something," she said and sat next to Michael. On the screen, ten picture thumbnails. Michael opened three photos taken during the game. In one of them, her father was taking an open shot to the basket. He'd been a massive young man, taller than the five other players shown in the picture, broad-shouldered, with a very muscular, athletic physique. His face displayed the high stakes and the intensity of the moment, hardened with focus and determination.

The next three photographs had been taken at the postgame celebration. Her grandfather stood amidst the crowd in one of them. He would have been, if her math was right, about fifty-one years old at the time.

Then came a photo of her father and her mother, kissing under the bleachers—Anna recognized her instantly from pictures she'd seen in family photo albums.

"Whoa, that's my mother!"

"What a precious find!" Michael beamed a triumphant grin at her.

"Yes, it's remarkable." Her words choked down to a mumble.

"Something wrong?"

"It's just"—she hesitated—"I thought Mom was in college when she met Dad."

Maybe she shouldn't have told him that. One reveal can lead to another.

"Did they attend the same college?"

"No, my dad never went to college. He started running the properties my grandfather put to his name right after high school."

Michael's face lit up. "A living inheritance—how lucky for him, to be set for life like that."

"I guess so. He had it easy. That's for sure." Set for life? That was one way to look at it. Living a cheap imitation of his father's life—that seemed more accurate, and pathetic.

"So, he was already wealthy when he began dating your mom?"

"Yes, I guess that's right," she said, wanting to cut short that subject. Why would her mom not want to tell her that she'd dated him in high school?

"Well," Michael kept on, "he still wasn't rich in high school."

"It doesn't really matter, does it?" Surely, Michael would take a hint now and drop it.

"Right, it doesn't. If anything, it shows that your mom liked him even before he had all that money," he stated, as if arriving at the logical answer to a math problem.

He probably meant no harm by it, just one of those ill-advised remarks that people can make with the best intentions at the worst times. A moment of silence would suffice to make him abandon that thread of conversation.

"Let's see another one," she suggested and pointed at a picture thumbnail. "I believe my father is in this one. I think I see him there."

Michael brought up the photograph. Sitting on a patch of grass, her father wore his St. Mary's sweater and a gold medal around his neck. Another young lady had her arms wrapped around him from behind, her hands on his chest, her lips kissing his neck.

The image struck her like a freight train. She felt her face instantly freeze in shock, desperate not to let any emotion show through.

That wasn't just any girl.

Michael started to say something, but he stammered and stopped.

She couldn't think straight. Michael must have already inferred that her father had been a player, a stone-cold womanizer like many men before and after him, but she had managed not to reveal the most awful part—that girl in the photograph was her mom's sister.

Aunt Marlene. It was her, without a doubt.

Anna broke the silence abruptly. "You can close it now. I don't need to see any more pictures."

Would Michael have the sense to not ask her about it?

The memory from Sunday at her parent's house came rushing back to her like an angry nightmare. That morning, she'd been in the kitchen making an omelet, and her father had left his mobile phone on the counter nearby. The phone vibrated and startled her. She laid her eyes on it by mere reflex.

A text message had popped up from her aunt: "You and I are both to blame for this, and we shall be judged in the end."

Alarmed, Anna hastened to finish her breakfast and hustled into the living room.

A few minutes later, her father came upstairs from the basement, went straight to the kitchen, picked up his phone, and stared at it for a moment. Anna pretended to be watching a TV show while spying on him out of the corner of her eye. With the phone in his hand, Victor glanced at Anna with a grave frown, but she fixed her gaze on her food, pretending to be oblivious to her surroundings.

Anna had not yet mentioned the disturbing incident to anyone. She could tell her older brother, Frank, who had always been her confidant, accomplice, and personal hero. But Frank could be very volatile and had not been on good terms with their father for a very long time. His father was to him the very incarnation of evil, a loathsome man who'd done nothing but wrong them their whole lives.

How quickly then would Frank come to the worst possible conclusion if he knew about the message? If he saw that photograph? He would become prosecutor, jury, and judge, right then and there, the hot-headed crusader that he was.

And what could Frank, in such a wrath, be capable of doing? It all led to a very dark place.

As if awakening from a trance, Anna realized how somber and pensive she must have appeared to Michael a moment ago. "Thank you so much for taking the time to help me with this silly search of mine. I really don't want to waste any more of your time," she said in a dignified tone and stood up.

It would be best for her to leave at once and not risk revealing anything more to Michael; yet she couldn't help feeling disappointed, as she had expected this encounter with him to end up much differently.

Anna shuffled her feet toward the door, as though being pulled against her will by an extraneous force.

Michael spoke, "I, um," he stuttered. Anna stopped and turned around. He continued. "I had hoped to take you out to lunch. Are you hungry?" His face didn't show much confidence.

She probably hadn't seemed very friendly a moment ago.

Maybe she could clear her head and enjoy Michael's company. Chances are he wouldn't even mention the photograph.

Or would he?

Was it worth the risk?

Yes, it was. There was something about him. A warmth. It was strange, she'd just met him, but she felt at ease with him. And his cute awkwardness was just delightful.

"Um, sure, I could eat," Anna responded with a deliberately revived smile. At least for now, she would lock her woes inside a black box and hide the key.

"Great!" Some color returned to Michael's face, and he stepped closer to her. "I know a great place for lunch just across town, by the district court, Emma's Bistro. You might know it."

"I love their paninis."

"I worship their Reuben sandwich. I might also try to interest you in sharing a bowl of loaded nachos."

"And you might succeed." Anna held his watch-bearing wrist and lifted it closer to her face. "It's a quarter to noon. We could still beat the crowd," she said to Michael, who wore an amused expression, never pulling his arm back. She set it down slowly, savoring the moment.

"I'll drive," Michael said eagerly. He taped a note on the glass door, and they left.

His red Mustang awaited outside—felt good to be right.

With juvenile enthusiasm, Anna asked if they could open the convertible top—he was happy to oblige. Instantly, the wind began messing up his hair, giving him a markedly relaxed appearance, much to her delight. Her hair, too, was blowing in the wind wildly, and she scrambled to gather it all into an improvised ponytail.

On their way to Emma's, they drove through the picturesque town center, with its historic buildings, chapels, antique and specialty stores, taverns, and coffee shops. Michael commented casually on the history of some of the buildings they drove by: one had been the county jail until

1946, another the site of a horrific massacre in 1972, and yet another rebuilt after it burned down in 1968, an incident suspected to have been a case of racially motivated arson.

Impressive as it was that he knew all these facts, it seemed as if there was only room for tragedy and gloom in the town's historical archives; or was it maybe him whose selective memory, consciously or unconsciously, latched on to dreadful events? Surely, the town must have had some history beside hateful crimes and prisons.

Ah, she was probably making a fuss out of nothing, overcomplicating things again. The guy just wanted to show off a little, not the worst thing.

They got there by noon. The place didn't look like much at first, but the interior was surprisingly appealing, featuring a classic look with dark-wood dining tables, perhaps mahogany, and an elegant cocktail bar. Instrumental jazz was played. Less than half of the tables occupied—just perfect.

A very friendly waiter, Wendy, offered them something to drink; both wanted a beer. A Reuben sandwich for Michael; Anna went with the pesto chicken panini. She let Michael order the loaded nachos as an appetizer.

It was way too much food, but what's life without the occasional excess? Every so often, she liked to do something to prove she was truly free, even from the limits of reason.

"So what do you do when you're not visiting empty libraries?" asked Michael. They were briefly interrupted by Wendy, who brought them two tall glasses of icy cold beer.

"Cheers." Anna clinked her glass with his. She sipped her beer, a local brew chilled to perfection. "I'm a school psychologist."

"Really, a psychologist? Oh no!" Michael exclaimed mirthfully.

"I'm basically a school counselor. But, yes, you should worry," she joked.

"I better hide that crazy boy inside my head."

"Oh no! Does he whisper terrible things to you?"

"Mm-hmm. Always wanting to do reckless, daring things." Michael adopted a playful air.

"Oh, do tell more. Like what?"

"Well, he dared me not to let you go today without at least getting your phone number." He flashed her a cute smirk.

"Well played. Yes, you can have my phone number."

His eyes lit up.

"So, what reckless, daring things have been tempting you? I want to hear more about that," Anna said spiritedly, inviting him to jump in with both feet. As long as she kept him talking, she wouldn't have to talk about herself.

"Oh, I don't know about reckless. Courageous, perhaps." He took a big gulp of beer and confided, "Mostly, I think about quitting my stupid job, getting the hell out of here, starting a new life journey."

"Is that what you want? I mean, you're the director of archives at a respectable institution. That doesn't sound bad at all." She hated how conventional that came out.

"A title is all it is. I go there every day and mostly do nothing. I'm a glorified librarian every day, a guide somedays, and an inconsequential local history writer every two or three months. What title would you stamp on that job description?"

Anna didn't answer that question, but his job would have driven her insane.

"Why don't you do it then? Why don't you quit?" she asked.

He looked at her like a man who is gathering the courage to open a door, not knowing what lies behind it. The nachos arrived. They asked Wendy for another round of beers.

"All right"—Michael's face twitched uneasily—"the thing is, I feel constantly in conflict with myself. Let's call these conflicting perspectives the boy versus the man. Do you like that?"

19

"Sounds like we are going deep. A psychologist's treat."

"Well, I aim to please. So, the boy is the dreamer within; an inspired, audacious creature; the best part of me, stubbornly resisting extinction. The man, on the other hand, is plagued by doubts and justifications built over the years. While the man fears defeat and heartbreak, the boy anticipates success and adventure. The man remembers past mistakes, while the boy only remembers times of unbridled happiness."

"You could easily pass for a psychologist yourself, or a philosopher, or both. But what you're saying in such an apt and eloquent manner, Mr. Donovan, sir, is that you're afraid." This had just started to get interesting, and nothing was more attractive to her than a bare soul.

"You're so right. I've been afraid of failure. When I first landed this job, I had big plans. After saving money for a couple of years, I was going to get into a PhD program, become a college professor, conduct research, publish my work in academic journals, and maybe even do some field research. Heck, I wanted to become the guy Indiana Jones is at the beginning of his movies, before the Nazis try to kill him. This damn thing was supposed to be temporary. Rotting away in a library was never my plan."

"But you'll do it, I see it in your eyes. The boy is gaining the upper hand."

"I like that. I like that very much." Michael's countenance was much like that of a sinner absolved by a priest, ready to pray ten Hail Marys.

Experiencing his vulnerability and his strength at the same time was addictive. Here was a man who had already decided to change his life, even if he didn't quite know it yet. In his head, thoughts were already in motion that would inevitably lead to conclusive action, and she was witnessing that revolution. She was not just attracted to him—she was intrigued.

After sharing their sandwiches, Michael and Anna drove back to the historical society. Along the way, Anna asked if he knew of any houses where anyone famous had lived. Michael was able to point out a tiny blue house where a very popular three-term mayor of the town had lived for twenty-five years and a brick house where a famous ballet dancer, who was at present a member of one of the leading classical ballet companies in New York City, had lived with her mother until the year 1999 or 2000, that he couldn't remember precisely. It was a relief to learn that great people and success stories were also part of the history of their town, and that Michael knew about them just as well as the gloomier facts he had recited before.

Back at the historical society's parking lot, they exchanged phone numbers—felt like being back in college. The time came to say their goodbyes. Anna wondered if he might try to kiss her on the lips. Instead, he kissed her on the cheek, in a very gentlemanly fashion. She liked that—this had only been their first date, after all, if it had been a date. It sure felt like a date.

Lost in these thoughts, Anna walked back to her car. Her phone rang, startling her as if getting a call had been unthinkable. Could it be Michael already? She pulled out the phone. It was not Michael who was calling, but her brother, Frank.

At that very moment, she remembered the black box in which she'd hidden the dreadful secrets. She'd locked them up in there until later, and that time was now—the key was in her hand, and her hand was shaking.

CHAPTER III

Standing by her car, Anna stared at her ringing cell phone with Frank's picture on the display, her index finger hovering nervously over the bright-green circle with the word Accept under it, agonizing over whether to take the call. What would she say to him—just act casually? Or instead tell him straightway that she needed to talk to him about a very delicate matter? Yes, that would probably be best.

But by then, she'd thought about it too long; the call went to voice mail. She could have called him back that very moment, but once the phone went quiet, she no longer felt compelled to do anything.

It was scorching hot inside the car, so she turned on the air conditioner at full blast and cracked open the front windows. A text message from Frank arrived: "Haven't seen you in weeks. Want to come by tonight?"

She couldn't say no. What excuse could she give him?

Five days had gone by already. How much longer could she keep him in the dark? Soon enough, she'd have to tell him everything: about the picture, Aunt Marlene's text message, and that godawful little chat with her mother.

Closing her eyes now, she could see it as clearly as if it had happened minutes ago. Scarcely an hour after the incident with the text message in the kitchen, her father had gone back to the basement—his man cave—and her mom had gone outside to water her garden.

Anna headed to the backyard. She and her mother started to chat at first about random things, but Anna subtly steered her to discuss family matters. Anna waited for her to make a remark about her father.

"Victor never was very interested in spending time with my parents, and to be honest, the feeling was mutual—your grandpa always hated his guts; your grandma still does," she said.

It was Anna's perfect opening—she jumped in at once.

"How about Aunt Marlene? Was Dad also distant with her, or did they get along just fine?" she asked her naturally, not even making direct eye contact, but keenly aware, studying her every move, dissecting every word she uttered.

Her mother's face suddenly paled and stiffened, as if holding back tears. She turned away from Anna, looking down at a rainbow of daisies, and mumbled her response, "With, um, Marlene, he was all right. They've usually been on good terms." She appeared to take a deep breath. "Well, you must remember Marlene and your cousin Diane came to visit us often, before they moved to Maryland."

Anna felt a cold shiver. She'd been sitting in the car for over five minutes with the air conditioner on full blast. She turned it down, buckled her seatbelt, put on her oversized sunglasses, and drove away.

She wouldn't go home; didn't want to be by herself. No, she'd go back to the town center, to her friend Stephanie's bookstore. She could say hi, grab a coffee and a book, be around other people, and organize her thoughts.

Stuck at a traffic light, her mother's words still bounced in her head like a distant echo. Something she'd said came in a flash, "your cousin Diane."

How could she have forgotten about Diane? She also had a right to know. Whatever came of this, she couldn't hide it from Diane any more than she could hide it from Frank.

If only she hadn't been in that kitchen.

If only her father had not left his stupid phone out in the open.

If only she could've turned a blind eye. What force had compelled her to dig deeper?

But how could she ignore potential evidence of an affair between her father and her mother's own damn sister?

She couldn't. However terrible the consequences might be, she'd do her duty as a decent human being, and as her mother's daughter.

Then again, maybe nothing really happened. It could all have been a series of fateful coincidences the universe had concocted to torture her.

Truth be told, though, her father wasn't a man who couldn't be suspected of such a hideous act; if there was something Victor Goddard had proven not to be, that was an exemplary husband and father.

Anna heard a loud horn from the car behind her and noticed that the traffic light had turned green—maybe a while ago—so she stepped on the gas pedal while making an apologetic gesture with her hand.

A few minutes later, she drove by the house where the famous ballet dancer had lived as a child. Michael had said specifically that she had lived there with her mother.

She conjured up the image of a little ballerina alone with her mother, fatherless. Immersed in her vision, she couldn't help but wonder who had had it worse, the ballet dancer, who grew up without a father, or her, who had a father, but a heartless, cruel one who seldom showed her any resemblance of love.

Had the ballet dancer been given a choice, would she have preferred to have a father, any father, however uncaring, bitter, and cruel? But before the ballerina could give an answer, Anna had to push the brake pedal hard to avoid hitting the car in front of her that had stopped for a pedestrian. Her car stopped just a few inches short of impact, then everything was still but her heart pounding with sudden vigor. She took a deep breath as all preceding thoughts abandoned her.

A moment later, she arrived at her friend's bookstore. This particular street had a distinctive old-town charm, inviting its visitors to pause their everyday lives' nonsense, sip a coffee, read a good book, maybe even light up a cigar.

Luckily, she found a parking spot right across the street from it. The building itself looked like something one ought to find in the midst of an enchanted forest. Nestled between an ice cream parlor and an antiques shop, the storefront presented nicely harmonized purple-and-blue accents, and a pale-pink door, like a dollhouse.

Crossing the street, Anna could see through the store's large glass window a small group of happy customers having, by the looks of it, a rather amusing chat. On top of the window sat a big sign with the name of the shop, Stephanie's Books & Coffee.

The moment she opened the door, a glorious tsunami welcomed her with irresistible aromas—coffee, cinnamon, vanilla, sweet pastries, and warm butter croissants. For now, it would just be a coffee for her, but she might get a lemon tart later.

There were quite a few customers sitting at small tables, couches, and lounge chairs; chatting, reading books, all having either coffee or tea. A well-organized interior made the most of the available space, with the majority of the bookshelves flush against the walls, allowing for more seating areas throughout the store.

Anna came up to the counter, where Stephanie herself came to say hello and take her order. "Hey girl! How's the novel?" she asked Anna.

It was all right. "It's great, very suspenseful."

While making Anna's double-shot latte with skim milk, Stephanie promised to check on her later.

Coffee on hand, Anna went and picked up a copy of H. P. Lowell's newest novel. Nothing better than the smell of a new book or that moment of childlike wonder turning the pages to chapter one.

She sat on a green lounge chair at one of the narrow ends of a long coffee table. On the chair at the other end of the table sat a middle-aged man in business attire with a serious, inscrutable expression, his attention closely fixed on whatever he was typing.

Between them, an unoccupied brown leather sofa where a couple with a little boy had been sitting a minute ago. Farther out, gathered around small tables, were little groups of younger people, chatting gleefully and enjoying their coffees, teas, and frozen drinks.

Anna spent the best part of the next hour reading. She looked around and noticed there were considerably less customers than before. The serious man had left too.

Stephanie left a young barista in charge of the operation and came to sit next to Anna, on the corner of the brown leather sofa.

"How are you liking this one?" Stephanie asked enthusiastically.

"It started out great. How's business?"

"Oh, I do all right. I have a modest but faithful clientele; and luscious young Brad over there has been good for business, too, you know."

"You devil."

"You know it. There's a younger crowd coming in lately, as in, since Brad works here, and they spend good money on their lattes, mochas, macchiatos. and frozen coffee drinks."

"I'm happy to hear that." Anna heard her phone again and glanced at it. "My brother's texting me."

"How's Frank, other than very fine?" Stephanie asked, her eyes narrowed, sparkling with mischief.

"Stop it. He's doing well. His music school is growing."

"Good to hear that."

"And he's pretty serious with his girlfriend, Sarah."

"Oh, do you think he'll propose to her soon?" Stephanie asked.

"I think so, yes."

"Oh poop." Stephanie let out a muffled laugh. "I'm kidding. How exciting!"

"I know. It's hard to imagine Frank married. But Sarah is really nice."

"Oh, you're going to cry like Mary Magdalene at his wedding."

"Yes, I think I will. You know, our whole childhood it was Frank and me against the world." Anna felt she was starting to tear up and tried to conjure up funny thoughts to wall off the onrushing wave of emotions.

"Yeah, I know. Has he made peace with your father yet?"

"I doubt he ever will, and I can't blame him. There was something about him that Dad despised, and he let him feel it every day of his life."

"Sorry I asked," said Stephanie. "I know you don't want to talk about that stuff."

"Sometimes, it's good to talk about it. It does more damage bottled up inside."

"Well, you know you can tell me anything. It's all as safe with me as it would be with a priest, and I won't make you pray no Hail Marys."

"That's terrible," Anna said. She'd take Stephanie over any priest, over the Pope too.

The bookstore was now empty except for two old men sitting in a corner playing chess.

"It's always slow at this time of the day," Stephanie said.

"It's kind of nice like this too—different." It reminded her of Michael's empty library. "Of course, I'd rather see it full of customers, but this gives us a chance to chat."

"Yes, it does." Stephanie sat back, crossed her legs.

An unusual moment of silence demanded to be filled with anything. The memory flashing in Anna's mind right then somehow became spoken words coming out of her.

"There's one night I can never forget. Frank was playing with his favorite video game. He must have been eight years old and I seven. The game looked so fun—I wanted him to let me play, but he was close to reaching the next stage or something.

"I started crying bitterly, trying to take the controller from him. Mom was in the shower upstairs. The front door opened, and Dad came in, already fuming. When he asked what was going on, I wanted to say, 'It's nothing, Dad.' But I was terrified and what came out of my mouth was, 'Frank doesn't let me play.'

"Frank thought Dad was going to hit him; I saw him recoiling in a corner of the couch. Instead, Dad yelled, 'I'm sick and tired of this shit!

27

This ends now!' He yanked the game console in one violent movement and slammed it against the wall.

"The plastic casing cracked, and little parts came flying out of it in all directions. What I remember most is Frank's face. I don't know if he felt more rage or heartbreak at the moment, but I think he was no longer a kid after that night. I've carried that guilt with me ever since."

Stephanie held her hand. "No kid should have to go through what you two had to." She sat there shaking her head, breathing out slowly.

"I wanted to love Dad—I did. But he didn't even seem to want us. It's like we were these things he'd gotten stuck with, like we stood in his way.

"And Mom, well, I could never understand why she put up with so much emotional abuse. I remember how he used to belittle her and humiliate her in front of us. It was awful."

"Did Frank ever stand up to him?" Stephanie asked, a slight frown forming on her face.

"He did when he was fourteen or fifteen. I can't remember exactly. That's an even more awful story."

"What happened?" Stephanie asked anxiously.

"I'll need another coffee before I tell you that one."

"I got it—this one's on the house."

Stephanie went over and talked to the young barista. A moment later, she returned with two coffees.

Anna took her cup from Stephanie. "Oh, you didn't have to—thank you!"

"No problem." Stephanie sat back, legs crossed, coffee in hand, ready to listen.

"Um, okay," Anna began. "This happened on a Sunday. Frank had made plans to play the guitar, at six that afternoon, in a band he and his friends had just formed. Trouble started when my father unexpectedly decided to mow the lawn midmorning.

"We'd been in Frank's room and came downstairs about twenty minutes before eleven a.m., expecting to see Mom and Dad dressed and ready for mass. Instead, we found our dad in the kitchen, all sweaty and with grass clippings stuck to his jeans, drinking a tall glass of water. That's when our father announced the change in plans—we were going to mass at six p.m.

"Frank flushed and muttered, 'I have a thing in the afternoon.'

"Dad didn't even look at him when he answered, 'Yes, you have a thing, and it's called mass.' I thought Frank would drop it right then, but no—he decided this would be the day to stand up to him.

"He said something like, 'Our band plays at six. It's been planned for a week.' Then he said, 'I'm not going to burn in hell for missing one mass, am I?' I was petrified!

"Dad stared down at him, stunned at first, but then enraged, and yelled, 'You little shit! I couldn't care less about your stupid band. We've never missed mass, and we're not starting today, so help me God!'

"Frank gave him a defiant glare and opened his mouth to say something, but right then, my father's hand came flying down and slapped him so hard I thought his head would fall off.

"That should have been the end of it, but, no, Frank was possessed. He pushed Dad, eyes on fire, and yelled, 'You, fucking ignorant jerk! Do you really think God forgives the hell you put us through every day just because you show up at church and bow, kneel down, and repeat the same prayers every Sunday?'"

"Your dad must have gone berserk," said Stephanie.

"Oh, he lost it. He dragged Frank across the house, saying, 'You'll respect me, you little shit, even if I have to kill you!' Even then, Frank was cursing him every step of the way.

"Dad pushed him out to the backyard; meanwhile, I could hear my mom frantically running down the stairs. Dad grabbed a broomstick and took a vicious swing at Frank, hitting him on an arm so hard that the broomstick shattered—he fell to the floor, writhing in pain. Dad stood by him with a merciless, hard expression, as if he might kick him in the

29

ribs. That's when Mom ran in—she fell to the grass, holding on to Dad's legs and crying, 'Stop, Victor! Stop, for God's sake! Don't hurt him!' He turned away and stormed out of the house.

"Mom lied to the doctor about what happened, and she told us to lie too. That's messed up, huh?"

Stephanie was speechless. Anna sipped her coffee.

"Luckily, Frank didn't have a broken bone. He stayed home, nursing a nasty bruise, and couldn't play with the band that day, but he didn't go to church either—or ever did again. You could say that was Frank's Independence Day."

"I don't even know what to tell you, girl." Stephanie tapped her hand tenderly.

"Thanks for listening to my horror stories."

Stephanie reached across and hugged Anna. "I better go help Brad." From one moment to the next, a line of five or six customers had formed at checkout.

"I'll walk with you."

Anna paid for her newest book and a lemon tart, said goodbye to her dear friend, and stepped outside.

It was a pleasant Friday afternoon, sunny and breezy. Next door, people were coming out with ice cream cones, kids were walking with their parents, couples were sitting on benches, laughing, and kissing. Anna crossed the street and got into her car, then remembered she still hadn't replied to Frank. She took out her phone and typed, "I'll be there at seven. Got something to tell you." She took a deep breath, read the message again, and sent it.

CHAPTER IV

Frank lived only two blocks away from St. Mary's and within walking distance of his new music school. His walk-up apartment was small and would have been quite uninteresting except for the three guitars, one acoustic and two electrics, he had hung on a wall in the main living area, and a piano, wedged in a corner, on top of which there were two curious brass table lamps. A black vinyl sofa and loveseat; a modern, also black, center table; and some sparsely arranged basic decor completed the space where, around fifteen minutes past seven, Frank received Anna with a kiss on the cheek and a long, warm embrace. He must have started using a new shampoo; he smelled like a stroll in the forest—the commercial would say.

"It's good to see you, sis!" he said.

"How's my big brother today?"

"I'm so good it's scaring me."

Anna followed him to the kitchen. "Funny. How do you come up with those answers?"

"Just things the voices tell me."

Cutting a flatbread pizza into near-perfect squares with the meticulousness of a brain surgeon, Frank asked her the usual questions. How's work? How've you been? Have you talked to Mom? He got the usual answers too.

Anna scanned his apartment. "Is that a new guitar?" She pointed at the black-and-white electric guitar in the middle of the set.

"Ah, you noticed my new Fender. It's a beauty, isn't it?"

"It's gorgeous. What happened to the other one?"

"I sold it and bought this one. Doesn't it look nice up there, next to my Gibson?"

"It does. When can I see it in your hands?"

"I'd be happy to give you a little demonstration later." Frank finished cutting the pizza and now picked up two beers from the fridge.

Anna walked over to the piano, ran her hand over the smooth, black surface. Such elegance; an intriguing contrast to the wild guitars on the wall.

Frank gave her one of the beers, then went and placed the tray with the pizza squares on the center table.

On the TV, though muted, images from a developing story of a plane crash in Indonesia reminded Anna of the grim account of recent events she'd had to give Frank. Pieces of fuselage scattered out everywhere, no survivors. Would she soon be picking up the pieces of a disaster of her own making?

She sat down facing Frank.

He picked a pizza square, folded it. "You said there's something you wanted to tell me." He took a bite.

Anna's pulse quickened; she felt such a knot on her throat that she feared not being able to utter a single word.

Frank lifted his index finger, swallowed, and resumed speaking. "The thing is, I also have news to share with you, and I just can't wait. So, would you let me go first? You won't regret it."

Anna felt her throat loosen. Nearly gasped for air.

"Absolutely. I've waited this long. What's another few minutes?"

Her response, she knew, had been a bit odd, as a quizzical look on Frank's face confirmed. She added eagerly, "Go ahead. I'm on pins and needles here."

"Okay, I'm just going to come out with it," he said, putting down his pizza. He fiddled with his chestnut hair for a moment.

His eyes, as green as her own, gleamed with excitement. "I'm going to propose to Sarah. I'm doing it tomorrow." And having said that, he pulled from his pocket a little jewelry box that he opened to reveal a lovely diamond engagement ring.

Frank's keen expression hinted that he wanted Anna's approval of the ring, which she figured must have cost him at least a month's earnings—a dainty pretty item, to be sure, though not spectacular or in any way ostentatious. A fitting display of devotion from a man who was not wealthy, and who was proudly making a life for himself, unwilling to accept scraps from a cruel benefactor.

Anna edged forward and took his hand. "It's a beautiful ring, Frank. She'll love it." A rush of tenderness came over her. "Can I hold it?"

She held the ring close to her face, admiring it from different angles, and then, seeing Frank so happy, she teared up thinking of the darkness she'd come to cast over him. How could she tell him everything now and threaten to shatter this moment of happiness in his life?

"Are you all right?" he asked.

"I'm fine, just a little emotional. Oh, you look so happy."

"I am happy, and I'll be even happier when she says yes."

"How are you going to propose to her?" Anna needed to buy some time to figure out what to do.

"I won't do any of the cheesy classics—the fancy restaurant, or in front of a crowd, none of those. I'll take her to our favorite spot by the lake. She won't suspect anything. I'll wait until sunset; that's when I'll propose."

"I'm impressed—you've turned out to be quite the romantic."

"Who knew, right?" Frank grabbed another piece of pizza. "But the right girl can soften even the worst of ogres."

"Who said you're an ogre?"

"Well, I'm not easy. I know that much. Hey, you haven't touched the pizza."

"I'm not very hungry, but I'll have a piece." She picked up a pizza square. "You're not difficult, Frank, just strong-willed."

Frank sipped his beer. "Isn't strong-willed another term for stubborn, and stubborn the very essence of being a difficult person?"

"A strong will is what you need to triumph over adversity, as you've done."

"You're doing it too."

"Following your footsteps," Anna said.

"That's nice of you to say, but you've fought your own battles."

"You were the beacon I followed. Your grit was the only example I ever needed."

Frank smiled fondly, then said in a suddenly saddened voice, "Then I'm glad at least I was a good brother to you."

"At least? What do you mean?"

"I wish I'd also been a good son," he said with downcast eyes.

"To our horrible father?"

"No, to our poor mother."

Anna felt instantly irritated. "How were you a bad son to her?"

Frank's face sunk. "I left her at the mercy of that monster. I watched him slaughter her spirit and extinguish her happiness for years, and I did nothing."

"And what is it you think you could have done for her?"

"God damn it, I should have had the guts to stand up for her!" He leapt off the sofa and paced around the living room, waving the beer bottle in his hand precariously, his eyes gleaming with bitterness.

Anna hesitated—she hadn't seen him like this in a long time. "You remember how he was, Frank. He could have killed you."

"Or I could have killed him!" he yelled convincingly, like he meant every word—it gave her chills.

"And you would have thrown away your life!" Anna cried out.

"Maybe so, but she could have started a new one," he said in a more subdued voice.

"No mother wants a son to rot in prison."

Frank sat back down on the sofa and set down the beer bottle on the center table, then hunched over, and covered his face with both hands. "Perhaps, she would have left him if I'd done something, or at least said something."

Anna held his hand. There were tears on the corners of his eyes, which he hastened to wipe off with his free hand. "None of what happened was your fault. Who knows why Mom never left him? She might have been afraid not only of him, but also of being without him."

"Yeah," Frank said, his body slouched forward as if deflating, a bleak half smile crumbling on his face. He guzzled down what was left of his beer. "Listen, I'm sorry for that absurd rant. I didn't invite you over to depress you. It's Friday night—what the hell is wrong with me?"

Anna sipped her beer, relieved. "I think this is on the job description of a sister, actually. I read it somewhere—listen to your brother's incessant rants."

"I don't know about incessant. You may have added that part." Frank chuckled. "We should watch a comedy, or sing." He stood up and walked to the kitchen.

"I vote for singing. You can play the piano, and I'll be the lead vocalist."

"I could play a Whitney Houston or Celine Dion song to put you to the test." Frank held two beers. "Do you want another?"

"Sure, this one's warm." Anna went and grabbed the beer from him. They sat across from each other at the kitchen counter.

"Wait, what did you want to tell me before? You said you've waited long to tell me. It sure seemed important."

"Oh, Frank, I just don't think the moment is right anymore." She felt a shiver down her spine. "It will upset you. Had I known you were planning to propose to Sarah tomorrow, I would have waited. Let's…can I tell you later?"

"Anna, just lay it on me, whatever it is, and then we can sing the night away," Frank answered resolutely. "Come on, how bad can it be?"

"It's bad enough that you won't be in the mood for singing."

"Well whatever it is, now I'll be twice as miserable if you don't tell me."

"You better sit down, then."

Frank came around the counter and sat down next to her.

Anna could feel her knees shaking.

"I want you to promise me two things. First, that you will not interrupt me until I'm finished."

"And second?" he asked.

"That you will not leave this apartment tonight, and you will not make any phone calls either, no matter what you hear from me."

Frank's eyebrows jumped up, his head pulled back. "Oh, this is going to be bad." His hands went behind his head. "Sure. I promise."

"All right, then." Anna took a deep breath. "It's about Dad and Mom, and…" She choked before she could say her aunt's name, took a sip of her beer, and swallowed with some effort. "And Aunt Marlene."

Frank's eyes opened wide briefly, then his face became somber, his hands clasped together over his lap.

Anna narrated the events from the previous Sunday at her parents. First, the detonating incident, so to speak, when she unwittingly glanced at her father's phone at the exact moment when the fateful text message from Aunt Marlene had popped up.

A menacing darkness descended on Frank's countenance the moment Anna revealed the text of the message, word for word. He looked as if he might burst into flames at any moment.

From time to time he would fix his gaze on the beer bottle in front of him, glaring at it with such intensity that one might have expected the bottle to shatter into a thousand pieces. Anna observed him closely, dreading a sudden explosive reaction, but he only sat there and muttered resentfully, "With her damn sister!"

"We shouldn't jump to conclusions. It wouldn't be the first time that evidence seems to point to a wrongdoing, only to be disproved later."

Frank smirked. "Right, let's not jump to conclusions. What was the message again? 'You and I are both to blame for this, and we shall be judged in the end.' Holy shit! It has a biblical ring to it, doesn't it? I'm sure Dad liked that about it."

"Cool down. Should I go on?"

He rolled his eyes. "There's more, huh? Yes, go ahead."

"Yes, there is, and I'm afraid it doesn't get any prettier."

"I'm afraid to ask, but what the hell—let's hear it."

Anna shifted in her seat, crossed her legs, and let her mind fly back to her mom's garden once more. The summer heat, the mixed scents of flowers and moist soil, and the pain on her mother's face.

She gave Frank a thorough account of the odd exchange, describing in vivid detail how flustered their mother had become trying to answer Anna's simple question.

"That's disturbing," said Frank while rhythmically stroking his chin, his gaze distant. "Maybe Mom actually knows, or at least suspects, about Dad's affair with Aunt Marlene."

"Still, I could think of other reasons why Mom might be feeling cross with her sister."

"True, but the evidence is starting to pile up."

"And there's one more thing I haven't told you yet—something I did."

"Something you did?" Frank's tone spiked with surprise.

"As you'd imagine, I was upset after that awful day with Mom and Dad. I could think of nothing else for days. I kept dissecting that text message in my head—it seems incriminating, but it's also very obscure. It doesn't openly mention an affair."

Frank nodded rolling his eyes ever so slightly.

Anna continued. "I couldn't prove that Aunt Marlene and Dad had had an affair, and that's a heck of an accusation to make without evidence. But I wasn't going to ignore what I saw. And that's how I decided to do a little digging myself and see if anything turned up."

"I see you have a little Sherlock in you. And what did you do?"

"You might recall that Grandpa once told us that he had donated some pictures of our family to the Blake County Historical Society, and how we were now part of the history of our town and all that."

Frank sneered. "Just to hear you say it makes me want to puke all over again. Like this town needed to remember his son, Victor Goddard the Great!"

"I'm right there with you, but I figured there might be something in one of those pictures—a furtive lustful look between them caught on camera by mere chance or them dancing too closely in the background on a picture taken at some black-tie event. I didn't know what I might find, if anything at all, but I didn't have any better ideas."

"So, you went to the historical society then?"

"Yes, I went there yesterday"

"And?"

Anna smiled. "I may have found a boyfriend, but I'll tell you more about that later."

"Oh, really? We'll definitely circle back to that later on."

"But I also found two pictures," said Anna, her voice regaining a sober tone. "They were taken the night St. Mary's won the basketball championship in 1984."

"Ooh! They snatched those up before National Geographic?"

"Funny. In one of them, Dad was kissing Mom under the bleachers."

"A high school classic, huh?" Frank's voice brimmed with sarcasm.

"Yeah, but Mom's always said that she was in college when she met Dad."

"Mm-hmm." He seemed unimpressed. "And the other picture?"

"Well, that's the kicker, Frank. In the other picture," Anna responded somberly, "Dad was with Aunt Marlene."

Frank's face contorted with bewilderment; his eyes fixed on Anna appeared on the verge of bolting out of their sockets. "You mean he was with her, as in…"

"Yes," Anna interrupted. "She was wrapped around him, kissing his neck."

Frank snapped, "Ah, that fucker!"

A moment later, he resumed speaking in a speculative tone. "Mom must have found out about it. That's why she reacted the way she did when you asked her about Aunt Marlene and Dad. There's your answer. They got along just fine."

"Maybe she did find out, but then she still married him, right?"

"Sadly, she did." Frank took a big swig from his beer. "Although she may have only found out about it after she married Dad. A nasty fight, I would imagine."

"Yes, I guess so." Anna liked this theory instantly. If all this had been about something that happened decades ago, and the whole thing had already been out in the open, then there would be nothing more to be done about it, and she could carry on with her life.

"Can I see the pictures?"

"I don't have them with me, but I can get them."

"You didn't get copies at the historical society?" Frank asked, squinty eyed.

She should have, of course. "I was going to, but I froze when I saw Aunt Marlene savoring Dad's goddamned neck. I wasn't by myself. This guy I met there, Michael, was showing me the photos, and I felt so embarrassed—I just wanted to leave."

"Yeah, I get it. So, Michael, huh?" Frank's face softened a little.

"Yes, Michael Donovan. He's the guy in charge of the library and archives department there."

"I must say I'm intrigued. You haven't dated anyone in a while."

"I'm not easily impressed."

Frank's intensity came down a few notches. "So, tell me about this guy."

"Well, he's devilishly handsome, smart, witty, and interesting. I think he's a dreamer, and a bit of a nerd too." She laughed. "He's a real history buff."

"I kind of like him already. Sounds like a fun dude."

"Yes, I think you'd like him." Anna stood up. She'd been sitting on that hard stool for a while now, all tensed up. "So anyway, next time I see him, I'll ask him to send me those pictures."

Frank got off the stool and went to sit at the piano. "I feel like playing something angry and depressing on account of having a sack of shit for a father, but I also feel like playing something romantic. What's your pick?"

"The night is young; why not both?" Anna stood next to him, with her back leaning on the wall.

Frank smiled faintly at her, then suddenly became very pensive.

"What are you thinking?" asked Anna.

"You know," he said, "even with the whole high school love-triangle thing, I mean…Aunt Marlene's message couldn't have been just about that. At least, I don't think so. That was ages ago, and her message was too ominous. There must be something they did much more recently; something a lot worse than dating in high school behind Mom's back."

Frank stood up and slowly walked back to the kitchen counter, where he grabbed and raised for visual inspection the bottle Anna had abandoned with more than half of the beer still in it. "How about a fresh beer?"

"Actually, I'd rather have a water," Anna responded feebly while sitting down on the piano bench with her back to the keys. Her fleeting fantasy about a quick-and-easy resolution to her current predicament had been crushed in an instant. She knew right away that Frank was right, and she'd been naive to think differently, even for a minute.

Frank came back with two water bottles.

"So, we are back to them having had an affair, then?" Anna asked.

Frank leaned against the wall. "It's the only thing that makes sense to me. Aunt Marlene wrote, 'You and I are both to blame for this.' You're quite sure about that, right?"

Anna nodded, slightly annoyed by his question, "Yes, I'm sure, those were the exact words. What are you driving at?"

"See, that wording is very important. She wrote 'for this' when she could have written 'for that' or 'for it.' If the object of her shame had been in a distant past, she would have used different wording."

A malicious smirk formed on Frank's face. He paused for dramatic effect—he liked to do that sometimes. "'For this' means now, the thing is present, staring at her with all its ugliness and baring its fangs. She prays for God to make it go away, but it just won't—not until judgment day, as she herself eloquently put it in her message."

"Gosh, Frank, do you have to make it so creepy? Are we talking about demons now?"

"In a way, we are. Guilt is the cruelest of creatures."

"All your bizarre drama aside, you may be right," Anna admitted. "She must have been responding to a message from Dad. I'm stepping on a ledge here, but they might still be having an affair. Ugh, just to think of it makes me cringe! I bet Dad wants to continue the affair."

"Of course—he could rob an orphan toddler of his only toy and sleep soundly at night."

"But Aunt Marlene, on the other hand, ridden with guilt, as you've so vividly conveyed, wants to stop."

"We have our theory," said Frank. "Now, if only we could get a hold of his phone to read their entire conversation, we would have this mystery solved in no time."

"You almost made that sound easy. We aren't hackers, so we would need to somehow steal his pass code first—already a daunting task."

"And then we'd need to set up some kind of situation that would make him leave his phone unattended. And everything would probably have to be done pretty fast."

"A lot of things could go wrong with a plan like that," Anna concluded. "I think it would be very risky."

"Would it? It does sound like a grand adventure. I wouldn't mind being the one to unmask the beast. That would be something, huh?"

Anna stood up, as her neck had started to hurt from looking up at Frank. With her left hand, she played three random low notes on the piano, for no reason whatsoever, and then an idea hit her.

"There's another option—Aunt Marlene. She would have the same conversation stored on her phone."

She couldn't believe that she was actually encouraging Frank's crazy ideas about playing detectives and stealing phones and pass codes, yet there was something liberating in this scheming with her brother.

"But how would we get our hands on her phone? It's about a four-hour drive to Baltimore, which is fine, but we haven't visited her, or even seen her in years. It would be pretty odd to show up there, just out of the blue."

"Maybe Diane could do it, if we told her everything—which we should—but then again, who knows where she's been for the last couple of years."

"Diane, huh?" Frank seemed interested. "I bet we could find her. She must have some kind of presence in social media or at least left a trace somewhere on the internet."

Anna paced to the kitchen counter and back, recalling her previous efforts to locate their cousin. "I looked her up a few months back on all the social media platforms I know and couldn't find her. I think she doesn't want to be found."

Frank looked puzzled. "Why would someone want to disappear like that? You don't think she's evading the police or something, right?" He laughed. "I do remember she was a bit of a wild child."

Frank's remark evoked in her memories of the little troublemaker that was Diane back in the day. "She was spirited, for sure! Anyway, I've heard nothing about her since she had that big falling out with her mom years ago. Seems like she got rid of her phone, email—everything."

"Yeah, she vanished, just like that. Quite a trick to pull off, right?"

"I'm not sure that it would be that difficult, if you really wanted to." Anna wondered what that might be like; to leave everything behind, disappear without a trace, maybe even change one's name, and live a whole new life far away from everyone one knew before. It didn't seem so terrible. A rather alluring idea, actually, going somewhere new—but leaving her mother behind, could she do that?

"Well, anyway," Frank declared, "since she's cut off all contact with Aunt Marlene, maybe she wouldn't be of much help to us."

"But we really can't be sure about it," Anna said. "We are making wild guesses about her state of mind, feelings and intentions, when we haven't talked to her in at least two years."

"Wild guesses are all we have, about everything," said Frank. "Doesn't mean we are wrong, though."

"Anyway, finding Diane might lead us somewhere. What if she knows something?" The thought hadn't occurred to her before—some sleuth she was!

"That's true. You know, the last time I saw Diane was at Grandpa's funeral. That drive to Baltimore was also the last trip we had together with Mom and Dad. I remember Mom was crying quietly the whole way, looking out the window, never looking at Dad."

"Gosh, you're right. I was, um, seventeen, at the time; Diane is three years younger than me, so she must have been fourteen. I can't believe it's been that long. After that I only spoke to her on the phone, and not very often. I guess life happened. I don't know."

Anna felt a tinge of sadness and the sting of guilt.

Frank seemed immersed in a thought, then asked, "When you looked her up, did you try different variations of her name?"

"I did—tried Diane Jennings, then Diane Wilde, then hyphenated, Jennings-Wilde. Same result."

"Jennings," Frank repeated with a curious look on his face. "I'd almost forgotten Uncle George. Do you remember him?"

"Only vaguely. I was still pretty young when Aunt Marlene divorced him, and then I never saw him again."

"Yes, I know. He was actually very nice."

Anna chugged down some water. "So anyway, I'll give it another try tomorrow—finding Diane, that is."

"All right, I will too. Call me if you find anything, and I'll do the same."

"I think you have more important plans tomorrow. Let me do the searching; and I want to be the first you tell when Sarah says yes."

"It goes without saying, little sister." Frank moved off the wall and walked toward the spot with the guitars. "And trust me: with or without Diane, we are going to get to the bottom of this awful business."

He took his brand-new Fender electric guitar from the wall. "But right now, let's give it a rest—we're done with that ghastly thing for the night. I owe you a rocking guitar solo."

Frank made his guitar cry, laugh, and scream, skillfully and passionately. They rocked the night away, playing some of their old favorites. When it started getting too late for the kind of noise they were making, they switched to mellow rock ballads.

Anna left Frank's close to an hour after midnight and went straight home. She felt lighter, relieved—she'd done well with Frank. He hadn't stormed off to confront her father, he'd been reasonable—and now, she wasn't alone in this.

She could have sworn the car drove itself home. She was half asleep already when she made it to her bedroom. She took off her shoes and dropped like a rock on her bed with her clothes still on. Her last conscious thought—tomorrow she'd search for Diane fanatically, in the darkest corners of the internet if necessary. She wouldn't leave a rock unturned.

CHAPTER V

When Diane Jennings clocked out at 4:00 p.m., she had plenty of energy left to make the most of her Saturday evening. The bus station was a short walk away from the large hospital just outside of Boston where she had begun working as a nurse three months ago. She got there a few minutes before the bus arrived.

Diane texted her friends Stacey and Camila and made plans to meet them at a tapas bar in two hours. It hadn't been a bad day at the emergency room; better than most days anyway—it could get pretty scary there sometimes, especially at night.

She worked nights Monday through Thursday and had Friday and Sunday off, with Saturday's day shift stuck in between—a bizarre, impractical schedule. Friday had been demoted to a mere parenthesis in her week—nap day. The closest thing to a weekend she had started after work on Saturday evening and ended midafternoon on Monday.

From her stop, Diane walked five minutes to her apartment complex. In another forty minutes, she'd taken a shower, blow-dried and combed her hair, and done her makeup.

She inspected the final result on the mirror and was very pleased with her look—the makeup was just right, making her blue eyes pop out; and her dark-brown hair, complemented with caramel highlights, looked full and lustrous. She got into a tight black dress, one of her favorite pieces of clothing, and completed her outfit with a pair of black high-heel shoes.

Having some time to spare, Diane took her laptop computer, crossed over to her tiny living room, and sat on the couch to check her email.

This was a new email account. She'd closed her old one two years ago along with her social media pages; a fresh start. She'd only used this one in her job search and to write to her father—she made him promise not to share her contact with anyone, especially not her mother, his ex-wife Marlene.

Sifting through the piles of digital garbage that she'd accumulated over the last few days; she saw a new email from her dad and hastened to open it.

Hey kiddo!

I am going to New York in two weeks for a marketing-and-sales conference my boss wants me to attend. It took a little arm twisting, but I finally accepted the burden of going to the Big Apple for five nights, weekend included, staying in a luxury hotel, eating and drinking to my heart's content, all paid by the company, and, sure, sitting in on a few entertaining presentations and collecting business cards from pretty ladies.

So I was wondering if you would like to meet me in New York. I checked the train schedule from Boston and the last departure on Saturday is at 6:30 p.m. It gets to New York by 11:00. I can pick you up at the station, and if you're not too tired, we can go to a piano bar or something, anything you like. Then on Sunday, we can take in the sights of Manhattan, go for a walk in Central Park, take the subway to Times Square. The last train to Boston from New York departs at 7:00 p.m., so we would have almost the whole day for ourselves. It will be great.

It goes without saying that you won't have to worry about expenses. I'll pay for your train tickets and won't let you spend a penny of your own money in New York. It's the least I can do for my daughter. It was so wonderful seeing you in Boston last year, and we had such great fun. We are due for another great time like that. So, just say yes, and I'll buy your tickets.

One more thing. I promise not to upset you or anything during our time together in New York, but maybe over a glass of wine, just for a few minutes, I do want to talk to you about your mother. I would very much like you to let her back into your life. She needs her daughter, and you need your mother. I know you've always blamed her for our divorce, but love is a lot more complicated than that. The heart cannot be compelled to love or stop loving. If nothing else, I'm thankful to your mom for giving me the best gift I could have hoped for, you!

Love,

Dad

Tears came streaking down Diane's face. Her makeup would be ruined, for sure, but she cared little about that now. Her mind was flung into a storm of thoughts and feelings which she couldn't altogether comprehend—tenderness shrouded in melancholy, resentment entwined with regret, and even a tinge of compassion for her mother, burning faintly under a timeworn layer of pride.

How could her mom have stopped loving this saint of a man? Even now, he defended her and pleaded on her behalf, with nothing to gain from it. The perfectly natural thing would be for him to resent her, if not for the breakup, at least for the time stolen from a life together with her daughter.

Diane's memory of the divorce was painfully clear—she'd just turned eight years old. Soon after, her mother decided that they would move to Maryland, hundreds of miles away from her father. Even then, her father managed to visit her at least every other month, staying in cheap motels nearby just to spend a weekend with her.

The more she had to wait to see her dad, the more memorable their encounters became; and by contrast, the more awful her bitter, nagging mother seemed to her every day.

By the time she became a teenager, Diane already avoided talking to her mother as much as possible, and when they did talk about anything but the most immaterial of trifles, one of them, or sometimes both, would wind up in bitter tears, such was the rancor that Diane had bottled up, like the foulest of wines.

After high school, she got a cashier job at a home-improvement store and got the hell out of her mother's house. They exchanged heated, hurtful words at the time.

Then she left town, cutting off communication with everyone but her dad. He'd always been an angel in her life. In fact, she was able to complete her nursing degree program in no small measure because of her father's support.

Diane wiped off her tears with the back of her hands, smearing her makeup and getting it on her hands too. She began typing up her response.

Hi Dad,

That sure sounds amazing. Let's do it. You go ahead and buy them tickets. Thank you so much. I'll be looking forward to it. I always look forward to hanging out with you.

I would hang out with you at the edges of hell—and I think we have, haven't we? Kidding! But Manhattan, well, you've really outdone yourself this time.

Now, about that other thing—I'm not sure that Mom ever deserved you, or that she deserves your kindness now, but you sure deserve that I listen to all you want to tell me. We can talk at that fancy piano bar you want to take me to.

Hugs and kisses,

Diane

After sending the email, she went back to her bedroom and, as quickly as she could, removed her smeared makeup using two towelettes, and started the process again.

It was now just about time to leave if she wanted to get to the tapas bar by 6:00 p.m., though she knew her friends would not really be annoyed if she got there a few minutes later.

All she needed now was to find her small black-and-white evening purse, which she knew must be somewhere in her bedroom, but where? She looked in the closet, where it would normally be, but it wasn't there.

She searched around the room impatiently, went to the living room and back, then sat on her bed to think with her eyes closed, and that's when she recalled that, for no apparent reason, she had put it in the bottom drawer of the dresser.

She dashed there, opened the drawer, and there it was, her darling little evening purse, which had been a birthday gift from her father and always reminded her of happy times with him. Beside it was a letter she had last opened almost a year ago, a letter from her mother—she'd sent it to her old address in Maryland just before the postal service's mail-forwarding period expired.

Diane never called her or wrote back.

She felt drawn to the letter now, the reason why she couldn't have articulated, but sure enough she lifted it from the bottom of this drawer that contained nothing but the purse and the letter itself.

It occurred to her that this bottom drawer was special as it only contained items of nearly magical qualities—beloved, dreaded, or despised, but special nonetheless. This was no longer a place to store socks, panties, shorts, camisoles, or trinkets of any sort. Hereafter, the price of admittance into this drawer would be tears, whether joyful or bitter. An engagement ring, a child's handprints, or the last train tickets, only those sorts of items would prove worthy of entry into this reborn bottom drawer.

She took the letter out of the envelope slowly, as if seeing it for the first time. As she opened it, she wondered if she might find new meanings in her mother's letter.

> *Dear Diane,*
>
> *I pray to God that you get this letter and that you're well and happy. I suppose there must be a reason why you have decided to shut me out of your life, disappearing like this without notice and without as much as a trail of crumbs to follow. You must think me your enemy, an ogre from which you must run away and hide. I guess I may have done and said some things to earn your resentment. I know damn well that I have made more than my fair share of mistakes in this life.*

You might find this hard to believe, but ensuring your well-being and happiness was all I wanted to do ever since I first felt you moving around in my womb. It's very difficult for me to accept that I was so bad at being a mother that you must hate me so much today.

Allow me to give you a few words of wisdom. You will find, hopefully not the hard way, that life can be as treacherous as it is beautiful, and sometimes, you're not quite sure which side of the coin you're on. There are almost infinite ways to mess up your life—some, like dating gangsters, are very obvious, but there are much subtler dangers, teeny bad choices that lead to other bad decisions, slowly leading you astray until one day you're left wondering what the heck happened to your plans and dreams.

You would do well to remember that the devil always comes wearing its best colors. I must admit that I stepped on a few landmines myself when I was younger than you're now, and so I may have obsessed with preventing you from making the same mistakes. I'm sorry that I didn't always have the level-headedness to give you advice the right way, as I should have. It's just that you have learned all too well how to push my buttons. There's too much of me in you, I guess.

About your father, I won't say much, only a couple of lines, because enough has been said already. He's an amazing person and the best father you could have had. For that, I will forever be grateful to him, and I hope you always keep him involved in your life. Such a great man deserved to be truly loved by his wife, and I just didn't have that to give to him anymore. He has that now, and I am happy for him. Love is a mysterious thing that doesn't obey any rules we might want to impose upon it. That is all I can coherently say about that.

I hope you will at least give me some peace by letting me know that you're doing well, wherever you are. I would have wanted a college education for you, and I was shocked and disappointed when you just up and went to live on your own. I felt you were throwing your life away; but you're smart and determined, some might say stubborn too, so I know you will accomplish whatever you set out to do.

I miss you terribly. A mother should not be estranged from her daughter. My sincerest desire is that we mend our relationship. I will be here, waiting with open arms and requiring no explanations. Please know that however imperfect a mother I may have been, I have always loved you above everyone and everything else. I know you must know that.

Love you always,

Mom

Diane was again on the verge of tears. She wasn't filled with spiteful rage like the first time she read the letter. What she felt now was entirely different—a muddle of pain and resentment, yes; but also sorrow, pity, and remorse; and a nagging feeling that she had taken her vendetta too far, becoming the villain in her own story.

Diane started as her phone rang loudly—it was her friend Stacey. Clasping the phone between her cheek and shoulder, she hastened to put the letter back inside the envelope and into the bottom drawer of the dresser. She grabbed her small purse as she listened to Stacey's directions. In another moment, she was requesting her ride from an application on her phone.

A few minutes later, she arrived at Sevilla's Lounge & Tapas. The place was remarkably busy, so it was a good thing that her friends had arrived early and gotten a table. As Diane walked in, she thoroughly enjoyed the assault on her senses from the intoxicating smell of spices filling the air and the loud, lively chatter from the crowd mingling with passionate flamenco music playing in the background.

Following Stacey's instructions, she walked all the way to the back, then turned right, took a few more steps, and glanced over, scanning people's faces, looking for her friends. Then she saw Camila and Stacey beckoning to her from a dimly lit corner table.

They ordered cocktails and a variety of tapas to share. Seafood dominated the table—shrimp, calamari, mussels, and codfish croquettes.

Camila seemed to notice something rather amusing at another table.

"Stacey, that man over there with the blue shirt is eating you up with his eyes," she said in a hushed voice, as if the man might be able to hear her from afar in spite of all the noise.

The man had a fairly athletic build and was handsome enough, with a strong jawline and a masculine appearance, though probably too old for any of them. He seemed to be alone.

With an impish look on her face, Stacey crossed her legs, letting her skirt come up just high enough to reveal a teasing sliver of silky caramel-mocha skin from her thigh. The man straightened up in his chair, squinted his eyes slightly, and tightened his lips, for a brief moment contorting his face into a distinctly lascivious stare.

Right then, a tall, slender, blond woman who gave every indication of being the man's wife, came and sat down in front of him. Who knows what words they exchanged, or if the woman even noticed, or acknowledged, the embarrassing moment? But the man certainly seemed very uneasy all of a sudden, looking down at the menu, barely opening his mouth.

"I feel sorry for that poor woman," Diane said while stirring her drink. "Is that what we have to look forward to, marrying a guy who after only a few years will be salivating after any hot, young chicks he crosses paths with?"

"All I heard is that I'm a hot, young chick. Thanks, Diane," said Stacey before bursting into laughter.

"I love your optimism, Diane," Camila remarked with a hint of mockery, her lips twitching from trying to hold in a laugh.

"Do I sense sarcasm?" asked Diane.

"No, never. You really are optimistic." Camila slurped the last of her strawberry daiquiri, making a loud, exasperating sound. "You think that your future husband—a charming, witty, super sexy dude, of course—will spend a few years married to you before he starts looking at other women. Girlfriend, I hate to break it to you, but he'll notice every hot chick at your wedding!"

That punchline got the full-on laughter it deserved. Diane herself almost cracked a rib laughing. "Oh, that's terrible. Hopefully, not every man out there is a pig."

"Honestly," said Camila, "I can live with the idea that most men are probably pretty disgusting on the inside, but hopefully, I can find a man with enough class to keep the lid on all that stuff."

"To well-behaved pigs!" Diane said, raising her glass. They clinked their cocktail glasses, already giggling before Diane snorted like a pig; and then they were laughing hysterically to the point of tears.

The three friends spent the rest of the evening immersed in sprightly conversation. For a moment, Diane felt joyful and untroubled by any woes. She would've wanted to slow down time and stay in that moment, but quite to the contrary, four hours flew by like they were nothing.

Thoughts of her dad and her mother returned to her on the ride back home. She went up to her apartment, took off her shoes, placed her purse on top of the kitchen counter, opened the fridge, and got herself some water. Having quenched her thirst, she wondered if her dad might have replied to her email.

She sat on the couch with her computer and opened her email inbox, scanning for her dad's name, but there wasn't a new email from him. Instead, she saw in there something entirely unexpected, and unnerving, like a phone ringing at 3:00 a.m.—it was an email from her cousin, Anna Goddard.

CHAPTER VI

Saturday morning had come for Anna in what felt like the blink of an eye. An unwelcome ray of light slipped through the curtains and, with great precision, found her unsuspecting eyelids. It was early, too early. She rose from bed annoyed and with a throbbing headache. The time was 6:35 a.m., and she had barely slept five hours. She could have sworn that she'd been singing with Frank one hour ago.

Nonetheless, after taking pills for the headache and brewing her compulsory morning espresso, she was ready to put on her Sherlock Holmes hat and search for Diane in the vast expanse of the internet with unwavering resolve—and that she did for hours on end, knocking on every virtual door, running into walls and dead ends, exhausting all options she could think of. She searched for her under her actual name and every variation she could conceive, in every social media site, in online forums and chat rooms.

At one point, she thought she might have found her in a forum where several people had been discussing the resurgence of right-wing extremism. One of the participants identified herself as Diana Jennings and related a story of a black student who was given a beating by three white supremacists in the Baltimore area. It was the most promising lead Anna had bumped into in over four hours.

She went back to the beginning of the discussion and read every entry Diana Jennings had posted, only to find out from one of her earlier comments that she'd graduated from high school in 2002, so she'd be about thirty-four years old now—she had hit another wall.

That last setback took some air out of Anna, and she decided to take a nice long lunch break. She warmed up a chicken noodle soup in the microwave, brought it back to the living room, and turned on the TV. She streamed an episode of a show she liked, in which a charming middle-aged gentleman traveled to different countries to explore the culture and the food.

For this episode, they went to Croatia. Anna watched in awe the splendid images of the stunning old city of Dubrovnik, the capital city, Zagreb, Hvar Island, coastal and mountain landscapes, surreal lakes, and waterfalls. The local seafood looked amazing: baked octopus, grilled squid, prawns, sardines, and seafood pizza.

Anna was spellbound. What an amazing job to have. What a dream it would be to see the world, experience other cultures, meet new people, listen to their music, learn their language, eat their food, live like them.

She'd been saving money hoping to take a trip to Europe. The sounds from the TV seemed to fade as Anna envisioned her future travels, her mind taking her on a high-speed train from Paris to Barcelona, then Florence, Rome, Venice, Budapest, Vienna, Prague, Munich; and she would have made it to Amsterdam and back to Paris had she not heard a phone call coming through—it was Michael.

"Hey, Michael."

"Hi, Anna, how are you?" His voice seemed a bit huskier than she remembered.

"Not bad at all. A little guilty about eating all that food yesterday."

"I know. I'm feeling it too. But it was so good, wasn't it?"

"Everything was great."

"Everything?" he asked with a peculiar intonation.

"I wouldn't have changed a thing." The words glided off her tongue like silk sliding off a bare shoulder.

There was a pause on his side. She pictured him running his hands through his hair, a big grin on his face. The thought made her smile.

"I really enjoyed your company." Anna pictured him with eyes closed, hoping for…

"And I yours."

She awaited his next move, which came after another little pause.

"So, I was wondering," he said, "how do you feel about the music from the nineties?"

"Oh, I love it. I grew up listening to rock bands like Nirvana and Pearl Jam—my brother Frank was a big influence there; and then stuff like the Cranberries, No Doubt…"

"Then I have a treat for you. There's a nineties-rock tribute band playing at the Fox's Den next Thursday night."

"I know the place. Frank took me there once. About a half hour east on the freeway."

"That's the one," he said.

"Did I mention that my brother plays the guitar and the piano?"

"No, you hadn't. Sounds like a cool dude."

"Yes, you'd like him."

"I bet I would…um, will like him." She liked Michael's little leap of faith.

"So, how about it? Do you want to go?" he asked.

"Yes, I do. Sounds like a lot fun."

"All right then. Pick you up around eight?"

"Sure. I'll text you my address," she said.

"I'm looking forward to Thursday," he said.

"Yes, me too." Anna paused, then added, "Oh, hey, I just remembered, you know those pictures of my dad we found? Any way you could send them to me when you get back to work on Monday?"

"Yeah, sure. Do you want all of them?"

"Yes, the ones you showed me. I figured they are worth keeping, those pictures of their younger selves."

"Sure, I'll send them to you."

"I really appreciate it." That was easy. Like a gambler who'd just won a hand, she got greedy. Before she could restrain the thought that had taken hold in her mind, words were coming out of her mouth, as if she were a mere spectator. "Hey, one last thing. This may sound strange, but do you have any idea how to find someone who's gone off the grid?"

"Huh, that's an intriguing question. Who are you looking for?" Michael asked, sounding both curious and amused.

Anna was already regretting her indiscretion, but she was growing desperate. Because of his training, she reckoned Michael would likely be adept at researching just about anything, digging into buried documentary evidence to uncover clues, much like a detective.

She'd cracked open her Pandora's box, and all she could do now was try to keep the lid from being flung wide open.

"It's my cousin. Her name's Diane Jennings. I've been trying to reconnect with her for some time now. She disappeared about two years ago without telling anyone where she went. She had been angry at her mother."

"And do you know that she's all right?" Michael asked with a note of genuine concern.

"Well, I don't really know, but the one indication we have that she vanished on purpose is that all her email and social media accounts were canceled, and her phone number was disconnected. Clearly, she must have done that herself."

"That makes sense. And how soon do you need to find her?" he asked.

"Well, I've been searching for her on the internet all morning because her mom's birthday is tomorrow," she lied, "and I was hoping to convince her to at least send her a message, anything, as a first step toward reconciliation."

"That's very thoughtful of you. I might be able to help you. A few ideas come to mind, but I'll need you to tell me quite a few things about her. For starters, I need her parents' names, her age, where she went to school, if she has had jobs that you know of, where and what did she do.

Also, if she ever told you about cities or states she wanted to visit, professional interests, or even hobbies and sports; any of those things could lead to something. Oh, and also her best friends and any recent boyfriends you might know about."

"That's great. I'm getting an education here," she said. "It's quite something to see your mind at work. You came up with all those research avenues in a minute."

"You're making me blush. Don't be too impressed. I've just had some practice digging up the past, often things that not many people are interested in unearthing."

Anna spent the next ten minutes telling Michael everything she could remember about Diane, without telling him too much. He didn't seem interested in scrutinizing her, but rather, appeared bent on impressing her with his ingenuity. And she was impressed.

Knowing that she now had a capable researcher on Diane's trail, and feeling exhausted from her previous efforts, Anna put her computer aside and laid down on the couch to rest her eyes for a little while. She felt quite comfortable, resting her head on a nice, downy pillow she had bought a few months back.

The sounds around her started fading, becoming more and more distant as she dozed off, then everything was calm, and she sank into nothingness. Time, matter, space, all her senses and thoughts vanished, as if death held her prisoner. Whether she had slept for hours, or only a few minutes, she couldn't tell afterward.

She was awakened by three loud knocks on the front door. She sat up on the couch, disoriented and alarmed, wondering who could be there. She noticed that the TV was turned off, yet she was almost certain that she had left it on—it gave her an eerie feeling. She looked about her and felt around the couch for her phone and couldn't find it. Another three, louder knocks, made her start for the door in haste.

"Who is it?" she asked, but no one answered. Anna got to the door and silently looked through the peephole, which, oddly, seemed higher than she remembered. She was downright dumbfounded to see her father's annoyed face on the other side. He stood so close to the door that she could only see his penetrating blue eyes, his wide, bulbous nose and his small mouth, with those remarkably thin lips that nearly disappeared when he tightened them in anger or stretched them to form a grin.

Her father had never come to her house, which made this a rather strange and upsetting visit. She took a deep breath and opened the door. There stood her father, though not his current self, but rather the younger man she remembered from the time when she was an eight- or nine-year-old girl. A young, radiant, stunning Aunt Marlene was beside him. In her father's strong arms, sound asleep, was her little cousin, Diane. Anna stood there, bewildered, paralyzed, in utter disbelief. She opened her mouth but was unable to speak.

Her father spoke first, "Anna, what are you doing here?"

She was going to say, "What do you mean? This is my house." But suddenly, she felt unsure about everything, as if the fabric of reality was being ripped apart before her very eyes; unfathomable and frightening revelations slipped through the cracks of her shattered certainties.

She looked behind her, and her home was no more. Instead, she was standing in the foyer at her parents' house. Dolls were sitting on a white upholstered chair, but they were not hers; they were Diane's. Horrified, she turned around and faced her visitors again. Behind them, the street was no longer there, nor were the neighbors' homes; but instead, there was the front porch of her parents' house and nothing but greenery in the background.

Anna looked at her own feet, and they were small, and she was wearing a kid's sandals, her sandals—she recognized them. She looked at her hands and, perplexed, saw that they also were a little girl's hands; then she looked at her father again, and he seemed much taller now—in fact, he was enormous.

He brushed her aside sullenly, and he and Marlene walked into the house. As her aunt walked by her, she gave her a pitying glance. Her father kept on walking briskly, and a moment later, she heard his heavy steps as he took Diane upstairs.

A moment earlier, Anna had been convinced that she was dreaming, but the little girl she'd turned into wasn't so sure. It all seemed so dreadfully real that she was almost ready to believe that her adult life had been the dream and she had now awakened, still a child.

She shut the front door and ran to the kitchen, where she'd heard the metallic clattering sound of pots and pans being hurriedly taken out of cabinets. When Anna got there, she stood facing Aunt Marlene, who appeared to be getting ready to prepare dinner; they looked into each other's eyes intently, but before either of them said a word, her father had come back downstairs and walked into the kitchen.

He grabbed Marlene by the waist, pulled her toward him, and kissed her decadently, shamelessly, while his hands slid down to her thighs.

"Where is my mother?" Anna asked him, but she was disconcerted to hear her own shrill, childish, powerless voice. Still holding Marlene, who looked positively ashamed, her father looked down at her with a chilling, malicious smirk on his face.

"Oh, Anna, why would I know your mother's whereabouts? She's not my problem anymore, and quite frankly, neither are you. Why are you here? She must have dropped you off while we were out, didn't she? Is she trying to abandon you already, that weak, pathetic excuse for a woman?"

"I...don't know," Anna whimpered, feeling scared, confused, angry, and hopelessly heartbroken.

"Look, maybe I should get you a cab to your mother's. I want to be alone with my new woman, Marlene. You shouldn't really call her aunt, you know, because that's weird." His little mouth contorted into a re-volting grin. He looked at Marlene, but she'd turned her back to them and was grabbing and moving things around, with exaggerated move-ments, clearly pretending to be busy cooking.

He added, "See, your mother was a mistake—I simply chose the wrong Wilde sister. Marlene was always right for me; I see that clearly now."

"What's happening? I don't...what am I supposed to do now?" Anna was overcome with sorrow and could hardly breathe; she felt tears streaming down her face.

"Well, you can't stay here. I'll give you money, but I don't want you here. Tell your mother I can give her more money. I don't want her sending you sad, dull children here. You're dull and pathetic, like your mother. The lot of you make me want to blow my head off."

Anna couldn't take it anymore. She ran out of the house, slamming the door on her way out, then stood at the front porch, sobbing uncontrollably. She was alone, unwanted, a forsaken, wretched little creature put on this earth to weep.

Not knowing where to go, she stepped out and walked around the house toward the backyard. She sat down on a wooden bench under a big oak tree. A gentle, soothing breeze caressed her face. She closed her eyes, breathing in and out, trying to think of nothing.

She remained like that for a moment. Then she felt something cold and moist touching her right hand, which startled her. She opened her eyes, and there she saw Bo, her beloved chocolate Labrador, alive and well once more; and her joyful tears mixed with the bitter tears she had shed before.

Evidently, Bo also was overjoyed to see Anna again; he stood on his hind legs, wagging his tail vigorously, his mouth wide open and his expressive eyes fixed on her. He gave her two gentle barks, skipping in place excitedly. Anna jumped off to the grass, hugged Bo, and rolled over with him.

Bo eagerly showed his devotion and affection, thoroughly licking her face, licking off her tears. She laughed and hugged him, pressed her face against the top of his head, smelled him and kissed him; then she closed her eyes and new tears came rolling down for Bo to lick off.

A moment later, Bo appeared to have seen something just around her mother's garden; he barked repeatedly looking in that direction and then ran over there, disappearing behind a row of azaleas in full bloom. Anna followed him to the garden, first walking, then running when she heard Bo whimpering.

She made the turn at the azaleas and slowed down, then stopped altogether. A spine-chilling feeling came over her. The garden was cast in an unnatural, ethereal light, and she sensed that it had acquired a sinister nature. She took a few more hesitant steps, went around a thick evergreen tree, and came in full view of a harrowing image.

Her mother was lying there, on a patch of lawn surrounded by flowers of every imaginable color, with her eyes closed and her hands on her chest, holding a bouquet of daisies. She was her younger self and looked like an angel, beautiful and peaceful, wearing a pretty blue summer dress. Bo was licking her bare feet.

Kneeling on the grass beside her was Frank, just a boy, crying his eyes out. He looked up at her. "We did this, Anna! We killed her!" he wailed dreadfully. Anna stepped back in horror, wanting to cry out, to beg for forgiveness, but no words would come out, and she couldn't breathe either.

Taking another step back, she stumbled and fell backward, yet she never hit the ground, but rather kept falling through what felt like an endless dark void. She finally plummeted to her couch—that's how it felt—and opened her eyes in a panic, gasping for air, with tears in her eyes.

She was back in her living room, awake, alone, and fully grown up. Her TV was on, and her favorite world traveler was sailing in Greece— the bastard. She turned it off.

She felt a sudden impulse to call her mother to make sure that she was fine; but then she came back to her senses and reminded herself that dreams don't carry any foreboding messages, but rather are just a hodgepodge of one's thoughts and memories colliding in the sleeping brain.

She felt ashamed to have entertained such an irrational notion, even for a fraction of a second. She was trained in psychology, for God's sake! The only meaning to be found in her dream was that she was worried sick about the consequences of exposing an affair between her father and Aunt Marlene.

What would her mother do if she found out, if she was confronted with clear evidence of the wicked treachery? Would she just ask him for a divorce; or would she finally blow up, go mad, smash things around the house, hurl vicious insults at him, slap him, punch him?

And how would he respond? Frightful were the possibilities, without a doubt—he could indeed kill her, couldn't he? Anna took both hands to her face and shook her head, as if physically trying to get those thoughts out of her mind.

She picked up her phone, which had slipped between the cushions of the couch. She looked at the time, and it was almost 6:00 p.m. She had slept for nearly four hours.

Anna went to her bedroom. Sunnier thoughts—Frank could be proposing to Sarah right now. From the window, she saw a clear blue sky with hints of yellow and orange on scattered clouds over the horizon. Just perfect. She'd worried about bad weather ruining Frank's momentous occasion with Sarah.

She undressed and got in the shower. Flashes from her nightmare still haunted her intermittently, and she kept fighting an absurd fear that at any moment she could blink and become the little girl again and be back in that frightening dream world. She tried to think of Frank, getting engaged to Sarah with a spectacular sunset as backdrop, but instead conjured up the image of little Frank kneeling by their dead mother. She shuddered.

Anna deliberately shifted her thoughts to Michael, picturing him alone with her in a room with dim lighting, wearing a black leather jacket over a tight white shirt, with a scruffy beard and ruffled hair; and her stroking that dark hair, and pulling it back as she kissed his lips. The image had the desired effect—she immediately felt freed from superstition and nonsense, in control of her mind.

She toweled dry, brushed her hair back into a ponytail, slipped on a long comfy blouse, and ordered her favorite Chinese takeout.

She was enjoying her chicken lo mein when she received a picture and a message from Frank. Him and Sarah kissing ever so sweetly and, behind them, an absolutely flawless sunset over the lake. The message— "She said yes!"

Anna was so happy for him. So happy. And worried. What if she ruined it for him?

She replied to Frank with cheerful congratulatory remarks and an assortment of ecstatic emojis; finished dinner, picked up her book, and sat down intent on reading chapter ten. Her phone rang. It was Michael.

"Hey there, how are you?" He sounded rather cool and confident.

"Just reading a book. It's a good one, though."

"Do you read a lot?"

"Mostly novels. Romance stories, mainly, but I also like mystery and suspense."

"I'll be sure to remember that," he said friskily. Anna put the phone away to laugh quietly without him listening. She couldn't make it that easy for him.

"Are you planning to buy me a book anytime soon?"

"Maybe, yes. I would welcome the challenge of getting to know you well enough to pick a book for you."

"Hmm, I think I'd love to see you try."

Michael chuckled, "So, listen, I have something for you."

"Oh, and what would that be?" Anna asked blithely.

"Your cousin, Diane—I found her," he declared triumphantly.

"Really? That's amazing. Where is she? And how did you…" Anna was stunned. How good was this guy.

"She's in Boston, and she's a nurse."

The troublemaker, a nurse? Anna would have never guessed it. "A nurse? Wow, that's good. That's, um…huh."

"Let me explain the part about how I found her. After spending an hour attempting different searches in various sites, I figured that I was going about it the wrong way. You always start with a motive—what does she want, what is her current pursuit in life?"

"This is getting interesting."

"So, Diane is a rebel who wants to stick it to her mom, right?"

"Sounds like her," Anna said.

"So, how does she do that? Well, she could throw her life away—that would be one way to do it—or do the exact opposite, make something of herself, get ahead in life without her mother's help. That means starting a career, so she'd need to put together a resume—a resume with contact information."

"Great instincts. But how did you get her resume?"

"That's where I would have run into a wall, but I remembered that I have a friend who's a recruiter—he calls himself a headhunter, which does sound cooler."

"Does it?"

"Anyway, this guy has access to a bunch of resume databases, and the guy owed me a favor. So, long story short, Diane sent her resume to a job board and agreed to make it searchable by potential employers and recruiters; and that's how my guy found it, and I have it, and you will have it in three, two, one, and…you have it now."

"This is amazing. I really appreciate it, Michael. There, I just got it." Anna briefly looked at the document she had just received from him. It really was Diane's resume. She'd listed her two sales jobs in Baltimore, and the end date of her last job coincided with the approximate time she disappeared. Soon after that, she enrolled in the nursing program from which she'd graduated only four months ago.

"Yes, this is her, no doubt about it. Look at that. I have her phone number and email address right there. I owe you one."

"Ah, it's nothing," Michael said. "It was fun, actually, like solving a case. I don't often get that kind of excitement. I love the rush of making a discovery."

"I'm happy you enjoyed it."

"Hope all goes well with Diane, and that you can convince her to end her estrangement from her mother. Maybe you'll tell me about it when I pick you up on Thursday?"

"I sure will."

"All right, well, you have a good night now, Anna," he said softly.

"Sweet dreams," she said, and ended the call.

Anna looked long and hard at Diane's phone number. She agonized over what to do next. Was she really going to call Diane, out of nowhere, on a Saturday night? Would she even answer the call? And if she didn't, what then, leave her a voice mail? Ugh, she always felt so weird leaving voice messages.

An email could be the way to go, at least as a first attempt.

She opened up her email application, copied Diane's email address from her resume, and began writing, quickly in the beginning, but then more slowly, stopping periodically to think, replacing words that she thought Diane could misinterpret or deem objectionable.

Hello Diane,

I hope that this message reaches you soon and, most importantly, that you're happy and doing well. When we get to talk, I'll be sure to explain how I managed to find your email address. For now, I'll be brief, as the intent of this communication is simply to reach out to you. I'm sure that we have so much catch up to do that we could fill up two or three evenings, and I would love to do just that. We could start with a phone call, whenever you're free for a half hour, and then we'll go from there.

I do want to talk to you about something that concerns both your mother and mine.

I came upon something that caused me to worry, and I just want to chat with you about it and see what you think. Don't fret too much about it, though. I'm hoping that, together, we can clear up the matter and that it ends up not being much of a big deal.

That's all for now. I do hope to hear back from you real soon. Call me anytime, or write to me, either way.

Take care,

Anna

She included her phone number at the bottom, under her name. Satisfied with the message, she sent the email. Now, it was just a matter of waiting and hoping for a prompt response from Diane. If this failed, she could still try calling her.

Anna picked up her book and went out to the deck. She would read the next chapter al fresco. There was a very pleasant, lulling breeze. She looked up and saw dark clouds racing under a bright, near-full moon.

"Howdy, neighbor!" a voice startled her. It was Michelle.

"Oh, hi Michelle. How are you?" Anna walked toward her.

"Enjoying the little things, you know? What are you reading?" Michelle lit a cigarette.

"It's a novel. A little suspense, some romance."

"I see, but on a Saturday night, a gorgeous girl like yourself—how come you're not out there living the romance?" She gave Anna a clever little smile while exhaling smoke upward through a tiny gap between her lips.

"Actually, I think I might be 'living the romance.'"

Michelle smiled. "Well, good for you."

"How's Ashley doing in college?"

"She's loving every minute. I just spoke to her. Oh, you remembered her name."

A flash of lightning crossed the sky just then, and a resounding thunderclap followed. A few drops of rain had started falling. Michelle said, "Well, we better take cover. Looks like a storm is coming."

"Yes, yes, it does," Anna said more cryptically than she had intended. Michelle looked at her funny. Anna just smiled and went back inside.

A rainy night such as this, Anna thought, will be ideal for sleeping—and dreaming. She went to the front door and made sure it was locked. She had an impulse to look through the peephole but felt a chill down her spine—she didn't dare. A big crack of thunder shook the house. She stepped back from the door, sat down in the living room, and turned on the TV, wondering what country she and her world-traveling friend would visit next.

CHAPTER VII

A little bell rang, seemingly very far away.

Then another one, closer.

The next one dinged so close it could have been inside her head. It had come from her phone on the night table. Anna rolled over and stretched her arm to grab it.

Still groggy, she opened her eyes wide to see the time—already 10:30 a.m., and Michael had sent her three messages.

"Morning! Wondering if you're a fan of big Sunday breakfasts."

Followed by, "Just in case you woke up hungry and in the mood for eggs, bacon and pancakes."

And last, "So, breakfast for two then?"

Funny guy. If he knew how much she loved lavish Sunday break-fasts, he might not even find it cute. But they already had plans for Thursday. Too much, too early?

Nah, go for it. Whose rules are these anyway?

"Sure, why not? Always hungry on Sunday morning. Pick me up in one hour," she replied and quickly sprang into action. She needed her first cup of coffee of the day, like medicine, so she brewed it and drank it unceremoniously in the kitchen, then jumped in and out of the shower, blow-dried and brushed her hair, and put on some light makeup. She slipped into a teal summer dress and added a pair of rose-gold hoop earrings for the final touch. Ten minutes later, Michael came to pick her up.

The rain clouds from the night before had all but dissipated, and the sun blazed overhead unfettered in the bright blue sky. "Looks like it will be a hot one," Michael said as Anna got in the car.

Was he talking about the weather?

"That dress was made for you. You look gorgeous," he said before driving off.

"Thank you. You don't look half bad yourself." That black shirt did look great on him.

"Have you been to Rosemary's Diner?"

"Is that where we are going?" Anna asked. Of course, she knew the place—one her mom's favorite escapes. She used to take her and Frank, and she would sketch their portraits on napkins while they waited for their food. "I've been there for lunch, but never for breakfast."

"They have the greatest pancakes. And we got to have some bacon. It's the best."

They arrived in another ten minutes. Michael opened the door for her, and she stepped in, greeted by the mouthwatering smell of sizzling bacon, but also the aroma of freshly brewed coffee and the alluring smells of maple syrup and butter.

They were quickly shown to a table in the back and their waitress, a skinny brunette named Liz, went over the menu in detailed fashion, pointing out the diner's all-time favorites and specials of the day. She came back a few minutes later to take their order—scrambled eggs and bacon, sausage too, and toast, buttermilk pancakes, French toast, orange juice, and coffee; they wanted it all.

"We may have gone overboard with the food," he said, beginning to laugh. "Do you have a dog? They love bacon."

Anna shook her head. "I had a Labrador when I was a kid. How about you, any pets?"

"We had a Persian cat. My older sister, Allison, named her Jasmine, like the princess from the movie *Aladdin*; she was our Persian princess. Cute, right?"

"Very cute. Do you have other brothers and sisters?

"No, just her," he said.

"So, you and I are both youngest siblings."

"Yes, we are probably spoiled brats." Michael leaned forward as tiny wrinkles formed at the corners of his eyes. "Isn't that what they say?"

Liz came over and served their coffee, which smelled fantastic.

While putting brown sugar in her cup, Anna said, "I've read that youngest siblings tend to be more confident and willing to take risks. That could make one seem like a spoiled brat."

"So, we're not insufferable after all, then?"

"Well, you might be."

"Ha!" Michael's jolt of mirth rocked the table, coffee swaying perilously near the brim in both cups.

She loved a man with a sense of humor.

"But seriously, spoiled brats are made by parents who overprotect their children and hand them everything on a silver platter." She sipped her coffee and added, "I don't know about you, but I don't remember getting a darn thing on a silver platter."

"No, I don't either." Michael became pensive. "I'm sure Mom and Dad would have liked to hand me the world, though. They were great, just had terrible luck."

"Oh, I'm sorry. What happened to them?"

"My dad was a steelworker. All the overtime he could get, he worked, just to pay the bills and put food on the table. My mom had a few jobs but couldn't seem to hold on to any one job for long, and then she got sick. She was just forty-eight when she died from cancer; and Dad just…it just broke him."

Michael shifted uneasily in his seat. A smile tried to break through the fog clouding his face but retreated; his glassy eyes avoided a direct encounter with hers.

"Losing your mom so young must have been really hard for you. I can't even imagine that kind of heartache." As her words came out, Anna tried to imagine what it would feel like to lose her mother. Would it be sorrow, regret, anger? And her father, what would she feel if he dropped dead right now? The answers frightened her.

"Is your father still alive?" she asked.

"He died last year. He was sixty-nine. Went to bed one night and never woke up—heart failure. At least, he died peacefully. That's how I like to think about it."

"It's a comforting thought. May we be so lucky when our time comes."

"I have good memories of both Mom and Dad. We had our time together. We humans can't ask for more than that, right?"

Anna nodded. How could she avoid having to talk about her parents?

Michael gazed at her inquisitively while blindly pouring copious amounts of sugar into his cup of coffee.

"Whoa, should I go get some insulin?" Anna joked.

They laughed like kids laugh.

"I just like sweet things. Can't help it," he said with a charming little smirk.

"Is that right?"

How she loved his nerdy, awkward charm. Nothing like the witless dudes she'd made the mistake to date before. Some of them could've not named five US presidents.

She felt a sudden impulse to go over to his side, without saying a word, sit on his lap, and kiss him long and slow. So strong was her instinct that she could almost feel the warmth of his face pressed against hers.

Though she hadn't even moved, Anna wondered if her gaze could have given away her impish thoughts. Embarrassed, she looked away, pretending to check out the place. The entire time, she sensed Michael's eyes on her.

If only she could read his mind. There was an attraction between them, that much she knew; but could this be the beginning of a meaningful relationship? Was his interest in her only skin-deep, or was he craving to peek into her soul?

Was she even letting him peek, though? Of course, she wasn't. Why not tell him right now about that awful dream? Nothing's more intimate than one's fears.

Okay, that's insane, she now scolded herself. Yes, go ahead and tell him everything—that your father is the devil incarnate, and your mother a tortured soul. That's the hot mess where you came from, a dysfunction supernova. Let him take a peek at that and see what happens. He'll run like a gazelle that's just stared into the eyes of a hungry lion.

A subtle smile crept up on Michael's face.

"What?" Anna asked. Gosh, had she had a funny look on her face or something?

He leaned back, running a hand through his hair. "Just enjoying watching you lost in thought, holding your cup of coffee, your gaze set on some distant point, and that intriguing intensity in your eyes."

She laughed nervously. "Wow, that's…the way you described me…you, um, seem to be rather perceptive."

"I can be, but only if the subject truly captures my interest."

"So you find me interesting then?"

"That would be an understatement." Michael grinned, one hand behind his neck. "But I think you already knew that."

A warm flush rose from her chest to her neck and cheeks. She let out a sound of mild surprise.

"Hope that wasn't—"

"I liked it," she interrupted him.

Michael's face lit up. He picked up a saltshaker from the table for no apparent reason.

A moment of silence. Not uncomfortable but somehow intimate.

"You know, it was nice hearing about your childhood," Anna said.

"I bet yours was very different."

"So very different, yes. I envy yours."

"Really?" he asked.

"Mine was the complete opposite. Money was never an issue. That, we had plenty of. And yet I bet that your family, your home, your childhood, were much happier than mine."

Michael leaned forward with his arms on the table and his eyes wide open, fixed on her.

Anna continued. "You know who my father was, but all you have is a name—Victor Goddard, son of Charles Goddard. Big fish in a small fishbowl. But the man, the husband, the father; that's a whole different matter. He's my father, and it pains me to speak ill of him, but the plain truth is that I only remember him as a deeply selfish, arrogant, and cruel man."

Anna paused to sip her coffee, avoiding eye contact with Michael. She could feel her hands beginning to shake.

"I'm so sorry that you have to feel that way about your father," Michael said. "No daughter should have to feel like that about her dad."

His thoughtful words were comforting. Reassured, she carried on speaking.

"He poisoned my childhood." Anna tried stave off the tears that she already sensed were on the way. "He made Frank and I feel like burdens he was forced to carry, unloved and unwanted. I could never understand it. He seemed constantly disappointed in us. Frank got interested in music, not sports, which is what Dad would've wanted. And me, well, I don't think he ever wanted a daughter at all. I disappointed him right at birth."

"That's so sad," he said.

"With other people, he's a different person, always preoccupied with his public image. I remember how he faked fatherly pride, even love. He painted a smile of contentment on his face, made us hold hands, and never missed church, constantly posing for a postcard picture someone might be taking."

"How about your mom? How did he treat her?"

"I have some early memories of him happy with Mom, but they are rather foggy, and I often wonder if I imagined those moments. Mostly, I remember Dad treating Mom like she was his property, and not a highly valued one at that. He humiliated her constantly. I don't want to go into all the grimy details, but he was awful to her. Still is."

Anna had told him much more than she had intended. She'd flung the door wide open.

"I can probably only begin to understand the full tragedy of it all. It's not fair what they did to you."

"They?" Anna asked, resenting the judgment on her mother.

Michael looked down at the table, as if searching for the answer there, then looked her in the eye. "No doubt your father was the villain, but your mother should have stopped it, for her own sake and yours. She could've divorced him. She could have sought help if she was scared…I'm sorry, I feel like I'm overstepping here. I don't want to upset you."

"I get what you're saying. And you're right. Mom should have done something."

Liz had just arrived with their bountiful breakfast—it was a sight to behold. The two stacks of pancakes looked amazing, golden, and fluffy; the French toasts also looked delicious, the scrambled eggs were soft and creamy, and the bacon was crispy perfection. With a sunny smile and careful, delicate motions, Liz put everything nicely on the table, went back to the kitchen, and returned a moment later with the coffee pot to top off their coffee.

"They didn't disappoint," Anna said, biting into a strip of bacon. "Oh, this tastes like heaven."

"I know. It's so good." He poured lots of syrup on his pancakes, cut a wedge from the stack, and put it in his mouth. He closed his eyes in ecstasy.

"Here we go, pigging out again," Anna said, breaking into laughter.

"No half measures; let's pig out like royalty," Michael said. And indeed, they ate greedily and unabashedly, laughing at their own gluttony without a care, as if they had known each other for years.

Between bites, they got to talk about Frank. Michael seemed rather curious about him, probably because she held him in such high regard. She described him as a highly principled man who at the same time could be cynical, quick to anger, and impulsive—a combination of attributes that Michael found rather interesting. Anna herself often thought him a puzzle, a singularity that could only have emerged from the flames of his childhood. From time to time, she also pondered how that same furnace might have shaped her.

Time flew by. Soon every face around them was new, and they were all having lunch. She was stunned to realize that it was past 1:00 p.m. already.

Getting ready to leave, Anna saw that she'd received a message from an out of state phone number. "Anna, this is your cousin, Diane. Could you call me around 2 pm?"

"Everything all right?" asked Michael.

"Just perfect, actually. It's Diane—she just texted me."

"Wow, that's great. You could still get her to call her mother today, on her birthday."

Anna instantly felt terrible about that lie she'd told him only the day before, but she reasoned that to come clean now would only make matters worse. To remove a lie, one must be willing to show what that lie has been hiding, and Anna wasn't quite ready to tell Michael the real reason why she'd urgently needed to find her cousin.

They'd just walked out the diner's door. Anna stopped and turned to him. "I'm so grateful for your help finding my cousin."

"I'm very happy I did," he said, his lips curling up into a smile. She wanted to kiss those lips. She imagined the kiss and could almost taste it.

Would he try to kiss her? He looked like he wanted to, and she wouldn't have stopped him. But the moment had passed, and they were walking to the car.

It was a quiet drive back to her place. She kept thinking about that kiss that didn't happen outside of the diner. Michael seemed lost in thought; his eyes were on the road, but his mind was somewhere else. A moment later, they arrived at her house, and Michael pulled into the driveway.

"This was wonderful. I had a great time," Anna said, leisurely taking off her seatbelt.

"I truly enjoyed this time with you. I can't wait until Thursday night."

"Yeah, me too." She leaned toward him for a kiss on the cheek. He leaned toward her, and they met in the middle. She kissed his cheek softly and started to pull back slowly, feeling the stubs of his beard brushing against the side of her lips and chin. She felt him slowly turning his gaze toward her, until they were face to face, staring into each other's eyes, their noses nearly touching, and then they were kissing. Anna finished up with a gentle tug on his lower lip as she pulled back.

"Best breakfast ever," she said in a smoky voice.

"I'm afraid to wake up right now, alone," he said.

"You too, huh?"

"I'll be counting the days till Thursday."

"Me too. Until then," she said.

"Until then."

She got off the car and walked straight to her front door, not looking back, smiling all the way until she was inside. There she stood for a moment with her back to the door reliving the moment.

The thought of Diane intruded into her mind, like an alarm going off. She saw that it was past 1:30 p.m. and hastened to send a reply to her cousin, "Hi Diane, it's sure great to hear from you. I'll call you in half an hour."

The minutes dragged on as Anna sat around waiting for the clock to strike two. She tried to read, but she couldn't really focus on the story and kept having to reread entire passages. She fell to fretting about what she was going to say to Diane. I believe your mother had an affair with my father—would she say it like that? Seemed awfully raw.

The moment she realized that she needed more time to work out how to soften the blow to Diane, time seemed to speed up. Two o'clock came, and Anna wasn't any closer to deciding how to tell her cousin about her appalling suspicion, but she made the phone call anyway. They'd have plenty to talk about before she addressed the dreaded subject.

The first part of their conversation went as one might expect from two cousins who had not talked for over two years. Anna explained to Diane, though rather cursorily, how she got a hold of her resume, a story Diane found remarkable.

"I'm sorry you had to go to such lengths to find me," Diane said with a note of shame in her voice. She didn't offer any explanations regarding her vanishing, though.

Anna didn't explain right away her sudden need to locate her. Instead, they chatted for a long while about Diane's decision to become a nurse, her job at the hospital, and about Boston. Also Frank's engagement to Sarah—it was too important not to mention.

Eventually, their small talk ran out of steam and Anna had the opening she'd been both looking for and dreading.

"Diane, there's something I need to talk to you about."

"Yes, you said so in your email. I've been wondering about it. Judging by the way you downplayed it in your email, I expect it is rather serious. Am I right?"

"Yes, you might be, although my sincere hope is that I'm wrong about everything. There's nothing I'd want more than to hear you say I'm being ridiculous."

"Holy shit. Okay, Anna, let's hear it then."

"I don't know how else to say this, so I'm just going to come out with it." Anna paused and took a deep breath, then closed her eyes and forced herself to say the words, "I have reason to believe my father and your mother may have had an affair."

Silence, a frozen vacuum of anticipation.

Anna braced herself for an over-the-top emotional reaction from Diane. Instead, her brief silence was followed by a deep breath and a collected response, "I'd be lying if I told you I don't believe it's possible. Sadly, I know my mother is capable of very selfish actions; and from there, it's a short, downhill path to wickedness."

"I was afraid you might say something like that."

"So, what makes you think this affair happened?"

Anna wished she had this chronicle recorded so that she could just hit play and have Diane listen to it, instead of having to relive the whole darn thing all over again.

Her mother's text message made quite an impression on her. Anna's conversation with her mother in the garden, on the other hand, didn't impress her much.

The matter of the high school photographs seemed to stir Diane considerably.

"Okay, that's really creepy," she said. "When do you think this affair between them may have actually happened?"

"We think it happened recently."

"We?"

"Frank and I."

"Frank knows about this?" Diane asked.

"Yes, of course."

"And why do you think it happened recently?"

"Because your mom's message seems to refer to something they've just done."

Diane seemed suddenly agitated. "But they may have been lovers for years, for many years, in fact. I mean, they dated in high school. Had you not thought about that?"

Her words stung a little. "You're right—it's possible. I guess I didn't want to believe it could be that bad."

"I'm sorry to have talked to you like that just now. You're just the messenger here. You didn't ask for this crap."

"It's quite all right," Anna responded, moved by Diane's show of compassion, a quality she didn't recall her displaying ever before. "This is pretty heavy stuff I'm laying on you."

"Yes, it is," Diane said. "I wish I could tell you that you're crazy and laugh it off, like you wanted me to, but the evidence is distressing." She paused. "Listen, I must tell you there's something I saw once. At the time, I thought it was bizarre, but I didn't have anything else to connect it to. I was only fifteen.

"My mom and I had been arguing about something, pretty much like any other day. I remember she was talking to someone on the phone and locked herself in her room. A while later, she came out, dressed up nicely. I was sitting on a rocking chair we had, listening to music. She walked past me and told me that there was food in the fridge and that she would be back in a couple of hours. She didn't say where she was going. I thought she seemed restless, but I was mad at her right then and said nothing.

"Then I heard a car pull over in front of the building—our apartment was on a second floor. I went to the balcony and saw Mom getting into a black car with a man, a blond man that looked like Uncle Victor.

"I was never sure, though. I asked Mom later who she'd gone out with; someone from work, she said. Seemed annoyed that I even asked. I supposed it couldn't have been Uncle Victor. It just didn't make any sense to me. I figured it must have been some other blond guy who just happened to look like him."

"Was the car a Mercedes Benz?" Anna asked.

"It may have been. I don't know. It was a nice car."

"Dad has a black Mercedes Benz. He's had it for at least ten years. He loves that car."

"That's messed up. Now, I think it really was him," Diane said.

"This is a nightmare. What are we going to do? We can't just turn our backs on this thing, don't you think?"

"No, you're right, it is too awful. We need to get to the bottom of this. Should we just confront them with what we know?"

"Most of it is inconclusive if you think about it," Anna explained. "Your mom's message is the most solid piece of evidence we have, but only I saw it. Frank and you only have my word. The high school photographs don't prove that they've had an affair, but only that they dated in high school. My chat with Mom, strange as it was, is even less consequential. Your memory of your mom getting in a black car, which may have been a Mercedes, with a blond man, who may have been my father—that could be really something, if you were certain."

"But I'm not," said Diane.

"Exactly. And confronting them without conclusive evidence could backfire. We could end up looking pretty stupid, and then we'd really have to let the whole thing go."

"You might be right. So, what now?"

"I'm not sure, but I think the three of us—Frank, you and me— could figure it out together. What do you think?"

"Yes, I think so. Should we do a three-way call later?" Diane asked.

"No more calls. Let's meet. I want to see you anyway. It's been over two years. Plus, I've never been to Boston, and it is high time I started going places. I'm sure Frank would love the idea. How does that sound to you?"

"I'd be very happy if you visited me, even if we have to deal with this nasty business. My apartment is tiny, but—"

"Oh, you need not worry about that," Anna interjected. "We'll stay in a hotel."

"Really? Because I could—"

"No, really, we'll be fine."

"Okay then," said Diane. "How about next weekend? I get off work around four p.m. on Saturday, and I'm free on Sunday."

"Sounds good. I'll talk to Frank."

"Great, I'll send you my address. I'm glad you tracked me down, Anna."

"Yeah, me too."

The instant Anna ended the call, she sent Frank a string of text messages about the conversation with Diane and the proposed trip. She laid back on the couch, mentally exhausted. She worried that she might fall asleep and wake up in some bizarre dreamscape.

She jumped off the couch, grabbed her book and some water, and headed to the deck. It was nice out there. The memory of that kiss in Michael's car interrupted her reading, but the intruder was quite welcome.

CHAPTER VIII

Thursday finally came. Anna put in her time at work and said goodbye to the school. For the next three weeks, she would be on vacation. She'd visited Frank the night before, mostly to plan their upcoming trip to Boston. Sarah would be joining them, Frank announced. He also suggested, though Anna thought it may have been in jest, that she should invite Michael. She hadn't even considered that possibility—seemed too early for that.

She was filled with anticipation about her night out with Michael. She had even bought a pair of black ankle boots—they'd look perfect with black jeans and a white blouse with open shoulders.

He came to pick her up right on time. Anna received him at the door with a little kiss on the lips and asked him to come in for a moment; she'd been finishing up her makeup.

They left the house at eight fifteen. The night bestowed upon them ideal conditions for a leisurely drive with the top down; they had clear skies, a pleasant, balmy breeze, and even a full moon, casting an ethereal light over all things, making it all absurdly beautiful. Holding down her hair with one hand, Anna took furtive glances at Michael, studying his moonlit figure. His eyes riveted on hers a few times.

They arrived at the Fox's Den just before nine. Moving past the place's minimalist facade, they came into a spacious interior, delightfully decorated with guitars and various memorabilia. On a small stage the nineties cover band seemed about ready to begin. A large crowd had already gathered, but they were able to grab a table in the nick of time.

Anna started out with a margarita, and Michael got a mojito. Shortly thereafter, the band started playing Pearl Jam's song "Jeremy," a song Frank had played for her many times. She started singing along, and Michael quickly joined her. He did his utmost to imitate the deep, soulful voice of Pearl Jam's lead singer, Eddie Vedder, which Anna thoroughly enjoyed.

His singing voice really wasn't all that bad; she could envision him putting on a good show on karaoke night with Frank and Sarah. She surprised herself a little, already thinking about Michael in that way.

Meanwhile, the band had started playing Nirvana's "About a Girl." Other timeless classics followed—The Smashing Pumpkins' "Disarm," The Offspring's "Come Out and Play," and Collective Soul's "Shine." Anna and Michael sang together every song. While the music made meaningful conversation nearly impossible, she felt that they were connecting at a much more primal level.

The band's female guitar player stepped forward, taking the place of the lead singer. The crowd erupted in euphoria as she began playing the distinctive guitar intro of the song "Zombie" by the Cranberries.

Anna loved that song—she knew it by heart and sang it from beginning to end. The entire time Michael watched her absorbedly and, she imagined, lustfully.

The dim light enshrouded him in a veil of mystery.

Another mojito. Another margarita.

She was starting to feel a little tipsy, so she'd better take it slow. They announced that the band would be taking a brief break.

"This band is awesome. Thanks for bringing me here," she said.

Michael mixed his drink, sparkly eyes alternating between her eyes and her bare shoulders. "I'm having a great time, and I could watch you sing all night."

"How's your work?" she asked, instantly regretting bringing that up.

"Dull as hell," he said, laughing. "But on a related note, I've started writing an article that I hope to publish in a journal."

"That sounds exciting. What is it about?"

"You might be surprised because it's a far cry from the local history articles I've written before, you know, the ones nobody reads."

"Ooh, I'm already interested." Anna set her elbows on the table, chin resting on her thumbs.

Let's listen to the handsome professor.

"Okay, the article is…about a what-if scenario—what if F. D. Roosevelt had lived another four or five years. And, of course, it's as much about Harry Truman as it is about Roosevelt, because Truman only became president in 1945, at the worst possible time, because of Roosevelt's death. Two radically different men, at a time when it mattered too much who was president of the United States.

"I'm convinced that Roosevelt's death and the rise of Truman changed this country, and the world. To be honest, others have already argued both sides of this debate, but I will do so with a special angle, inferring from Roosevelt's decisions during his time as president the decisions he might have made in 1945 and beyond. Hope I'm not boring you."

Anna sipped her margarita. "Not at all. Sounds like a great article, very compelling. I'd like to be the first to read it when it's finished." She fiddled with the top button on her blouse as though she might undo it.

Laying his arms flat on the table, Michael inched closer to her. "Or better yet, you could critique my first draft."

"I'm flattered," she said.

"You're obviously very smart, and I could use the free labor."

Anna leaned a tad closer to him. If he breathed hard, she'd feel it. "Oh, I'll be sure to get something in exchange."

"Whatever you desire," he said softly, slowly, like honey dripping off a spoon.

"Are you quite sure? I'm a greedy girl."

"Greedy?"

"Greedy for life, if that's a thing," she said.

"I get it. You want more from life—more intensity, more adventure, more freedom."

"And how do you know that about me?"

"You favor new adventures instinctively. You have none of the brutal pragmatism of a conformist. You want life with the top down."

"Clever. The poet strikes back." Anna pulled back a little and took a sip of her margarita, never taking her eyes off of his. "I do want more. If we only get to live this one life, I want to feel alive every day, not just wake up still alive every day."

"And what would make you feel alive every day?"

"I'm not sure yet, or I'd be doing it," she said. "I think I need to leave this place, though."

"There's got to be more to it than a place. What do you need that you can't have here?"

Anna had to think for a moment. What a profound question that was. "A clean break," she said. "Living here, walking these same streets, I'm but the second chapter in the story of a sad girl. I want to become a new book, full of crazy, unexpected chapters."

"I know exactly what you mean. I myself sometimes daydream about having a whole different life; not that I'm suggesting that you're a daydreamer too."

"But I am, and it's nothing to be ashamed of. Daydreaming is how the soul rehearses for happy moments. What have you been daydreaming about lately?"

Michael looked keenly at her, running a hand through the back of his head. "Respected scholar has been a recurring alter ego of mine."

"I like it. Respected scholar: it has a nice ring to it. Is that why you're writing a scholarly article with the intent of getting it published in an academic journal?"

"Actually, I've been toying with the idea of applying for admission to a PhD program next year. Having one or two articles published could really help my chances."

"Bravo!" Anna gave his hand a little squeeze. "Of course, you should. Obviously, it's what you want to do, so go for it."

"How about you? Is getting out of here something you might do anytime soon?"

Anna leaned forward, looked him in the eye and replied with playful emphasis, "Hmm, I don't know. Do you think I should?"

"It's what you want, but I'd really hate it," Michael said in a voice that got lower and huskier toward the end.

"Would you really, really hate it?" she said, infusing her voice with both innocence and seductiveness.

"I'd hate it so much," he whispered, leaning in toward her until their faces were perfectly positioned for a kiss.

Anna closed the distance to within a breath of his lips and locked eyes with him. Michael cupped her cheek in his hand and met her lips with his. He kissed her delicately at first, but there was a raw intensity, an urgency, building up behind his tenderness and restraint. She parted her lips, inciting his invasion, which rushed in like a river of sweetness. She lost herself in the lingering kiss. She felt weightless, as if floating away, and her body tingled all over.

A blaring guitar intro startled Anna back into full awareness, and she was reminded of the crowd that surrounded them. She gently pulled away from Michael. No words came from him, but a smitten look on his face told her everything she needed to know. Anna didn't intend to spoil the moment with needless commentary either. She let their eloquent silence simmer a while longer.

The band closed out their show with a string of popular songs from the likes of Soundgarden, Radiohead, Oasis, and Alice in Chains. They also played Alanis Morissette's "You Oughta Know," which Krista—that was the name of their female guitar player—sang with searing passion, convincingly radiating the raw emotions that her audience craved. The band was done playing around midnight.

They stayed for almost another hour and talked about their favorite artists and songs, favorite movies and series. Anna's most adored movies were romantic dramas like *Pride and Prejudice*, while Michael loved high-octane espionage movies such as *Mission Impossible* and *The*

Bourne Identity, but they also had some favorite movies in common, like *Jerry Maguire*, which they planned to watch together sometime soon.

They kissed again in the car before leaving the parking lot. This time, his hands got a little busier, coming down from her neck and shoulders to wander up and down her back, and sliding under her arms, where a disoriented thumb crossed the forbidden frontier to the edge of her breast. The thin, silky fabric of her blouse did nothing to stop the jolts of electricity that his fingers sent rushing through her skin.

On the way back to town, Anna's anticipation turned into sweet, intoxicating tension. She felt like a college girl all over again. Life with the top down, he'd said—indeed, she wanted that, she wanted it now, with him.

What they talked about in the car Anna would hardly remember later. She'd been thinking about what would happen fifteen, then ten, then five minutes later when they arrived at her house. And then they did.

Michael pulled into her driveway. Not two seconds later, they were kissing with an unmistakable hunger. Her hand was resting just above his knee, and then it was moving, as if commanded by a force beyond her control, very slowly and delicately up his thigh.

"Do you want to come in?" she whispered in his ear. He uttered his acceptance in a soft, breathy voice and carried on kissing her lips, her cheek, and her neck. Melting in his arms, she barely managed to regain control and pull out of his embrace. "Come on," she said, getting out of the car.

Anna fumbled with her keys for a moment, found the right one, and opened the front door. The lights had stayed on from when they'd left earlier. Michael walked in behind her and locked the door.

They gazed at each other in silence. She wanted him. She hadn't wanted anyone like this in a long time.

He came close to her and would've said something, but Anna silenced him with a sweet, long, sensual kiss that progressed into a hungry exploration. Michael's hands avidly explored her waist and hips. She pulled on him and pressed her body to his while deepening her kiss.

As if by an unknown law of physics, they had pushed and tugged their way almost to Anna's bedroom. She was now with her back to a wall. He grew bolder and undid the top button on her blouse, and then another, and another. His hands now eagerly explored her body while he kissed her and tasted the bare skin of her neck and shoulders. Her senses were overwhelmed; she felt warm all over.

She pushed Michael against the opposite wall and looked into his eyes boldly, almost defiantly, while she unbuttoned his shirt and his pants. She kissed him slowly and deeply as she ran her hand from his neck, shoulders, and chest, down to his abdomen, and then lower. She pulled back from his lips to look at his face and his eyes. He was conquered, lost in sweet surrender to her touch.

She pulled him into the bedroom and pushed him onto her bed. With deliberate movements, she removed her boots and slipped off her jeans. The way Michael looked at her made her feel like a goddess sent down to Earth to possess his body and soul. She invaded him in bed, and they became a single, perfect symphony of lustful abandon.

Afterward, Anna laid next to him, wrapping her legs and arms around him, giving him little kisses on the lips, cheeks, and neck. They must have been like that for a few minutes when, on the verge of dozing off, Anna asked him, "Would you like to go to Boston with me this weekend?"

CHAPTER IX

"Finally, I get to meet you, Michael, the historian," Frank said warmly, approaching him with his hand outstretched, which Michael quickly met in a firm handshake.

"And I get to meet Frank Goddard, the rock star," Michael said.

"Oh, come on, just call me Frank…Sinatra!" They both laughed.

Anna would have loved to have cameras recording the scene for her to analyze later. Never had Anna seen her brother more excited to meet a boyfriend of hers. He'd seemed ecstatic when she told him the day before, a bit embarrassed, that she'd invited Michael to go with them.

Meanwhile, this was the first time Anna had seen Sarah since her engagement to Frank. They dashed toward each other and met in a heart-warming embrace.

"I don't even know what to say," Anna said. "We were already friends. Now, we'll be sisters."

"Oh, thank you Anna. I'm so happy." Sarah's voice was full of emotion. When Anna stepped back from their embrace, she saw that her future sister in law had teared up. She was truly a gentle soul. What a great complement for the raging storm that was Frank.

"Here, let me introduce you to my…um, boyfriend?" She lowered her voice for that last part, not wanting Michael to hear it. She was suddenly embarrassed. "We're definitely dating, but it's still pretty new," she said, still in a hushed voice.

"Ah, not to worry. Labels are a clumsy thing. You like him, he likes you, and here you're together. And can I just say, good job, girl. He's cute."

"He isn't bad looking, is he?" For a split second, Anna giggled like a schoolgirl. "Well, come on, I'll introduce you."

Michael had been sharing a laugh with Frank about who knows what when Anna and Sarah joined them.

Anna said, "Michael, this is Sarah, Frank's fiancé; Sarah, this is Michael."

"It is a pleasure to meet you," said Sarah.

"The pleasure is mine," said Michael.

Frank held his fiancé in a way that would've made for a perfect picture had she been ready to take it. Sarah was a beautiful woman in her own peculiar way. Hers was a petite, slender body, though not devoid of curves. Her skin was quite pale. She had really big hazel eyes, framed by black hair as dark as a raven's feathers, a large forehead, and a curious nose that was very thin—some would say too thin to stand between those huge eyes of hers—and appeared to point slightly down. Her lips were full and seemed constantly eager to smile. These unusual features gave her a quirky look, but that's what made her especially pretty, like a porcelain doll.

"We better get going," said Frank.

"Yes, we can talk in the car. It's a long way to Boston," Anna said, starting for the door.

They went downstairs and toward Anna's car. She unlocked the doors and got in first. Frank and Sarah got in the back seat, which left Michael with the front passenger seat.

"Whatever you hear back here, don't look back," Frank said as Anna backed out of the parking space and drove away.

"He's kidding, of course," Sarah said.

"No, I'm not. It's a long trip. I'm bound to get hungry, and you smell delicious."

Anna tittered. Michael also laughed. *This started well,* she thought. She looked at Frank through the rearview mirror and saw him looking back at her with a clever smile. She gave him that same look she'd given him a thousand times before, the one meaning, *Are you going to be trouble?* She knew that he was bursting with energy and would get talkative, which could go in any direction.

"Michael," Frank began. "Which time and place in history you've enjoyed studying the most? Which one you find most fascinating?"

"I don't know if I would call it fascinating, but I'm fairly obsessed with World War II."

"Hmm, I agree, lots of angles to explore, right?"

"For sure." Michael turned his head and shoulders, attempting to make eye contact with Frank, but he was sitting right behind him.

Frank had his topic picked out for him. "I've always been intrigued by Hitler's rise to power, as a sociological phenomenon. I mean, Germany today is a very progressive country. And yet that same country—what?—eighty years ago supported Hitler's dictatorship and his war."

"Actually, it's rather complex how that came to be. It took Hitler a lot of political maneuvering, deception, and intimidation of his opponents to finally ascend to power. But, yes, he did manage to amass considerable popular support. What's most scary is that this was a country that already had democratic institutions and a diverse society before the rise of Hitler."

"Exactly, so how did he do it?" asked Frank.

"Well, he knew how to exploit people's fears and frustrations; and he managed to silence a divided field of political opposition. He was a cunning politician, and a bully."

"There's a lesson for us there, don't you think?" Frank asked.

"Oh, definitely. Something like that could have happened anywhere, could happen again, and could happen to us. All you need is enough frustration, fear, ignorance, and hatred. The cunning manipulator is just the final ingredient."

"Irrational thoughts are the strings by which the puppeteers control their subjects."

"That's very true," said Michael. "Who wrote that?"

"I just came up with, but really, you did."

"Well, you sure summed it up perfectly."

"There's irrational thinking aplenty in our own country," Anna interposed, suddenly overcome with an impulse to challenge the oracles. "How come we haven't seen an oppressive regime installed in America?"

"Would we even know if we were sliding into one?" Frank asked.

"Good question," Michael said somberly.

"Michael, would I be correct in saying that the only way to guarantee social progress is to eradicate irrational thinking, which engenders anger and hatred?"

Anna looked through the corner of her eye at the rearview mirror and saw Frank looking at Michael, awaiting his response. He'd keep this up until his curiosity was fully satisfied. He wanted to measure him up. Hopefully he wouldn't take things too far.

"It would be amazing if we could do away with most of the irrational thinking that plagues us, but whenever we start talking about eradicating a group's perspectives, however backward they might be, we risk becoming a version of what we are trying to defeat."

Anna tried to suppress the little smile creeping up on her face. If this was going to become a debate between these two men, some primeval ritual disguised as intellectual exchange, she must remain neutral.

"Maybe eradicate is too strong a word," Frank said. "What I mean is that we must fight disinformation with facts, and irrationality with reason."

Michael nodded. "True, and that's an uphill battle because irrationality and zeal tend to go hand in hand."

"Ah, brilliant. The more unreasonable and absurd the beliefs, the more irrevocably attached to them people become."

Michael chuckled. "You have a way with words, Frank."

Frank kept on, "Religious fundamentalism is the most glaring example. Believers encapsulate themselves in dangerous fantasy worlds where it's okay to deny even the most basic scientific facts if they threaten their literal interpretation of scripture. Some have even taken their kids out of school so that they won't learn science. Some contributors to society they are creating!"

Michael laughed heartily. "Yeah, I get you man. That stuff bothers me too—it does. But how do you combat that without attacking religion in general?" A warm, earnest tone of voice had replaced Michael's scholarly manner.

"Well, sometimes, I wonder if religion itself must be overcome for humanity to achieve its true potential. All it does is divide us. Think of all the wars and violence religions have justified throughout our history. It's a hefty price we have paid just so that people can ease their anxiety about death."

"I take it you're an atheist, then."

"Yes, I certainly am. Aren't you?"

Michael answered after a brief pause, "A historian being a true believer of religious dogma would be every bit as contradictory as an evolutionary scientist being one."

Anna felt like partaking in the conversation. "I still think that someone or something must have pushed the red button on that big bang that got everything going. I don't know. Maybe God grew tired of us a while ago. Who knows? Maybe he's busy creating a better version of us on some other planet."

Michael had a quizzical look on his face, half amused, and half stunned.

Frank threw himself back and laughed hysterically, like a mad hyena. "Ah, that's funny, and dark, and then funny all over again—like a layered dessert. Brilliant!"

Sarah shuffled in her seat and began speaking slowly with an inkling of subdued irritation. "Well, if it's my turn, I'm a harmless Catholic who goes to church occasionally and sort of abides by the teachings of the church; I'm not a saint, but probably a solid candidate for purgatory—ha! Now, Frank, stop torturing us with your atheist inquisition. I'm not quite ready to believe that when I die, that's it, like a bird or a dog."

"Oh baby, we are just talking. You said something important just now. We humans are cursed with the awareness of our own mortality, and it sucks! Our minds cannot comprehend not existing—it's terrifying. So religion came to fix that with promises of eternal life. Being an atheist is staring into the abyss without blindfolds."

"I think I'll take a nap now, while you guys decode all of life's mysteries," said Sarah.

"Ooh, you're feisty today! Come here." A loud smooch was heard. "We'll change the subject immediately, my queen. What shall we discuss next? Art, perhaps?"

"Talk about whatever you want. Just lay off politics and religion. Jesus! That's common sense, isn't it? Discussing politics and religion leads to disagreements and hurt feelings."

"It can lead to bruised faces and broken bones, too—I should know."

They were all silent for a moment.

"What was that about bruised faces and broken bones?" Michael asked.

"Oh, um, right…" Frank made eye contact with Anna through the rearview mirror. "Have you told Michael about…"

"About Dad?" Anna finished the question. "Yes, I've given Michael some idea of the not-so-great dad he was to us." She tried to communicate to Frank, with her eyes, the importance of steering off the subject as swiftly as possible.

"Yes, well, I don't want to go too deep into that rabbit hole, but let's just say that Dad was not fond of debate. He mostly enjoyed us agreeing with him on everything and didn't take well to his son challenging his opinion on religion, politics, or what to have for breakfast."

"And when you did, he beat you up?"

"Yeah, he did beat me up a couple of times. You could say I wasn't a fast learner."

"Sounds like you had it pretty rough. Anna, in your line of work, you probably see a lot of kids with tough situations that you can identify with, right?"

"Toxic parents. Abusive parents. Disgusting relatives. Yes, I've seen it all."

Anna paused for a moment, collecting her thoughts. "A few months back, there was this eleven-year-old kid that had been displaying extreme anxiety. Every time he got a C, or even a B-minus on a test, he would cry his eyes out. It just wasn't normal. It got to the point where teachers dreaded giving him any grade below a B-plus. So, I met with him a few times and he kept saying that his father was a very stern perfectionist and that he punished him for any bad grades. He wouldn't say anything more.

"One time, I asked him how his father punished him, and he looked down and thought for a while, too long, before responding. He said his father grounded him and took away his computer, but I knew that was a lie. And so, I asked the kid's father to come to the school to meet with me.

"The man came. He was short but built like a tank, and his face looked aggressive the entire time he was there with me. He gave me the creeps. I told him about his son's excessive anxiety over his academic performance and the crying fits. After listening for a long while to this guy's empty talk about building character and stuff like that, I asked him directly about how he reprimanded the kid. He recited scripture to me! He gave me a hideous righteous smile, and said, 'Do not withhold discipline from a child; if you strike him with a rod, he will not die.' I looked it up later; it's from the book of Proverbs.

"Anyway, the day after I met with his father, the kid shows up and asks me to please never ask his dad to come to the school again. I asked him why and he said that his father had gotten very angry. Right then, I noticed a red spot on the underside of his left arm, partially covered by the sleeve of his shirt. I asked him to pull up his sleeve, and that's when I saw a fresh, big nasty bruise.

"I talked to the school director, and we got the Department of Social Services involved in the matter. The bruise we saw was only the tip of the iceberg. This kid's father had repeatedly lashed him with a leather belt, and he had bruises all over his back. And that had been only the latest of several beatings."

As Anna concluded her story, she felt a knot on her throat, and her voice faltered. "Ugh, I really shouldn't have told you that story."

"Oh my God, that's horrible," said Sarah. "I don't think I could ever do what you do for a living. It would kill me."

Michael seemed stirred. "I'm not sure that I could, either," he said. "What made you want to be a school psychologist?"

"I just wanted to help kids learn to cope with the hard stuff life throws at them. I mean, a lot of kids have great childhoods, full of love and precious memories; but that, which seems like a human right to me, is denied to many children. Life is hard enough. A happy childhood should be part of the deal. You get one guaranteed happy season. Good luck with the rest."

"And that happy childhood was denied to you? Do you feel that way?" Michael asked.

"I do. I do feel that way. Very much so." Anna felt like a little girl answering Michael's question. The same strange sensation of vulnerability from her dream possessed her for a moment, and she sensed that she was wide open, that she had bared her soul, and now, all could see the sad, scared little girl, and her anger.

No one spoke for the better part of the next ten minutes. Anna kept looking straight at the road. She was well aware that Michael was looking at her, but she wanted to be left alone with her thoughts for a while. She couldn't help resenting Michael for that pointed question. She felt dissected, scrutinized, like one of his topics for discussion.

She peeped at Frank through the rearview mirror and saw him looking back at her with a smile that brimmed with approval, complicity, and satisfaction.

For the next couple of hours, they only had fragments of conversation, mostly initiated by Sarah, and focused primarily on the scenery and things of interest they passed on the road. They drove through some beautiful mountain scenery, which prompted Sarah to reminisce about a trip she had taken with her parents to the Smoky Mountains when she was sixteen years old. That got them talking for a good fifteen minutes. Anna and Michael took turns asking Sarah questions about the trip and her parents. She'd grown up an only child, and though she had evidently tried to play it down, it was clear that her childhood had been blissful, something to be envied.

As soon as they crossed the Massachusetts state line, Frank suggested stopping for lunch. "Am I the only one here who is starving?" he asked. He wasn't. Anna herself had had a light breakfast and was quick to endorse her brother's proposition. Sarah suggested stopping at a burger joint, an idea that appeared to be to everyone's liking.

Walking from the parking lot to the restaurant, Frank caught up to Anna and whispered to her ear, "I like this dude. He has substance, and Dad would fucking hate him." He sniggered heartily, hiding his face behind her, like a teenager.

They had their burgers and fries and milkshakes too. Later, in the car, Sarah leaned on Frank and dozed off. It wasn't long before Frank was asleep too. Michael leaned toward Anna and kissed her bare shoulder tenderly.

"You've been kind of quiet. Are you okay?" he asked.

"Yes, I'm...fine. Just lost in my own thoughts."

"Did I maybe say something out of order? I feel like I may have."

"Um, not really. I'm a bit complicated sometimes. You're liable to trip a booby trap every now and then through no fault of your own."

"So, I did say something, then."

"I guess I'm used to sitting exclusively on the psychologist's chair. I'm not too comfortable sitting on the opposite side, getting analyzed."

"Ah, I had a feeling that I had crossed a line. I'm sorry. I really am. I can get carried away with my curiosity, and as you must know, I am especially curious about you."

"It's great that you're curious, and even greater that you're curious about me. Don't censor yourself on my account. I don't want you to feel like you need to be walking on eggshells around me. That wouldn't be healthy. I'd rather we risked having an argument than risk being over-cautious and dull." Anna looked through the rearview mirror to confirm that Frank and Sarah were still fast asleep.

"So, I'll just have to live dangerously, then."

"That's right," she said. "After all, what's life without a little danger?"

"Indeed." She could almost read his naughty thoughts.

"Yeah, don't worry about your little transgression," she said. "I have plenty of ideas as to how you can earn your atonement."

He tittered and said in a lower voice, "Oh, I'm sure you do. Are you sure these guys aren't listening to any of this?" He turned around to look at them.

"I think so." She smiled. "Hope so."

It was just past 4:00 p.m. when they arrived at the hotel. Frank and Sarah had woken up a few minutes earlier when Anna hit the brakes hard at a traffic light that had turned red faster than she expected. They checked in and went up to their adjoining rooms.

Sarah wanted to continue the nap she had started in the car so that later she would be ready to party in Boston. Michael decided to visit the shopping mall across the street and maybe buy something new to wear later. Both of them knew in advance that Anna and Frank needed to go see Diane alone for an hour or two before they all went out together.

They were early, so Anna and Frank went down to the hotel's restaurant to share a glass of wine before heading out to Diane's. Sitting at the bar, Anna wondered what might come out of all this. What grand design could they conjure up to crack this case and get to the bottom of everything? In the end, she would either have to laugh at herself and blame her overactive imagination, or look into the bare face of evil, and call it Dad.

"What are you thinking?" asked Frank.

Anna sipped the wine that had just been served to her. "Mm, this is good wine."

"You look worried."

"Yes, I am. Why shouldn't I be? I mean, aren't you? What good do you think is going to come from this investigation of ours, all this scheming?"

"Justice, that's what, and maybe even a second lease on life for our poor mother."

"I don't know. It's not like Dad's just going to disappear and let us all live happily ever after. And now, we got Diane involved too. Should we prove that this affair did happen, she will never reconcile with her mother."

Frank set down his wine glass. "We'll deal with the consequences later. The truth must come out. The truth has value in itself; it isn't just a means to an end."

Anna covered her face. "I just feel sometimes like we are driving off a cliff."

"Mm, you're right—this is great wine. Hmm, driving off a cliff, sounds extreme, don't you think? Anyway, what is this happy family we would be breaking up? You and I, we are family. Mom is a prisoner we would be rescuing. And Aunt Marlene, well, Diane doesn't speak to her as it is; and if she was capable of betraying her sister so horribly, Mom should know. Whether she ever forgives her is Mom's decision to make. We have no right to take that away from her."

"Damn, Frank, must you always be right? I've always admired your principles, your moral compass; but sometimes, I fear your tenacity, your stubbornness. We humans aren't supposed to just ignore our doubts; often they are sensible reminders that we don't have all the answers, that we could be wrong. This thing could spiral out of control. Could you at least concede that?"

"Sure, we're not infallible. We cannot control how Mom might react, or what Dad might do. But we can control what we do, and we can plan for contingencies. First, we get to the bottom of this mystery. If our worst fears are confirmed, we don't have to do anything right away. We can talk to Mom first, alone, outside of the house, and not let her go back. I know that's what you're worried about, and for good reason, I might add. But don't fret yourself. We can and will be careful. And we will protect Mom, you have my word."

Anna had needed to hear those words. "Okay, okay, you're making much more sense now. Planning for contingencies, pausing, thinking, being careful—that's the language we need to use with Diane."

"And that's what we'll do." Frank sipped his wine.

"Good, I'm happy we got to talk first," she said.

"I love this wine. Oh, hey, we aren't bringing anything to Diane's. How rude of us. We should bring a decent bottle of wine to share with her."

"Good thinking," said Anna. "Let's get a bottle of this one."

As they departed the hotel, Anna felt a sense of clarity that she hadn't experienced since that awful Sunday at her parents.

CHAPTER X

Standing in front of the door with the number 707, Anna and Frank looked at each other in silence before he knocked. In Frank's other hand, a bottle of cabernet sauvignon. The door opened, and their young cousin Diane stood facing them, her face glowing, expressive eyes wide open as she spoke.

"Hey, cuz. You're here," she exclaimed as she wrapped her arms around Anna.

"Look at you," Anna said. "You were barely a teenage girl last time I saw you."

"I know. And Frank, good to see you."

Frank hugged her awkwardly. "Hey, troublemaker."

"Come in, you guys. I have some fresh guacamole. I made it myself. And here's some red pepper hummus which I…bought, of course." She laughed. The snacks were laid on the small table in her living room.

"The guacamole looks great. Here, we brought some wine," said Frank.

"Oh, thank you. You didn't have to." Diane grabbed the bottle from Frank and examined it curiously. "Ooh, this does not look like the cheap wine I buy." She chuckled softly as she walked to the kitchen.

Frank sat down and grabbed a chip. "Mm, I'm going to dig into this guacamole. These chips are nice too, restaurant quality."

"Yes, they are my favorite chips," Diane's words came from the kitchen, followed by the sound of wine being poured into a glass. "I got them at a store I like a lot. They sell authentic ingredients from different countries—at least, I think so; they could have me fooled and I wouldn't know any better—but I like their stuff."

"I bet these really are authentic Mexican chips," Frank said.

"I'm glad you like them." She brought glasses of wine for the two of them, then went back to the kitchen and returned with her own glass of wine and the bottle, which she placed in the middle of the table.

Anna had been watching the scene like a bystander. It all seemed somewhat surreal to her. This delightful young woman was her cousin, yet it felt a little like she had just met her. It was an odd feeling. She realized that she had not spoken in a while and hastened to say something, anything. "We better not get too full before dinner, or we'll have to deal with our annoyed significant others."

"Yeah, we don't want that." Diane smiled, sitting down beside Anna on the couch. Frank was sitting on a black leather chair that seemed out of place in that room but did create an interesting contrast in what would have otherwise been a rather plain space.

"You know what I just remembered, Diane? I wonder if you remember it yourself. You were little, like seven or eight years old. You were visiting us one day. I remember you were playing with Anna. I was watching something on TV. Then Aunt Marlene came asking if anyone had seen her car keys, because she couldn't find them. I told her I hadn't seen them. Mom asked her if she had checked inside the car. She said she had. They were not there, she said. Then I heard her asking you, and Anna too; nobody had seen those keys.

"She kept looking everywhere—under the furniture, the front porch, the grass in front of the house, under the car, inside the kitchen cabinets, even inside the fridge! Nothing, they were nowhere to be found. Then it got dark. She decided to stay for the night and look again in the morning. Oh, she was very frustrated! Then morning came, and after breakfast, she started looking everywhere for the keys again; only this time, Mom and I helped her as well. I went and looked inside her car one more time and, voila, found the keys wedged between the armrest and the driver's seat."

"I remember it well," said Diane, smiling mischievously as though she was once more a child. "But finish the story. You're doing great."

"So I brought the keys to Aunt Marlene and explained to her where I found them. She couldn't believe it; she was beside herself. She was sure that she had looked in there. She seemed more irritated than she seemed relieved to have found the keys. That was the end of it as far as everyone knew, and even to this date, that would be the official story."

Frank looked at Anna with a sly smile. "But before Aunt Marlene and our little cousin here left, Diane came to see me—I was alone—and she proudly confessed to me that she'd made the keys disappear. So cunning was Diane that she knew to hide the keys in an impossible place— inside one of your boots, in your closet, Anna—and then wake up before anyone else and put the keys inside the car, in a place where, conceivably, Aunt Marlene might've not looked well enough."

"Wow, I didn't know that story," Anna said.

How come Diane had trusted Frank and not her with that confession? And how come her brother never shared it with her?

Frank seemed to read her mind. "I knew that Diane didn't want another soul to know about it. If she could've told a mute kid, she would've. Am I right, Diane?"

Diane smiled and nodded. "And I found the next best thing— Frank. I swear you could've been a priest."

"Ah, that's ironic. But what's most interesting to me is that you really didn't need to tell anyone; you had gotten away with the perfect crime, so to speak—*prank* really would be the word for it. And yet…you told me. Why?"

Frank's eyes glimmered with mischief. He stroked his chin. "Well, I think I understand it quite well. What good is getting away with the perfect crime if no one knows about it—where's the glory in that?"

"Well, mister, you have me all figured out. I thought Anna was the only psychologist in the family." Diane paused, then continued in a more subdued tone.

"You know, I was eight at the time. Mom had just recently told Dad that she wanted a divorce, and he had moved out of the house only a few days before that day I hid Mom's car keys. I wanted to punish her in any way I could. I did other things too. Glasses mysteriously fell to the floor and shattered. Important letters got lost. Stuff like that."

Anna began to comprehend something of significance. Frank and Diane had shared a special connection in their childhood that she had not understood until now. They both became acquainted with rage, despair, and cynicism at a tender age; and in response to their painful upbringing, they had grown up rebellious, clever, sarcastic, fond of mischief, and almost certainly hostile to authority figures. Her own childhood would have been just as terrible but for the protection Frank afforded her. His defiant presence alone was enough to deflect her father's unwanted attention away from her, the same way the Earth's atmosphere shelters all life beneath from the fury of our Sun.

"If I remember correctly, Aunt Marlene and you left for Baltimore the year after that," Anna said while glancing at her phone. The time was now 6:30 p.m.—she darted a glare at Frank in an attempt to convey the urgency of discussing the main topic already.

"That's right," Diane said. "Pretty random thing to do, don't you think? No explanation. 'I got a job there,' she said and dragged me to Maryland, away from Dad."

"I liked your dad," said Frank. "Haven't seen him in ages."

"He's doing well. I'm actually going to hang out with him in New York next weekend."

"Oh, that will be amazing, Diane," said Anna. "I'm jealous."

Anna and Diane both took a moment to sip their wine.

"I do believe we have a most unpleasant matter to discuss," said Frank.

"The affair," said Diane.

"The affair, yes," said Frank.

"The suspected affair," added Anna.

Frank waved a chip in his hand. "Suspected, yes. That's precisely the matter at hand. We must either prove or disprove this seeming abomination, this…"

"Sin?"

"Nah, Diane, I'd rather keep God out of this," said Frank.

"I think he too wants to be left out of it," said Diane.

"Hmm."

Anna interrupted, suddenly getting impatient with her brother's knack for turning any conversation into a philosophical rant. "All right, guys, we better get on with it."

"Right," Frank said. "Before we begin let's make sure we have our facts straight."

"All right," said Anna. "There's the text message, of course—the pictures, and Diane's memory of someone who looked like Dad picking up her mom in a black car."

"You forgot to mention Aunt Lydia's reaction when you asked her how Mom and your dad got along with each other," said Diane.

"Yes, in the garden." Anna had left that out on purpose. "It just seems like that's the weakest piece of evidence we got."

"Don't be too sure about that," said Diane. "That incident alone might've been meaningless, but in view of everything else we know, it becomes significant."

Frank nodded in agreement. "It suggests Mom may have her own suspicions, or worse."

"Let's tackle the big question. How can we prove or disprove our suspicions?" Anna leisurely dipped a chip in the guacamole, anticipating the long silence that followed. Anyone can formulate theories. Now came the tough part.

Frank looked at Anna, then Diane, and then Anna again, giving them an opportunity to share their thoughts. Diane sank back in the couch, looked at the ceiling, and sighed. "Well, I got nothing. Let's hear your ideas."

Frank leaned forward. "I've come up with a few ideas myself, most of which I have discarded after playing them out in my head." He sipped his wine. "There is only one idea that I think could…should work." He sipped his wine again, placed the glass back on the center table and re-positioned himself in his chair—all this with deliberate movements that were infused with sophistication and suspense.

Frank's theatrics were testing Anna's patience. He seemed to be en-joying this too much. She leaned back, crossing her arms and legs. "Come on, Frank, tell us already. It's almost seven."

"I'll try to be brief, but I need to explain the idea well enough, or your instinct may be to reject the one idea I think will work."

Diane nodded, but her face was taut with apprehension. Anna her-self felt uneasy the moment Frank hinted that his idea might not be well received by them.

Frank straightened up in his chair and put his right foot over his left knee. "The first thing is to determine which type of evidence we could hope to get that would conclusively prove or disprove that there was an affair.

"Right at the top of the list, a full confession from either Dad or Aunt Marlene would be fantastic—I mean, it'd be horrible, but conclu-sive. Of course, trying to get a confession from either of them would be very risky."

Anna interrupted. "They'd probably just deny everything, and with-out evidence, we would have to drop the whole thing. I can't even imagine having that talk with Dad. And if it was you, Frank, who con-fronted him, I don't even want to think about how that would end."

"Agreed, it's a bad idea," said Diane. "What's next?"

Frank continued. "Questioning Mom crossed my mind, but I quickly discarded the idea. She could go and confront Dad alone, and that, we must prevent at all costs.

"Without a confession, the only other evidence we could get is the text messages. We must find a way to retrieve the entire conversation, their whole exchange. In the messages that preceded the one Anna happened to see by mere chance must lie the answer we need."

"You're right. I can't think of anything else, but how could we possibly do that?" asked Diane. She leaned forward and cupped her face between her hands, briefly fixing her eyes on something in front of her before darting an alarmed look at Frank. "We would be assuming that they've not erased those messages. Do you suppose that's something we can count on?"

"That's true," said Anna. "They may have erased them. I would've."

In that instant, Anna had to admit to herself that, deep down, she was still harboring some hope for a way out of this obligation, free of guilt, absolved by circumstances. It had not occurred to her that such an outcome could result from this gathering, but now suddenly, Frank's only feasible idea seemed on the brink of rejection. Indeed, his notion appeared to rest on cracked, unstable planks of wishful thinking.

Still, she felt ashamed at the thought of Frank noticing in her voice or demeanor any inclination to give up on the investigation.

Frank continued. "To be sure, that's certainly a possibility. They both could've erased the entire string of texts and, if that were the case, we would have nothing; no evidence at all. However, I would bet neither of them have done that."

"What makes you think that?" asked Diane.

"Psychology," Frank declared, glancing at Anna with a clever smile. "Of course, I'll defer to Anna's opinion on these matters, but I dare say that I understand enough about the human psyche to make some sound inferences. Diane, we'll start with your mother. Would you say that she's the suspicious type?"

"Yes, I would. She's a mistrustful person."

"I would've guessed that, but I couldn't really say why. So we can assume that she'd normally be inclined to erase from her phone a self-incriminatory conversation. However, she lives alone. She has no reason to fear that someone might get her phone and go through her messages.

And that's why I think there's a really good chance that, this very minute, that entire conversation is still in Aunt Marlene's phone."

Anna said nothing. She couldn't really disagree with his logic. Diane nodded in agreement.

"Our most interesting research specimen is, of course, our father," Frank said, glancing at Anna. "What is it like to be Victor Goddard? He's the Kaiser, king of his little kingdom, a man accustomed to do as he pleases, unchallenged. He's a predator at the top of the food chain. Everything and everyone orbiting around him exists to serve him. Why would the man I just described to you fear anyone, especially our victimized mother, the only person who lives with him, going through his personal messages?"

"He wouldn't," Anna answered, knowing that with those words she was extinguishing any hope of ending their dreadful enterprise right then and there.

"Quite right, he wouldn't. His arrogance and overconfidence play in our favor. I'm positively certain that he would keep the entire conversation and perhaps even go over it every night, the dirty bastard."

"All right," Diane chimed in, "let's assume then that at least one of them, if not both, have kept the conversation intact. Have you thought of an actual plan to get our hands on one of those phones long enough to find and read the messages, undetected? And let's not forget that they might have protected their phones with a pass code. That's a very common practice, of course, and we should not go as far as presuming they wouldn't take that simple precaution. Even wannabe dictators can lose their phone at the mall."

"Dad does have a pass code. I know that much," said Anna.

"I did think about that, and, yes, it might be a tricky challenge to overcome. I've thought out the rudimentary foundation of a plan, but I'm hoping the two of you can help me with the details, which have thus far eluded me.

"First and foremost, we must devise a plan that maximizes our chances of success by running simultaneous attempts on both targets—so to speak. Sequential attempts would be much riskier. Let's say, for example, that we decided Diane would attempt to get into her mom's phone; and only if that attempt failed, we would attempt to seize our father's phone. Should Aunt Marlene discover Diane trying to get at her private messages, two things would likely happen. First, Diane would be left having an awfully uncomfortable conversation with her mom. Any of us doing such an attempt must have ready an alibi, a credible alternate reason to be rummaging through that phone—preferably an emotional reason. In your case, Diane, maybe you wanted to see if your mom mentions you to other people. Not bad, huh?"

"You devil. That's not half bad. Mom would probably gobble that up."

"Thanks, Diane. I wish I had more good answers where that one came from, but I'm starting to run thin on ingenuity. See, that response will likely get you out of trouble, but not out of suspicion with your mother, which brings us to the second thing that's likely to happen in this scenario should you get caught red-handed. And that is, possibly in a matter of minutes, Aunt Marlene would delete from her phone the conversation we are trying to get at, and immediately alert our father, who might, as a mere precaution, delete the conversation as well. Even if he didn't, he wouldn't then leave his phone unattended for any reason.

"So that's why we must find a way to make both attempts simultaneously. It's the only way we are really going to realize the benefit of having two cracks at it. That's the first, rather vague notion I've come up with."

"It's well thought out," Anna said. "Now, we just need to figure out the details."

"We'd need to create some sort of controlled situation that gets us access to both Dad and Aunt Marlene and come up with tactics to get them away from their phones," said Frank.

Diane's face grew somber, her gaze suddenly dropping to the floor. "There's something you haven't addressed directly but is implied. If I'm to be of any help, I must first reconcile with Mom. How else could I get near her?

"As it is, I've been contemplating doing just that. I've begun feeling like enough is enough, that it's time to forgive…and seek forgiveness. Am I to do it now only as a necessity, to put in motion a scheme, a plan that may ultimately drive us apart for good? I just don't know if I can do that. That in itself seems as despicable and heartless as the betrayal of which she might be guilty."

The three of them remained silent for what seemed like a long time. It may have really been only a minute or two—time enjoys an uncomfortable silence.

Anna bounced notions and words in her head until, finally, she thought she knew what to say to Diane. "I think I can understand how you feel. I've been torturing myself with similar thoughts about causing irreparable ruptures in the family. I've thought about you too. Even now, sitting here, I feel somewhat guilty to have brought you into this; but it would've been even more unfair to keep you in the dark. In the end, we're only looking for the truth. If we find that nothing really happened, I'll be the first one to open a bottle of champagne."

Frank had been looking at Anna absorbedly while she spoke. An inkling of a smile flashed on his face before he turned his gaze to Diane. "Would you feel better about this if you weren't the one getting into your mom's phone?"

"Yes, I would. That would be easier. What would I do, then?"

"I think you could create the distraction needed to get her away from her phone. Then one of us could get the phone without her or anyone else noticing," he said.

"All right, that doesn't sound so terrible," said Diane.

Anna glanced at her phone. Michael had sent her a picture of a hardcover novel he had seen at a bookstore. She replied, "Christmas gift already?" Then she saw the time.

"Hmm, it's getting late, almost seven thirty. We should get going soon. Sarah and Michael will be expecting us to pick them up by eight. And we still haven't come up with our perfectly manufactured controlled situation."

"Right," said Frank. "Let's put our heads together here for a moment. What kind of event can we come up with where we could create situations, distractions, instances of controlled chaos, perhaps?"

Diane's face lighted up as if a voice had whispered the answer to her ear. "I got it. We need to plan a family reunion—at your parents' big house. That place will provide plenty of opportunities for controlled chaos, as you cleverly called it, Frank. Also, it's the only way to ensure that Uncle Victor will be there—he must be the host. And yet, all the work must be done for him. Um…Aunt Lydia, of course. We'll need to insert the idea into her mind, you know, like they did in that movie with Leonardo DiCaprio. She must be convinced that it was really her idea— Anna, it's time to earn your stripes as a psychologist."

"That could work. It really could," Frank exclaimed. His face too lit up. "Now, how do we make sure that Aunt Marlene shows up? It's a long drive for her. Should we get her a plane ticket to sweeten the deal?"

"No, that's not what will convince her to go," said Anna. "You, Diane, seeing you—that's why she'll make the trip. Through Mom, we can send her the message that you'll be there and that you want to see her, that the wait is over and reconciliation is at hand."

Tears suddenly came running down Diane's cheeks. "I'm sorry…I'm…I'm just a little emotional. You're right, Anna. That should work. It's a great idea. Oh God, is there any chance Mom didn't do this horrible thing? Please, God, let it all be a mistake. Please let me…forgive her." With those last words, she held on no longer and wept wretchedly. Anna held her in her arms, also tearing up. They were in that moment like kids again. They were family once more.

Embracing Diane, Anna felt both her cousin's sorrow and an almost inexplicable joy. Perhaps, there is a sort of happiness that can only be experienced by sharing grief. In any case, Anna could hardly get herself to pull away from Diane. When she did, she saw a faint smile in her cousin's face. She then turned her gaze to Frank, who had been rendered speechless.

She knew Frank desperately needed her to take over.

"I think that we have all the basic elements of our plan. There are, obviously, a lot of details that we still need to hash out, but we won't get there tonight. Don't you agree, Frank?"

"I do. It's a great start. We can talk again tomorrow or Monday and start putting more meat on the bones."

"All right, then. Let's get on to the fun part of the evening," said Diane, trying to smile.

"Yes, we should go now. Oh, look at the time. I'll send Michael a message."

"I'm texting Sarah," said Frank.

"Do you mind coming back this way to pick me up? I just need to fix my—"

"Makeup?" Anna finished Diane's sentence. "Of course, go ahead. We'll be back in twenty minutes, give or take."

"I can't wait to meet Sarah and Michael."

Anna and Frank barely talked on the way back to the hotel. They'd been driving for four or five minutes already when Frank remarked in a subdued voice, "We did very well, I think." Anna agreed impassively and commented no further.

She could've easily called it a night and just stayed at the hotel, but she abandoned that thought as soon as they walked into the hotel lobby. Sitting there were Michael and Sarah, chatting animatedly, electrified and ready to party.

They went back to pick up Diane, who promptly came down brandishing a sunny smile. They met up with her in front of the building. Sarah and Diane seemed to click instantly.

Within minutes, the crowded Volvo was heading down the freeway toward downtown Boston. Diane and Sarah's rowdy energy wound up rubbing off on all of them; even Anna got in the mood for a little fun. They went to some of Diane's favorite spots. First, she took them to the Theater District, where they had Thai food before going to a bustling night club.

After a few drinks and some dancing, they went for a change of scenery at the North End, Boston's Little Italy, where they did a little walking to earn the right to enjoy the best cannoli any of them had ever had; and finally, they took the train to Harvard Square for the last fun of the night. There, Frank and Michael played a game of pool that they may have taken more seriously than they made it look like with their carefree behavior and amusing banter. Michael eked out a win, making a tough, and probably lucky, shot in the end—his own face betrayed as much. Frank seemed to like him more every minute, and the feeling appeared to be mutual.

A train ride and a short walk later, they were back in the car, leaving the city. This was a distinctly happy moment for Anna. How glad she was now, observing them together, that both Michael and Sarah had come. Even accounting for the alcohol, it was clear that they all had become much closer—the way they talked to each other, their lighthearted laughter, the way Frank tapped Michael on the shoulder to share an inside joke, or the way Sarah leaned on Diane, laughing hysterically; all were signs of that proximity.

Perhaps—she thought—*on balance, life is still smiling at us. Could we not all move out here, like Diane did, and forget, leave behind all which threatens this newfound happiness?* The vision warmed her up, but only fleetingly. An image of her mother, left behind in darkness, flashed before her; and a shiver ran down her spine. It was then she felt the warmth of Michael's hand on hers.

CHAPTER XI

Things moved along at a dizzying pace for Anna following the trip to Boston. The second evening after their return to town, she and Frank called Diane from his apartment for what turned out to be a remarkably productive conversation. They devised an assortment of crafty strategies, tactics, and ploys designed to achieve their main two objectives at the family reunion. First, they needed to spy on Marlene and Victor as a means to obtain the pass codes to both phones. They presumed that, at least in theory, that task should prove the easiest.

The trickiest job, of course, would be to get each of them to leave their phones unattended long enough for someone to take them and look for the text messages—all of this undetected by anyone. But their explosion of creativity bolstered their confidence that they could accomplish this ambitious and risky undertaking. Frank, especially, appeared exceedingly pleased with their combined ingenuity.

Anna came out of their little conclave with a tough assignment which was quite fundamental: planting the idea of the family reunion in her mom's head. A failure on her part would spell disaster for the entire operation. She spent the better part of Wednesday awfully anxious about her mission, in no small measure because she regarded herself a terrible liar.

She resolved to call her mother and invite her to share a glass of wine with her in town, midafternoon the following day. She was very happy to hear from Anna and, to her invitation, she responded in a muted voice, "Um…okay, sure…where? The Courtyard…yes, I know where it is…three p.m., got it." She changed the subject abruptly, asked Anna if she had seen Frank, how was he and, "Have you seen Sarah lately? Such a nice girl. God bless them. Frank sent me a lovely picture the other day.

You do know that they are engaged now, don't you? Well, I hope so; this is no way to find out. Ah, good, good. Your dad says hello."

That night she went to the movies with Michael. They watched a scary movie, but it wasn't any good. More than anything, it was a good excuse to cuddle. The auditorium was empty but for them, so they did a little more than cuddling. After that, they went to Michael's apartment, where they finished what they had started at the cinema. More and more, she felt an intense connection to Michael, both on a physical and emotional plane; and from the way he looked deep into her eyes when they made love, she could tell that he too was all in.

She woke up on Thursday morning to the mouthwatering smell of sizzling bacon. She found Michael in the kitchen, already dressed up for work, and on the table, breakfast for two—scrambled eggs, bacon, toasts, coffee, and orange juice. What a guy! She gave him a little something to fantasize about at work.

Then, in the most nonchalant way possible, he just gave her a copy of the key to the apartment. "Take your time, just lock the door on your way out. Here, you can keep that one. It's a copy." Another big kiss and he was out the door.

Anna kept looking at her shiny new key; to her, it was much more than just a key to an apartment. It opened more than a door—it opened possibilities.

His apartment was small, but it was nicely furnished and very modern. She walked around looking at his stuff. She found a nice picture of him with his dad in front of a baseball stadium. It must have been from about ten years back. The resemblance was remarkable.

She left the apartment shortly before noon and went to her house. Close to an hour later, she drove to town, and having time to spare, she stopped by Stephanie's shop for a lemon tart and coffee, but mostly to see her friend and get her up to speed on her and Michael, Frank and Sarah, her cousin Diane, and their trip to Boston.

Time flew by with Stephanie and before Anna knew it the time was two forty-five. Anna hugged and kissed her friend and went out. The

Courtyard was only five minutes away on foot from Stephanie's. She got there with time to spare and picked a table.

While she waited, Anna kept rehearsing in her mind the things she was planning to say to her mother with the object of, as imperceptibly as possible, inserting in their conversation the idea of a family gathering. She looked down at her phone and saw that the time was 3:02. When she looked up again, her mother was coming in through the front door. Anna stood up and beckoned to her.

Lydia Wilde had been a woman of considerable beauty in her youth, and now, at fifty, was still quite attractive. By anyone's guess, she would not have looked a day over forty. Her figure was still rather youthful, and she carried herself with an elegance that seemed natural and effortless. Anna had her to thank for her striking green eyes; only in her mother, those eyes had acquired a permanently downcast appearance, even as she smiled, as she did now, approaching her daughter.

"Hey, Mom, it's great to see you." Anna hugged and kissed her. They both sat down.

"You look happy. What a rare pleasure this is, sharing a glass of wine in town with my baby girl."

"You look great, Mom. I really like that dress." Lydia was wearing a beige belted dress that reached just below the knees. Anna was struck by how well-toned her arms still were. She wondered why she hadn't noticed that before.

"Why, thank you, sweetheart. Surely, you must have seen it before. I've had it for a very long time, though I probably hadn't put it on in years. I don't go out much anymore."

"Yes, I know. It's almost impossible to get you out of that house." Anna opened the wine menu that had been brought to her a few minutes earlier.

"Yes, well, you know how your father gets." Lydia looked about her restlessly.

Anna sighed. "Yes, he's an egotistical control freak, but that doesn't mean it's right."

Lydia rolled her eyes, closed them briefly, put her hands together, and exhaled audibly. "It would be an awful waste if all we talked about was your father, don't you think?"

"On that, we can agree. One last thing, though—where is he today?"

"He said he'd be out all day inspecting rental properties. What do I care?"

"So that's why you could get out of the house today." Anna sensed a sardonic smile creeping up on her face and looked down at the wine list to conceal her dry amusement. A brief silence followed. Anna didn't look up until her mother spoke again.

"Could we talk about something else now? You must have interesting news to share if you invited me here."

"Sorry, Mom, nothing more about Dad, I promise."

"All right, then."

"And…I really don't need any special reasons to want to spend some time with my mom, I hope you know that. But I do have interesting and amazing news."

Lydia jerked forward. "Aha! I knew it. Come on, tell me already."

"Easy, easy. Let's order some wine first. Here comes the waiter. Take a look at the menu and see what strikes your fancy."

"Oh, I'll just have the same as you, as long as it isn't too dry."

"I think I know what you'll like," said Anna. "I've learned a thing or two from Frank—he's the wine snob of the family."

They shared a quick laugh.

"I was so happy to hear about Frank's engagement. Sarah's such a sweet girl."

"Yes, I really like her," said Anna.

The waiter, a fine-looking young man, was now standing beside them. Only when he had their full attention, he asked whether they were ready to order or if they needed a few minutes. Anna pointed at the menu. "We'll have a bottle of this Sonoma Valley merlot."

"Excellent choice," said the young man and started for the kitchen, walking at a brisk yet elegant pace.

"A whole bottle, Anna?" Lydia's eyes opened wide. She looked worried.

"Yeah, why not? Live a little, Mom. It'll be fine."

"Well, all right, but I don't know if I'll have more than the one glass."

The wine was brought over promptly, and two glasses were served for the ladies. "Would you like to order food as well? Maybe an appetizer?" asked the young waiter.

"It will just be the wine. Thank you," Anna responded. She turned to her mother, who'd just taken her first sip. "So, how do you like it?"

"Mm, it's really good. Fruity, but not too sweet."

"I knew you'd like it."

"All right, enough about the wine now. Tell me the news. I'm dying to hear them."

"I actually have two big news. I almost don't know which one to tell you first, but...well, here it goes." She sipped her wine slowly, looking straight into her mother's eyes, to build up the mystery—this she had shamelessly taken right out of Frank's playbook. "I'm...dating again. I met this great guy. His name is Michael, Michael Donovan."

"Oh, that's great Anna." Lydia's face lit up. "Gosh, I don't think you'd dated anyone in like, two years, right?"

"Right, so—"

"And you're so darn pretty. I'm sure there's plenty of guys attracted to you."

"Yes, well, nobody I liked much. But with Michael, there was an instant, mutual attraction, and"—she smiled—"things have been moving kind of fast."

"Huh...well, you know, you're an adult woman, obviously, but do be careful. You don't want to get stuck in a situation with a man before you're really sure he's the one for you." Her gaze dropped slightly as she said those last few words. An introspective look settled on her face for a fleeting moment.

"I know what you mean, Mom. Don't worry. This is a great guy. But, yes, I'll be careful."

"And what does Michael do?"

"He's the…" For a moment, she drew a blank. "Archives director at the Blake County Historical Society. He's a historian, a very smart, polished guy. Oh, you should have seen him and Frank together—they were insufferable." She chuckled. "They just feed off each other. They might like each other too much."

"You mean he and Frank are friends already?"

"They met only days ago, but they were instant friends. It was amazing. We just came back from a quick trip we did together—Frank, Sarah, Michael. and me. It was so much fun."

"Well, I'm intrigued. When do I get to meet this Michael?"

"That could be arranged…soon enough."

"And you say you went on a trip together? Wow, that's…great. Where did you go?"

"All right, before I answer that, I need to tell you the other big, big news." Again, Anna sipped her wine slowly for dramatic effect. Her mother's face was brimming with anticipation.

"Are you ready?"

"Come on, child, for God's sake, tell me already."

"We found Diane. We saw her. We were with her this past weekend…in Boston. That's where we went, to see Diane."

"Oh, dear God! Anna, that's amazing…amazing. How is she? Does Marlene know about this?"

"Not yet, she doesn't. I was thinking maybe you could be the one to tell her."

"I'd love to tell her that Diane is fine. She is, right?"

"Oh, she's doing better than fine. It's such a great story. You won't believe it—she went to school and became a nurse. She works at a large hospital in the Boston area. She has her own apartment. You know, she's really got her act together. I'm very happy for her."

Lydia appeared on the verge of tears. Anna had not expected this news to have such a profound effect on her mother. Her face worked with emotion. "I can't wait to tell Marlene. I'll call her tonight."

Clearly, Diane was the best card she had. The time to put her strategy in motion was now. She pounced at the opportunity.

"And that's not all, Mom. You know, I could really tell that Diane is more mature now. Maybe time has worked its magic; whatever the reason, she's changed for the better." Anna took a quick sip of wine. "She didn't say it like this, exactly, but I sensed that she's ready to reconcile with her mother. Now, listen, this is important. You can't just tell all this to Aunt Marlene. Both mother and daughter are proud women, so we must tread carefully; but we do have a chance to help them reconcile. We must think it through, though."

"Thank goodness, Anna. I'm so happy to hear all this. You have no idea how my sister has suffered. To be separated from her only daughter, without news, fearing that she might be living a hard life, not knowing if she's even alive—that's a slow death; it's what it is. If there's anything—absolutely anything—I can do to bring her daughter back to her, I'll most certainly do it. God knows she's suffered enough already."

Listening to her mother speak of Marlene as though she were some sort of martyr whose heavy cross it would be her great joy to lighten, Anna pondered how to reconcile those words with the indelible impression left on her that day in the garden. How could the mere mention of her sister one day make her mother's face pale and her voice falter, and yet now elicit from her such a heartfelt, compassionate response?

"What are you thinking?" asked her mother.

"Um, just wondering what that must have been like for Aunt Marlene, these last years. I guess up until now I had mostly seen the whole thing from Diane's perspective."

That was clumsy. Why did she say that? What could it accomplish?

"And how does it all look from her perspective? Because from a mother's perspective, what she did was cruel and undeserved." She darted a reproachful glance at Anna, as if it was Diane herself who was sitting in front of her.

"I think she'd agree with you now, though she might not use those same words. I think she'd say that her actions were those of a hurt, resentful girl. From what I gather, her main beef with her mother always was her divorcing her dad and taking her away to Maryland."

"Children perceive their world differently from their parents." Lydia grabbed Anna's hand, and a dejected smile formed on her face. "Sometimes, our kids fancy that there are certainties and intentions where there's really only doubts and fears. But kids need to believe their parents are strong; otherwise, their little worlds come tumbling down."

Anna was silent for a moment while her mother's words fully sank in. She looked her in the eyes and said earnestly, "I understand, Mom. I really do. And I think that's also what Diane has begun to comprehend."

Lydia patted Anna's hand, sat back and lifted her glass of wine. "Hmm, I'm sure Marlene would love to hear that from her."

"Yes, she would, wouldn't she? And do you think Aunt Marlene would be ready to forgive all and start over with a clean slate?"

"She would, absolutely. There's no doubt in my mind."

"Well, then, things are looking up. The only thing that worries me is…um, the distance between them. You know, I just wish they didn't have to have that first talk, after years of silence, over the phone. I've just seen too many phone conversations go wrong because someone said something clumsy. And then, if one of them hangs up in anger—you know what I'm saying?"

"You can't hug your daughter over the phone. That's what it comes down to. A warm hug can't be misinterpreted—it can only mean 'I love you and all is forgiven.' You're absolutely right about that. It's too bad that Diane lives so far from her now."

"Yes, it is. If only we could arrange for them to meet in person."

"Well, I really think Marlene would go to see her in Boston. Yes, of course, she would."

Anna sipped her wine reflectively. "Don't you think that she might take the unfortunate position that Diane should be the one to go to Maryland? Pride is a nasty, treacherous emotion. One never knows when it might come out and show its ugly face."

Lydia widened her eyes, eyebrows raised. "God, I don't think she'd do that at all, but…well, you seem to have been giving this some thought. I dare say that you look like you have an idea you'd like to suggest. If you do, by all means, tell me, because I can't think of a good solution for the difficulty that you have so well anticipated."

Anna had tried, to the best of her abilities, to bring up the idea of a family gathering in the subtlest way possible, but she knew that this was the end of the road. Her mother had seen through her, and the only way forward now was to reveal and openly suggest the notion. At least, Anna reckoned, she'd been successful in sparking her mother's interest and building a good argument, which thus far her mother appeared to be buying.

"You're right: a thought did occur to me. In fact, this idea I'm about to tell you crossed my mind a week before we saw Diane, when Frank and Sarah got engaged. I thought, *This is a great occasion that would deserve a small gathering at our parent's house.* I mean, has Dad even met Sarah?"

"No, he hasn't, and that might be a good thing too. You know your father and Frank would sooner be at each other's throats than sit down for a civilized dinner together."

"I agree that it's been that way between them for a long time, but if Frank's engagement to be married isn't occasion enough for them to bury the hatchet, at least for a day, then all is lost between them."

"That's a fair point. If only they would…but let's get back to Marlene and Diane."

"Yes, so that thought crossed my mind then, but soon other things occupied my mind, and I forgot all about it until I talked to Diane…"

Her mother interrupted her. "I've been meaning to ask you, how did that come about? How did you find Diane?"

Anna was instantly vexed at herself. What a rookie mistake this was, not thinking in advance how to answer that question. She tried to keep her face relaxed, "Oh, I…had been searching for her on the internet, from time to time, and I finally found her on a discussion board." Her heart was racing. That was a half-cooked lie. Would it be enough?

"Huh, how fortuitous," Lydia said with a quizzical look on her face. "Go ahead. Sorry to interrupt you. I was just curious."

"Oh, it's fine." Anna couldn't believe that her mother was letting her off that easy. She tried to calm herself down.

"Where was I? Ah, yes, we were in Boston with Diane. Oh, Mom, you have to see her. She got so pretty, like a doll! Anyway, we are there, talking, and I started picturing all of us together—a beautiful day, just like today, sunny, with a nice breeze; a big picnic table on the front lawn; Frank is there with Sarah, Grandma Rose is there too, and Aunt Marlene, of course; and here comes Diane, she hugs her mother—like you said, it's like you finished up my vision—they hug and all is forgiven, no need for words."

"Oh, I can almost see it, what a beautiful scene that would be." For a moment, Lydia's eyes were graced with a glimmer of joy. Anna knew right then that she had struck the right chord with her mother. This was what she had hoped for.

"But Victor won't…I just don't think that he would…" Lydia now spoke slowly, as if thinking out loud. The light had abandoned her eyes, which now seemed to stare into an invisible abyss in front of her. She suddenly looked exhausted. "Your father won't like this. He's gotten more and more reclusive, you know. He still goes to church and talks to some people there, but I think it's just a front, a character that he plays. He's just not interested in anyone, I think. I can't imagine that he would be the least excited about hosting a family gathering."

"But listen, Mom…" Anna felt success was quickly slipping away, soon to be out of reach. Desperation took hold of her.

"No, you listen. The more I think about it, the less I like the idea. You figure that my mother would come with Marlene, and you're right: I think she would. Well, your father hates her. Always has and always will. It will take him two minutes to start attacking her with his malicious, cynical remarks. Ah, such a delightful evening. And to have Victor sit down with Frank, and meet Sarah, his lovely fiancé—well, let me tell you something: that might just be a recipe for disaster. He could send that girl running for the hills."

Anna was swept by a torrent of irrepressible anger, and before she could get a hold of herself, she was already yelling at her mother. "He won't drive anyone away—he doesn't have that power, Mom. He only has the power that you give him. The power to abuse you, to insult you and belittle you in front of your kids—you gave that to him. You let him have it."

"You have no idea what you're talking about. Jesus, stop this embarrassment at once. I thought I'd taught you to have more class than this. People are looking at us."

Anna darted glances left and right. An older female waiter carrying a wine bottle looked at her sideways. She didn't look pleased. Anna lowered her voice, but not her intensity.

"Class? Yes, you taught me how to keep appearances, how to play a part as an extra in your husband's story. I wish you had taught me real dignity, Mom, some self-respect. I had to look for that elsewhere. Thank God I didn't become you."

A moment later, Anna was free of the anger that had possessed her, and she could see what she'd done. Not only she had messed up and put the entire mission at risk, but she had really hurt her mother. If only she could take back those cruel words.

Lydia looked from side to side before speaking again in a subdued voice, her eyes glassy with unshed tears. "Now, you've said your piece. I've always admired your candor, but please be reminded of where we are and that you invited me here to have a good time. Let's please drop this conversation for now. I didn't come here to argue with you. Let's enjoy this wine and try to have a pleasant talk."

"I'm sorry, Mom. I shouldn't have said that. I'm really sorry." She wanted to say more, but the words got stuck in her throat.

It took another five or ten minutes for their conversation to regain a semblance of normalcy. They spent the rest of the afternoon discussing Frank and Sarah, Diane, the trip to Boston, and Michael, a carefully edited, innocent, dull version of it all, anyway. Not another word of substance or consequence was uttered.

She had failed. On her way back to the house, she kept thinking how to explain to Frank and Diane that she had made a mess of everything. There was no good way of telling them. She would just come clean and take the blame. No excuses; there was dignity in that.

Her mind was in turmoil. Like a good chess player facing a superior opponent, she wondered what price she or others might have to pay later for her unfortunate misstep. Would the entire plan have to be scrapped? Was there even a way forward from this point? Would Frank resort to some alternate, riskier strategy; perhaps one involving a direct confrontation with their father? It would be her fault if he did—that much she knew.

Two hours later, at her place, Anna paced from side to side, recalling the conversation with her mother. She had to tell Frank. Who knows what dreadful nightmare she might have if she went to sleep with that worry hanging over her head? But she still had time. She tried to numb her mind watching her beloved travel series; then a standup comedy show—nothing worked. It got dark outside. She wouldn't put it off any longer. It was time.

Anna grabbed her phone and looked up Frank's contact. Her finger was hovering over the dreaded green icon, a millimeter away from placing the call, when the phone rang, startling her so that she almost dropped the phone. It was her mother.

"Hey, Mom, is everything all right?"

"Everything's fine, Anna. Why wouldn't it be?" She lowered her voice. "Listen, against my better judgment I brushed the subject of having a small family gathering here with your father. I told him about Diane and everything. I don't even know why I did it. I was expecting him to hate the whole idea, get angry, yell at me, burst into flames or something. Imagine my surprise when he said he loved the idea—loved it! Those were his words. Dear God, do I just not know the man at all anymore? Anyway, we are doing it. Can you believe it? I haven't been this excited about anything in a very long time."

Anna was stupefied. It took her a good five seconds to be able to say anything. "Wow, Mom, that's…amazing, and crazy, yes, that too—but wonderful, nonetheless!"

"Yes, well, I'll get on it right away. I'll call Marlene—can't wait to tell her. And Mom, I want to tell Mom too, tonight. I think Labor Day weekend would be our best bet. Everybody has that one extra day."

"But that's just in a little over a week."

"That's why we need to get started right away. Your job, Anna, is to make darn sure that Diane comes. And Frank and Sarah too. Oh, and Michael. Of course, you have to bring Michael! I want to meet him. Your dad too wants to meet him. He said so himself."

"You got it," Anna said.

"That's what I wanted to her. Okay, I have to go."

"I love you, Mom."

"I know. I love you too."

Anna felt dazed as she ended the call with her mother. She was half expecting to wake up on the couch all of a sudden, but not this time—this was real. There was only one thing left to do now. She started typing, "Success. We are on. Labor Day weekend, that's when it happens. Talk tomorrow."

She read the message twice. Her own words scared her—"that's when it happens," she had written. She didn't change a thing, however; just sent the message. She had somehow succeeded, and should have been relieved, yet she couldn't shake the feeling that their design already harbored some fatal flaw that would spell disaster in the end.

CHAPTER XII

Michael would always remember how gusty it was that Sunday afternoon when they arrived at the Goddards' family house. Thick white clouds raced across the bright blue sky over the big, old farmhouse. The sight somehow seemed menacing to him, but perhaps he had been predisposed to feel that way by Anna's stories about her father and her insistence that he bring his car so that he could leave anytime he wanted, should anything not be to his liking. He had followed Anna through a series of country roads to get there. Had Michael lost her trail, he would have never found the place on his own.

They parked their cars, side by side, about a hundred feet from where a large outdoor dining table had been meticulously set up on the front lawn. Walking briskly toward them came a sophisticatedly dressed, delightful lady who could only be Anna's mother. She came up and gave Anna a tender hug and a kiss before she flashed a big smile at Michael, extending her hand, "You must be Michael. I'm Lydia, Anna's mother. I'm so glad you could come. Come, come, let's get inside."

Anna's hand felt cool in Michael's as they followed Lydia; a chill spread through his body as the shadow of the old house eclipsed the sun. The wind howled, trees swayed, and languid creaky groans escaped from the weary bones of the abode.

Lydia looked back at them. "Everybody else should be here around five, so we've got an hour to kill. Michael, over there sitting on the porch is Victor, Anna's father. He's been looking forward to meeting you. The two of you can get to know each other while Anna helps me in the kitchen."

"Sounds good," said Michael, not meaning it at all. He was, how-ever, to a certain degree, curious to meet this man, the architect of Anna's miserable childhood. During the week leading to this day, as if preparing him for the encounter, Anna had related to him more and more stories about her father, and they just got darker and darker every time. They stole a glance at each other behind Lydia's back. Anna's expression was something like a warning. She appeared very tense all of a sudden.

The house now loomed large in front of them, appearing both splendid and tired. It retained much of its old glory, but it bore unmis-takable signs of wear and tear—must have been neglected for years. A two-story home painted mostly white, with a green roof. On the front facade, five windows of the same size and shape on the second floor, and a tiny window on top, presumptively one of those attics which, in mov-ies, are always scary places.

Climbing the steps to the house's wrap around porch, Michael saw Victor Goddard, in the flesh, for the first time. He was an intimidating sight, and a handsome devil too, despite some visible signs of aging. Vic-tor's icy-blue eyes, fixed on Michael, and Victor's sly little smile, unnerved Michael instantly.

Victor rose from his chair and acknowledged his daughter with a nod and a fleeting smile. "Hi, darling, how are you?" He could have been reading from a teleprompter. It seemed as if the star performer playing the father in this scene had become sick at the last minute and replaced by an understudy who didn't know his lines.

"Hi, Dad," Anna said in the same tone as a kid who has been forced to apologize.

"Victor, this is Michael, Anna's boyfriend," said Lydia.

"Ah, yes. You're Anna's boyfriend, huh?" Victor's low-pitched voice was imbued with the confidence of a lord who was dealing with peasants.

"Yes, Mr. Goddard." Michael glanced over at Anna, and her approv-ing smile reassured him. "It is a pleasure to meet you, sir." Michael extended his hand, which Victor met in a firm handshake. The man tow-ered over him. He felt like a rabbit under the shadow of an eagle.

"Welcome to our home, Michael. Do sit down. Let's have a beer. Lydia, would you be a doll and bring us two cold ones?"

"I'll bring them," said Anna. She and her mother went inside the house.

Michael sat down across from Victor at a small table. "It's a good-looking place you have here, Mr. Goddard," he said to break the ice but hated the sound of his own voice—he always felt this way at his stupid fundraising galas, complimenting those VIP assholes whose boots he was paid to lick. Victor's father had been one of them.

"Just call me Victor. This house, yes, it's something, isn't it? And old too. I hear you're a historian."

"On my best days."

"That's an interesting comment." Victor's voice rippled with amusement; his eyes appeared to get even smaller, like a cyborg's glittering blue orbs. "What are you on your worst days?" A smirk blossomed on his face.

Perhaps, Michael should have dodged the question, but what the heck—he wasn't going to tiptoe around the man. "A glorified librarian, to be honest." Maybe too honest.

Victor bent forward, his massive arms pressed firmly on the table, and looked him straight in the eyes. "Don't put yourself down, or people around you will see you as an easy target." For a moment there, Michael half expected Victor to call him "my young apprentice."

"Oh, it's no big deal. I've always had a good sense of humor about myself."

Anna came over with two beers, served on large, thick glass mugs. She gave Michael an uneasy look. "I'll be in the kitchen with Mom if you need anything." She glanced at her father, who dismissed her with a dull gesture that didn't quite amount to a smile—half a nod and a twisted curl of the lips, his eyes lifeless like a doll's. Anna's face stiffened like a mask, then turned around, and went back inside.

Victor tasted his beer absentmindedly, gazing vaguely in Michael's direction but as if he weren't there. In another moment, his eyes were once more set on Michael's face. He seemed as if perched atop a tower, looking down on him from a vantage point; his face reminded Michael of a deadly sniper in a movie he'd seen a while ago. "Lydia said you're a director of some kind at the historical society; is that right?"

Michael brought down the mug that had just barely kissed his lower lip. "Yes, director of archives and library." That stupid title again, poking its dumb fucking face in the door, waving to the camera.

He finally got to taste his beer. Strong, full-bodied, probably German. Quite fitting too. It would have been weird if this silverback of a man drank light beer. He looked like he should also smoke Cuban cigars and drink his coffee black, with no sugar—that's right, no sugar at all!

Victor nodded with his head slightly slanted, raising his chin. "Sounds like something you ought to be proud of," Victor said. "It's a nice enough title; it's a mouthful, sure, but sounds important."

"It does sound important—that's what inflated titles do best."

Victor's eyebrows ebbed slightly away from his piercing eyes, the corners of his lips arching up ever so slightly. "Are you familiar with the phrase, 'fake it until you make it'?"

Michael nodded. "Sure, I think everyone is."

"Well, you would do well to put it into action. Don't show weakness; stand tall, stand proud—discourage your enemies before they even think of taking a shot at you."

"My enemies, huh? Don't you think that sounds a little extreme?"

"Not at all," said Victor. "You sure as hell have enemies, whether you know it or not. Just look around you anytime, and you'll see someone who wants your job, your girl, your life. And if you make it easy for them, they'll take what's yours. You better believe it. There are only wolves and sheep out there."

Michael's response came out with unintended informality. "Oh, come on—you can't go around judging everyone that way. Surely, you don't mean that literally, in absolute terms, right?"

"I most certainly do, and if you fail to acknowledge that, you're already halfway to becoming a sheep."

Michael chuckled nervously. The sniper's face remained still, oddly contemplative. "That's, um…an interesting perspective, Victor. I'll keep it in mind." He chased that hard-to-swallow, thick roll of bullshit with a big gulp of icy-cold *bier*. "As for marrying Anna, well, we've been dating for only a couple of weeks, so it's really too early to say."

"Nonsense, kid. When you know, you know. It's like a chemical reaction. Sodium and chloride could be together for a thousand years, but they could never make water; their potential together is only to make salt."

"But hydrogen and oxygen only need an instant to make water, because they are destined to," Michael finished the thought. "That's actually a brilliant analogy." It was. He might use that later—a gold coin found in the gutters is still a gold coin.

"They told me you were smart." Victor observed Michael with a flicker of curiosity in his eyes while leisurely sipping his beer. "I'm starting to believe it."

"I'm flattered." He wasn't.

"Yes, you should be." Victor grinned, his lips stretching thin until they disappeared, leaving only his mountain of a nose and tiny eyes deep within a labyrinth of furrows. The sniper face was back shortly. "I can't believe you called yourself a glorified librarian, Michael. Don't say a thing like that again. Tell me: What is it exactly that you do in your job?"

"Well, let's see. I receive visitors—not a lot, but some—and I curate collections, prepare exhibits, sometimes organize events."

Victor sat back with an arm behind his head. "What kinds of events?"

"Community events, fundraising galas—that kind of stuff." *Ugh, more* bier *please! Hopefully, he'd stop already with all these questions.*

"And what is it about it that you hate so much?" the silverback sniper asked, eyebrows coming down, little wrinkles forming on his nose bridge.

"It's just not what I want to do. It's dull, mind-numbing work."

"And why do you keep doing it?" Great question—Victor had him square in his sight.

"The pay is good, I guess." A weak answer. So weak.

Victor's eyes gleamed maliciously. "See? You're a sensible man, after all. Pipe dreams don't keep the lights on, right?"

Michael had to play some defense; he couldn't just let the old man toy around with him. "I've written some articles, too. That's the kind of work I enjoy."

"History articles?" Victor asked, either interested or mockingly— Michael couldn't tell.

"Yes, usually about local history, but now I'm working on one for a national journal."

"What's your article about?"

Michael now had home-court advantage. Time to dazzle the sniper. "It's about the end of World War II and the beginning of the Cold War."

"That's major league history, huh? So what's your take on the whole thing?" Victor sounded genuinely intrigued.

"Well, my main argument is that if F. D. Roosevelt had lived longer, he would have not dropped the atomic bombs on Hiroshima and Naga-saki, and that might have changed history in many ways, for the better."

"So you think bombing the Japs was a bad thing, is that it?"

Oh boy, he called them Japs. "I try to stay away from making a moral judgment. From a military standpoint, though, it was unnecessary because Japan was all but ready to surrender before Hiroshima; and drop-ping the bombs made the Cold War inevitable." Michael chugged down some liquid courage. "And we do carry the stain of being the only nation ever to have used nuclear weapons in an act of war."

The chair creaked as Victor edged forward in his seat, beady eyes glimmering as his words came out with bridled intensity, like vicious dogs chained to a tree. "A stain? A stain you say. Oh, you're looking at it all wrong. You need to stop thinking like sheep. At a personal level, at a national level, it's all the same thing. Our show of strength with the

Japs, the Russians, and all that have come after is why we are on top of the world. Would you rather be at the bottom? I'd rather be on top, and you have to show your strength to stay at the top. It's not a stain, Michael; it's a badge."

Michael chuckled. *What a nutcase.* "I don't think we are going to agree on this, are we?"

"Probably not. You picked a good subject for your article, though. War—a guy like you chooses to write about war. I find that interesting."

"A guy like me?" Michael knew exactly what he meant—a sissy, a sheep. The question slipped out of him as a reaction.

"Let's just say I can't picture you with an M-16 strapped to your back, crawling through the mud under enemy fire."

"Oh, I didn't know you served," Michael said as believably as he could. Of course, he hadn't. For all his bravado, Victor Goddard had been but a beneficiary of his old man. He'd had an easy life, turning money into more money with little to no effort. And now, he spoke like a self-made John—fucking—Rambo!

"I didn't say I served," he responded, as though taken aback.

"Oh, I just…the way you described crawling through the mud so vividly, I thought…sorry, I misunderstood."

"Yeah, I get it." Victor glugged down what was left of his beer. "I wanted to ask you, how did you meet Anna?"

"Oh…um, I met her at the historical society." Michael remembered that picture—young Victor with that other girl—and Anna's face when she saw it.

"Really? So you were working then."

"Barely. It was a slow day." *They are all slow days.*

"And why was Anna there?" Victor slanted his head, eyes slightly squinted.

"Lucky for me, I guess she must have been especially bored that day."

"Yeah, lucky you." The sniper's eyes fixed on his empty glass mug, turned it clockwise full circle, then glanced at the front door as if expecting something—service, perhaps. "A psychologist and a historian—damn, you two would drive your kids crazy."

Michael forced his lips into a smile. "Yes, we probably would." Perhaps, he'd ask Victor about his own kids. He'd heard some pretty insane stories. His parenting advice might be dark comedy gold.

Victor shifted in his seat and brought one leg over the other. "Speaking of you being a historian, I'm sure you'd appreciate the history of this house. It was my father's. Charles Goddard was his name. Does it ring a bell?"

"The fact is I met your father years ago. He contributed generously to the historical society, as he did to several other institutions, from what I've been told."

"Sounds about right. He did care about a great many causes. He was a very wealthy man, as I'm sure you know."

"Yes, I figured as much," said Michael.

"At the height of his real estate empire, if I may be so bold as to call it that, he owned five different houses in these parts, each one as large as this one, and three apartment complexes. But what is really remarkable is this—whether because the old man was truly magnanimous, or because he didn't want any of us secretly wishing for his death, he gave money and properties to my brother and I in life, many years before he died, in fact. This house was his wedding gift to me—I was only twenty-three years old when I married Lydia. The house was ready for us when we returned from our honeymoon."

"That's really something. What a gift. This house looks like it must have been built in the 1920s. Is that right?"

"You know your stuff," Victor said. "It was built in 1922. It's really quite remarkable when you think about it. Sometimes, I like to picture a brand-new Ford Model A, or one of those classic Studebakers parked over there." He pointed at the front lawn. "A family lived here during the Great Depression. Then World War II. Then someone watched the news of Kennedy's assassination in the same living room where we watched the news of the 9-11 terrorist attack and live broadcasts of the war in Iraq."

"Yeah, it's something. The house is almost a century old."

"On this very same porch, the man who sold this house to my father might have hugged his son for the last time before he went to die in Vietnam. I don't know that, of course, but the thing is, if the house could talk, it would sure as hell have some great stories to tell."

"Yes, it would, wouldn't it?" *What stories would it tell about you, Victor?* The thought of asking that question popped up in his mind as though whispered by a devilish creature or, perhaps, Frank?

The idea of Frank seating beside him in invisible form, egging him on to raise hell, amused him. Half of the stories Anna had told him about her father in the last few days involved Frank, that heroic, defiant son of a gun.

Victor's gaze wandered for a moment; when it came back around it had hardened. "What did you say your last name was?"

"I didn't. It's Donovan."

"Donovan, Donovan…I knew a Donovan years ago. A tenant in one of my apartments. Patrick Donovan was his name. A relation of yours by any chance?" Clearly, this Patrick Donovan was someone beneath him, some loser who'd once lived within the fringes of his empire.

"No, most of my relatives live in Philadelphia."

"Philadelphia, huh? You look like you have some Irish in you. Am I wrong?"

"No, you're right."

"Oh, I'm good at this. Catholic?"

"I was raised Catholic, yes."

"Raised Catholic. I love that phrase. It leaves you in suspense. Is a but coming after that? I was raised Catholic, but I haven't stepped into a church in decades. I was raised Catholic, but now I worship the devil." Victor let out a burst of laughter. "All jokes aside, are you a Catholic, then?"

"Well, not exactly." *Shit! Not this topic with Mr. Come-to-Church-or-I'll-Break-Your-Bones!*

"What do you mean, not exactly?" The right tip of Victor's lips edged up, a crevasse running from his cheek to his chin like a dried-up riverbed.

Michael felt a droplet of sweat sliding down the back of his neck. This couldn't be over soon enough. "What I mean is that while I believe in the values professed by the Catholic Church, I don't subscribe to the supernatural aspects of the Church's teachings." *Yes, big words, Victor—because I'm a nerd—just leave it alone.*

The sniper's next words came out in an increasingly piquant tone. "So, what you're saying is you're a good guy, but you don't believe in God. Did I understand you correctly?"

"That's a way of putting it." *Bullshit, that's exactly right.*

"Simple but accurate, wouldn't you say?" A sardonic little smile crept up on his face. Michael felt a sudden impulse to grab a chair and smash it over his head. The sniper was quite right about his chemistry theory. He'd fallen for Anna pretty much on sight. He liked Frank instantly. And now, it only took him minutes to want to murder him. Loathing at first sight.

The sniper put his sight on the front door again; he seemed impatient, even angry. Then back to Michael. "And how did that come to be? You just stopped believing one day?"

"It didn't happen in an instant. I guess there must have been one first moment of doubt, but I couldn't tell you when that was. At some point. I could no longer reconcile science and history with my religious beliefs. I had to choose, so I chose hard facts over dogma."

"Dogma?" Victor exclaimed, his eyes as big as he'd seen them. "That's such an ugly word in the mouth of an atheist. It's so full of disapproval and self-righteousness. If Faith was a child, dogma is what the evil kids at school would call it sneeringly. I find it disrespectful, to be honest, but I'm sure you didn't mean it that way. Right?"

"I certainly did not, and I apologize if that's how it came across. Perhaps, I should have said religious beliefs instead. In retrospect, I think you're right. It is true that the word *dogma* is most often used by non-believers."

"Apology accepted." Victor's face twisted into a bizarre smirk, as though his body and his mind were having a disagreement. "We're just two men speaking candidly, and in an unguarded exchange one must risk getting a bruise or two." A long pause; his gaze drifted toward the spot on the front lawn where his imaginary Studebaker would have been. "And Anna knows this about you? That you're an atheist?"

"She does know I'm a nonbeliever. It somehow came up in conversation with her and Frank, actually." Michael immediately regretted mentioning Frank.

"Oh, Frank, ha! I bet he agrees with you on this one, doesn't he?" Victor brimmed with unconcealed disdain.

"Um, yes, yes, he does."

"To be perfectly candid, it does bother me a little."

"What does?" Michael asked.

"That you're an atheist; because the thing is, if you two get married and have kids; then, will you even want to baptize your children, my grandkids? Is Anna supposed to accept that their children will grow up atheists. Do you expect me to accept it?"

Was that a threat? *Yes, Victor, your opinion matters to me as much as the astrology section on an old newspaper*—that's what he should have answered. If only he didn't care about making a mess of things. Hell, Anna would probably like him better for it. No, perhaps she wouldn't. The angry silverback demon sniper could take it out on her mother.

"Honestly, I'd want to raise the child in a way that my wife would be comfortable with," Michael responded with poise. "I wouldn't just impose my view. If that means that the child grows up to be a devout Catholic, I'm fine with that."

His eyes narrowed, and his lips pulled back into a skeptical smirk. "You'd be willing to have your children raised with beliefs contrary to yours, in your own house?"

"That's right." *This better be the end of it!*

"Would you go to Church with them? Sing the hymns, pray aloud, stand when you're supposed to and kneel when you're supposed to, before a God you don't believe in?" A triumphant ugly grin crept up on Victor's face.

Michael chuckled, looked away from Victor's intense stare. "I guess I'll cross that bridge if and when we get there. There's no sense in racking one's brain with such questions now. Who's to say that Anna won't dump me next week?"

"That's just lazy, Michael. I was led to believe that you enjoyed a good debate."

"I'd gladly debate a topic not as emotionally charged as religion."

Victor sat back with his hands behind his head, biceps bulging up. "But isn't there a sort of hypocrisy in being willing to debate only topics that you can keep at a safe distance from your heart? What could be more important than your lack of belief in God and the afterlife?"

"Lots of things. That's just one aspect of who I am."

"I couldn't disagree more. See, Michael, you live your life believing that any day you could drop dead, and that will be it. You will—what?—be no more? Disintegrate? The heart stops, the brain goes dark, and your essence, nothing but chemical reactions and electric pulses, is lost forever?"

"That's actually very well put." Michael could hardly stop himself from laughing.

"Then how could that notion not govern every thought and every action of yours? Why deny yourself anything in this one life you have? Why risk your life for anyone or any cause when death is so final?"

"I believe good deeds are their own reward. They make me feel good about myself." *What else do you got, sniper?*

"And what comfort could you give anyone on their deathbed? Would you tell your mother, just before the end, that she's at the edge of a great precipice, an endless darkness from which she shall never return?" This was probably his best argument so far, not a bad jab.

Michael gave it some thought. "Um, my mother did die, many years ago; and, no, I didn't tell her about the great precipice." Michael chuckled in an attempt to lighten things up. "I didn't tell her anything. That's not how I picture death, anyway. I suppose there must be as much fear and suffering after death as there is before birth—none. Peaceful nothingness."

"Sorry about your mother, Michael. I didn't know." Victor ran his index finger around the edge of his empty mug; his face twitched as if, just then, he'd made a critical connection. "The joke is on Anna," he remarked, though it seemed more like he was thinking out loud.

"What do you mean?" asked Michael, feigning indignation. Anna didn't care for her father's approval, so why should he?

"Don't get all worked up, Michael. I'm actually somewhat impressed by you. You've proven to be far more interesting than I expected. You'll understand what I mean in a minute. See, I know that Anna has always seen me as an arrogant prick—and make no mistake, that's exactly what I am. But I have a right to be. And I think you do too, Michael."

"So, I'm an arrogant prick?"

"Yes, but that's a good thing. Men aren't really created equal, Michael. They feed us that bullshit since we are kids, but it's not true. Some men have what it takes to be lawyers, doctors, men of stature, even presidents; and some have what it takes to lick those other men's boots. Now, you should know that Anna thinks she dislikes arrogance, but I can see now, quite clearly, that she doesn't. She's attracted to the arrogance she wants to hate."

"You're losing me here, Victor," Michael interposed. "If there's something I'm not, that's an arrogant man."

"Yes, you are. Your stance on death, that's what gives you away. You've decided that you're strong enough to face an unforgiving death, oblivion, a vision of death almost no one could endure, a death without hope. You're at peace with it; yet you would not tell anything of that sort to your mother on her deathbed, and probably to no one else. Therefore, you must think that others couldn't face such a hopeless death as stolidly as you do. You must believe you're inherently stronger than them. In your own way, you're an arrogant wolf like me."

"A wolf, you said?" This Michael hadn't expected. Was this a good thing?

"Yes, you should embrace it. I'm a sovereign wolf, Michael. That's my nature, and I don't try to hide it. Doesn't mean we're evil, just strong, better. I've been plenty merciful with the sheep in my life, because I know God would want me to." There was something unsettling about the way he spoke. Michael would have loved it if Anna had come to grab him that very moment, but he wasn't so lucky.

"I guess whatever pushes us to be better is worth keeping, right?" asked Michael, attempting to return to shallow waters.

"You're quite right," Victor said impassively. His gaze wandered again.

The front door swung open. Lydia approached them; Anna was not with her.

"How are you two doing over here?" she asked.

"A little thirsty," Victor said with an edge in his voice, "but we are enjoying ourselves, aren't we, Michael?"

"Most certainly," Michael lied amiably.

"Truth be told," Victor said, putting his hand on Michael's shoulder for a brief moment, "this has been the most interesting chat I've had in a very long time." He looked at Lydia oddly, with a twisted smile that seemed sarcastic. "I'm seldom afforded the opportunity to converse with any real depth. It's been quite a treat. I wish I could do it more often."

Lydia blushed. She was beginning to turn around to go back inside but stopped abruptly and turned back to them. Her big, green eyes gleamed intensely as she said, "Perhaps, it helps that Michael, being our guest, need not worry about you, um...strongly disagreeing with him."

Not two seconds after she spoke, Lydia's expression had transformed, and it was dread, not anger, that her eyes now conveyed. Michael looked from her face to Victor's, which had contorted into a deep, menacing scowl. It was as bone chilling a countenance as he'd ever seen. Victor addressed her in a steely voice imbued with feigned civility, "Honey, please, we must maintain our decorum, especially in the presence of guests."

"You're right, of course. I apologize for the offhand remark. Would you care for another beer?" Her voice was now like a kitten's.

"Why, yes, that would be marvelous, honey. How about you, Michael?"

"Oh, I think I'll wait a little," Michael said, frozen in place. "Don't want to drink too much, too fast."

"All right," Lydia said. "I'll be back with your beer, Victor." The apologetic kitten went back inside.

Victor didn't speak for several minutes and would not even make eye contact with Michael. He just looked out into the vast front yard. Michael did the same. A strong gust of wind swung the branches of several large, mature trees and made a whistling sound that had a soothing effect on him. A moment later, Lydia came back with a glass of beer and, without uttering a word, placed it in front of Victor. He didn't look at her.

Victor waited until Lydia had gone back inside. "One must show strength with women, Michael. Remember that. They might think they want a sensitive, considerate, indulgent gentleman; but when they get one of those puppets, soon after, they are disillusioned and crave something else—they yearn for danger, excitement, even a little fear. It turns them on. Haven't you noticed that?"

Victor took a sip of his beer; didn't wait for an answer. "They want a real man, a strong man. Even Anna, modern and independent as she appears, in the end, I assure you, will want to have an apex predator by her side."

Was Michael that apex predator? That's what the sniper wanted to know, now looking down on him from his tower, measuring him up.

"There must be some middle ground between being a puppet, as you say, and being a dictator, don't you think?" Michael asked, perhaps with a brazen tone; he couldn't be sure how it came out.

"Wolves and sheep, Michael. You must decide which you want to be. Do you think I'm a dictator? Maybe you've been talking to Frank too much. That ungrateful prick, what a loser he would have been if I had been soft on him, if I had allowed him to disrespect me. Sometimes, a good slap on the face is the best gift you can give your kid. You don't think I took a couple good ones from my father? Oh, yes, good hard ones. But I'm sure I deserved them, and they made me a better, stronger man."

He gazed at Michael with amusement and interest. "Oh, yes, Charles Goddard, the patron of the arts and saint of all good causes, the philanthropist, he was no sheep, Michael. He was a wolf, a bigger wolf than I am. He just made sure to lick off the blood from his fangs before showing himself in public. I learned from the best. He was a shrewd, tremendously successful businessman—but you knew that. Sheep don't run successful businesses. Wolves, Michael, they run the world. I suggest you develop a taste for blood."

Michael didn't know how to respond to Victor's wild rant, so he didn't. He sat back trying to think of anything he could say to change the subject entirely, but he drew a blank. The best he could think of was to comment on the time. "Oh, look at that. It's almost five already." Victor nodded while silently studying him. No other words were spoken for a period that felt as unnerving as it felt long.

The silence was broken by the sound of glass or porcelain shattering inside the house. Victor rolled his eyes but didn't move. Michael was going to get up, but he heard Lydia's voice announcing, "Everything is fine, just a broken tray; we got it."

Adrift in a sea of awkwardness, Michael impatiently awaited to be rescued. Deliverance from his appalling host came to him a few minutes later. Someone in a small white SUV had come through the gates and pulled up next to Anna's car.

"Someone's just arrived," said Michael.

"Oh, good. Marlene is here." Victor took one last gulp of beer and leapt off his chair. "Excuse me," he said, not even looking at Michael.

As Victor went inside the house, Michael got up and leaned against a column. Two ladies emerged from the white vehicle. The youngest of the two, evidently Anna's aunt, came out of the driver's seat. A moment later, she and her elderly mother, Anna's grandmother, slowly approached the house. Anna's aunt was a strikingly attractive woman, perhaps two or three years younger than her sister, Lydia. She somehow seemed familiar to him. Where could he have seen her before? Surely, they had never met, but, wait, could it be?

An unthinkable idea took hold of him. It seemed ludicrous, and yet it made perfect sense. The moment she stepped onto the porch, looked at him and smiled, he was sure—this woman he was about to meet, Anna's aunt, had been the high school girl he'd seen with Victor in that photograph that had so disturbed Anna. No wonder she had not wanted to talk about it.

CHAPTER XIII

Anna had dreaded leaving Michael alone with her father. It was torture to think of the vicious, appalling rhetoric Michael was likely being subjected to at that very moment while she waited for a batch of butter rolls to be ready. Rectangular trays with clear lids, full of side dishes and appetizers, crowded the kitchen counter and the dining table. Her mom was planning to take them to the large picnic table out front just after five when the others started arriving. It wouldn't be long now, Anna thought.

Three more minutes for the rolls in the oven, and her mom would not stop talking about the most excruciatingly trivial matters. Perhaps, she feared that any moment not filled up with meaningless chatter could become one of those brief silences that often lead to genuine dialogue; and that could derail a perfect day of pretend family bonding. She was dying to take a peek at Michael. She shouldn't have brought him.

The timer reached zero, and she opened the oven. Golden perfection! The rich, buttery smell filled her nostrils, and she stopped thinking about Michael and her father for a whole minute. She had a roll, and so did her mother. Oh, they were scrumptious. Finally, something they could truly enjoy together. "I'm going to check on your dad and Michael, see if they need anything," said her mother. Anna followed closely behind her, and as she stepped out onto the front porch, Anna rushed to a window from which she could see them up close, looking through the blinds so as to remain unseen.

Michael smiled, but it didn't seem genuine. He looked rather uncomfortable. Her father must have been grilling him with insolent questions the whole time. He must have offended him in some way. If this did anything to damage her relationship with Michael, she would have no one but herself to blame for it.

Her mother approached the table. Through the thick glass, she could only make out a few words. Now, her father smiled and put a hand on Michael's shoulder. Anna tried hard to listen—something, "most interesting chat I've had," something, something. What the hell did he say? Was he being sarcastic? Of course. There was that face he always made. What was he saying now? She couldn't make it out, but clearly, it had been an offensive remark. She could see it on her mother's face—he had humiliated her in front of Michael, the same way he always did in the presence of her kids. The disgraceful scene made her cheeks flush and her fists clench. Anger and shame overwhelmed her senses.

What happened next was rather unexpected. Her mother turned around abruptly and faced her tormentor defiantly. Anna couldn't hear the words, but her mother's face was taut with anger, and her lips quivered as she spoke. Michael was evidently quite alarmed. Her father's face now grew menacing as he spoke. The expression on his face chilled Anna to the core. She had only seen it once before—the day he gave Frank that awful beating.

Her mother now looked downright scared; she uttered something submissively, averting his gaze, shrinking; her entire body cringing as if about to be hit by a tsunami wave. Could he actually hurt her? Had he already hurt her? Anna lowered the blinds, closed her eyes. A cold draft sneaked inside of her, blowing over dusty memories of her teary-eyed, red-faced mother, rushing to her bedroom, locking the door, her broken voice answering, "I'm all right, sweetie, just tired, just need a nap."

Anna started for the front door. As she reached it, so did her mother from the other side. She stepped aside to let her in. Once inside, her mother used the back of her fingers to stop tears from rolling down her face, and a muffled whimper broke through her trembling lips.

"What was that, Mom? What happened? What did he tell you?" As Anna held her, she could feel her mother's heart pounding vigorously.

Lydia took a big breath and pushed back from Anna. "Listen, I just…I need a minute, all right? We'll talk in a moment. Um, did you put in the second batch of butter rolls?"

Anna didn't answer. Butter rolls, that's what she was thinking about. Her mother's helplessness angered Anna. It always had. Anna wanted to shake her up, slap her, even, if that's what it would take to finally wake her mother up.

Lydia ran back to the kitchen and returned with a glass of beer. Anna couldn't believe her eyes. The beer was for her father—a servile gesture meant to appease the beast. Her humiliation would now be complete. The thought of snatching the glass from her mother's hands and smashing it against the wall played in her mind vividly. Instead, she watched her mother stride by with the master's drink.

Anna went to the kitchen and put the second batch of rolls in the oven. The sweet and savory smells that inundated the air now struck her as ironic and upsetting, like a circus clown at a funeral. Anna stood ready to get some answers from her mother, who came back looking rather weary.

"All right, Mom, now tell me—what hideous thing did that monster say to you?"

"He's your father, you know."

"Oh, screw that, Mom. What did he say to you?"

Lydia crossed her arms, squinted her eyes. "In front of your boyfriend, you forgot to say. Is that what bothers you most?"

"Sure, I would have much preferred that Michael wasn't subjected to a shameful scene like that. But bringing him here was my mistake, not yours. That's not what this is about, and you don't get to turn this on me. We are talking about you here—about your life, and your dignity. When are you finally going to stop taking Dad's abuse? Just leave him already, Mom, for goodness' sake."

Lydia sat down on a tall brown stool by the counter. Her downcast eyes darted from one side to the other before she took one more deep breath and lifted her gaze slowly, as though with great difficulty.

"This time I was partly to blame. Yes, he hurt me with a nasty, sarcastic comment. He insinuated I'm stupid…or boring." Lydia closed her eyes and a tear slipped through, but she captured it before it could carve a furrow through her makeup. "I saw Michael's expression of embarrassment and that made me feel the sting of Victor's insult even more. So, I lashed back at him with a little sarcasm of my own. It was quite unnecessary. I know that now."

"How you keep finding ways to blame yourself is beyond me. Unbelievable. Don't you think you deserve some semblance of happiness?"

"It's not always bad, you know. Your dad has his moments. When I was young like you, I also idealized love. If you're lucky, you get to live that fantasy for a short while, enough to create a few good memories. But life carries on, and things change. Soon, you realize that little moments are all one can ask for."

Had her mother been a smoker, surely, this would have turned into one of those classic moments of depressing wisdom served between plumes of smoke. Anna was reminded of her neighbor, cigarette in hand, pensive, lonely, missing her daughter, her little angel. Was she her mom's angel? Did she deserve the title? Was Frank more honest than her? That day in his apartment he kept crying, "I should have done something." Perhaps, she too should have done something. Should have seen something. Should have believed her eyes, her instincts. She sure as hell should do something now.

And she would. "And in between those scanty little moments, Mom, is it okay to get abused, belittled, mocked…maybe even hit by your husband?"

Her mother opened her eyes wide. "Why would you say that? Have you ever seen your father hit me?"

"Well, hasn't he? Because the way he just looked at you out there froze my blood—yes, I was watching, and I saw the fear on your face."

"You really shouldn't be meddling in our relationship. It's complicated enough as it is. But I know what he is, I know what he's not, and I've made my peace with it. My life is not as terrible as you might imagine, and your father is not the devil."

"Well, answer me then. Has he hit you, Mom?"

"What if he has? What would you have me do? Leave him, get a divorce, right? That's easy for you to say. I'm fifty and have never had a real job. What am I going to do? Live under a bridge? Try to get a job flipping burgers to survive? This isn't some movie, Anna, or one of your books. In real life, things don't always work out in the end for the good girl. So, wake up!"

"Mom, don't you know? In a divorce settlement, you'd probably get half of everything. You would be fine."

Lydia chuckled dejectedly, tragically. "Oh, you sweet innocent child. I've done a good job protecting you from some harsh truths. This little empire Victor has, he got it all from his father, the magnificent Charles Goddard, before he married me. Being the cunning man that he is, of course, he made me sign a prenup. We always lived in his world. It's about time you knew."

"Jesus, Mom. Why did you sign a damn prenup?"

"I was young and stupidly in love. He persuaded me that it would have been extremely unfair for him to risk half of his father's living inheritance when half of marriages end in divorce. So, I did that and then proceeded to become a housewife, get pregnant immediately with Frank, and then again with you, and no career. Just stupid, stupid, stupid."

"Wow." Anna shook her head in disbelief. This explained so much that she would almost have to revise her perceptions of her entire childhood. "I wish I knew what to tell you, Mom, but I'm stumped."

"Well, then we are finally talking. I'll answer your question now. Twice. He has hit me twice in almost thirty years. The first time, we had been married about four years. You and Frank were very little. We had a guest, a lady friend of ours. I was coming back from the kitchen with cookies I had baked, and right then I thought I saw something going on between them. They were looking at each other in a flirtatious way; at least that's what I thought I saw. I was very jealous back then, and your father was a hunk. He still looks great, for his age, but back then he couldn't walk into a bar without half the women turning to look at him. He was super athletic, and he had this sexy swagger—"

"Ugh, I get the idea. Please don't make me puke."

"I'm just trying to provide some context. Anyhow, that night I confronted him; I asked him directly if he liked her, if he wanted to…screw her. I was really mad, so I don't know what else I might have said to him.

But the next thing I knew, he had slapped me across the face pretty hard. I remember it so clearly because no one had ever slapped me before. It's like time stopped and everything went quiet. At first, he looked surprised that he had done it, but in a moment, his face hardened, and he just stormed out. I think only a minute or two later I started feeling that side of my face really warm and tender, and I had the salty, metallic taste of blood in my mouth. I did think of leaving him, then, but I was crazy in love with him, and I had two little ones, of course. So, I just didn't."

"How awful. Did he come back asking for forgiveness or some crap like that?"

"He said he was sorry, but he didn't beg or anything. Nothing was the same after that."

Was Aunt Marlene that flirty guest? Anna sensed she was close to uncovering the whole truth. "Mom, who was that woman?" The question came out like a bullet.

Lydia's face went pale, like that day in the garden. "Why would you ask me that? It's no one you know."

"Surely, you'd never forget her, that sleazy, treacherous woman. What was her name?"

"Um, Nancy, that was her name. A friend from college. Are you happy now?"

Lydia looked agitated. She stood up abruptly and, in doing so, flung back an arm which struck a fine porcelain tray and sent it flying off the counter. It hit the floor and shattered into a thousand pieces, making a remarkably loud noise.

"I'm pretty sure they must have heard that," said Anna.

"Yes, I bet they did," said Lydia, and then yelled out, "Everything is fine, just a broken tray; we got it." She stepped away and came back with a broom and a dustpan. "At least, it was empty," she said, while scooping up sharp chunks of porcelain from across the dining room.

"When was the second time?" asked Anna from behind the kitchen counter.

"What?"

"You said he hit you twice. When was the second time?"

Lydia came around to the kitchen and emptied the dustpan into the trash. She leaned back against the sink and gave a heavy sigh. "A month ago." She smiled despondently.

"What? A month ago? And you said nothing?"

"Of course, I said nothing. And now, you will do the same. I want you to promise me. Frank cannot know any of this. I didn't protect him his whole life to have him throw everything away now with some stupid, heroic act."

"You said a month. Is that four weeks today? Because I was—"

"Yes," Lydia cut her off. "You were here that Sunday. It was that night, after you left."

"How did it happen?" Anna's heart was pounding like a drum. If her mom said anything about Aunt Marlene, she would have to tell her about the text message. Then things could quickly get out of hand.

Lydia closed her eyes and sighed deeply. She snatched another tear before it could stream down her cheek. Then, looking down at the floor, she said with a broken voice, "I spoke to my sister on the phone after you left. She talked about Diane. She was crying, and...I told her that sometimes I feel...like I've lost my kids too, especially Frank, that my boy won't set foot in this house again because his father is a monster."

"You called him a monster?" Anna interrupted. "That's the first time I've ever heard you say it."

"Those were my exact words—and he was just around the corner, listening. I thought he was in the basement, counting the rent money." Lydia stopped another two tears from ruining her perfectly dolled up face. "The moment I got off the phone he was there. And...oh, he was livid! He accused me of slander—what a word, right?—and I don't know what else. I think he truly believes he was a perfect father, that he made you strong, prepared you for life, all that crap. I told him he was crazy and that I had said nothing but the truth. And that's when his hand landed on my face."

151

"Mom, you could come live with me. What are you waiting for? He's going to kill you one of these days. Did you see his face out there? It sent a chill down my spine. That's not a man who loves you. That's a man you should fear."

"And I do."

"Well, then do something. I'm serious. Leave with me today."

With misty eyes, Lydia gazed at her daughter in silence for a moment, then she threw her arms around her and hugged her tenderly. Anna teared up. Would this be the day she'd save her mother from a wretched life?

They heard the front door open and Victor's heavy footsteps approaching. Lydia stepped back and gave Anna a little shove. They both tried to look busy. "The butter rolls will be done in another two minutes," Lydia said just as Victor showed his face.

"Marlene's here with your mother," he said, coolly scanning both of them.

"All right. I'll be there in a moment," Lydia said.

Victor nodded, a jarring unfinished smile carved on his face, eyes like cobalt arrows. Anna had to look away; looked at her Mom, at her own feet—anytime now they'd become tiny, her hands too, and her voice would shrink, become a little girl's, shrill and powerless. When she raised her gaze again, her father had left without saying another word, his heavy steps moving away toward the front, then the sound of the door opening, indistinct chatter outside, door slamming, then silence.

Her mother spoke softly now. "We'll talk more after everyone leaves. Let's put on a good face and try to enjoy the company of the people who love us."

"All right, Mom. You go receive Grandma Rose and Aunt Marlene. I'll finish up here."

Her mother gave her a kiss on the cheek and left the kitchen. In another minute, Anna had taken the rolls out of the oven. She grabbed her bag and went upstairs to check the view from every window on the second floor. There was her old bedroom, her father's office, a guest room, and Frank's old bedroom. His electronic keyboard was still there. Memories started flooding in, but there was no time for that now.

She texted Frank, "Your old bedroom has the best view of the picnic table." The office in the back had the best view of the garden, of course, but surely, she didn't need to remind him of that very useful detail.

Anna peeked at the landing to make sure that no one had come upstairs. She opened her bag and took out a small pair of binoculars Frank had given her. She sent him another text, "Binoculars planted inside closet in your old bedroom."

She received a text from Frank, "Got it. On my way there. ETA 5:25." Her job there was done. Anna almost ran downstairs. It had been a while since she had last felt such an adrenaline rush. The time was 5:17. She took a few deep breaths, normalized her heartbeat, and headed out to the front porch.

Upon stepping out, she saw Aunt Marlene conversing cheerily with her parents and Michael. Grandma Rose came straight toward her with a big smile on her face. "Anna, my baby. Oh, am I happy to see you. Look at you. Oh, sweet Lord, you're just gorgeous." She gave her a warm hug and a kiss on the cheek. "I met your boyfriend. Goodness gracious, he's easy on the eyes, isn't he? And so proper and well-spoken too."

"Yes, I like him too, Grandma." Her grandmother laughed. Michael had been darting looks at her. Now, a smile from him reassured her. He seemed in good spirits, in spite of what he had been put through.

Grandma Rose went and sat down by herself in one of two rocking chairs that were close together, with a small side table between them. Anna joined the others. She gave Michael a quick kiss and whispered to his ear, "I'm so sorry."

Marlene wrapped her arms around Anna. "I'm so happy to see you. It's been too long." It felt strange being embraced by her aunt—Anna pulled out gently. Marlene continued. "I just met Michael a moment ago. He was telling us all about how the two of you met."

Crap. "Oh, is that right?"

"It's quite a story. I mean, you must have driven by that history museum a hundred times before and never stopped. Am I right?"

"Yes, you're probably right." Anna laughed to conceal her nerves. Could Michael have mentioned the photographs? "But there's only so much you can do around here, so I was bound to go there eventually."

"It just goes to tell there's such a thing as destiny. Who knew that you would meet this handsome, classy guy in there? I must admit that I've never as much as stepped into one of those local museums. Perhaps, I should have, right?" Marlene got a little laugh out of her sister and an amused smirk from Victor. Michael blushed.

"Well, now," said Lydia, "everyone else will be here shortly. Anna, would you help me bring out the food and get the table ready?"

"Sure, Mom."

"I'm happy to help as well," said Marlene.

"Great, this will be easy, then. All the food is in covered trays," Lydia explained. "We'll place them side by side at the center of the table, like a buffet line."

"I could help too," said Michael.

"Oh, I have the perfect job for you. See that cooler over there?" Lydia pointed to a large white cooler in a corner, close to where Grandma Rose had been sitting. "Hey, Mom, why are you sitting there all by yourself?"

"Don't you worry about me. I love this spot right here," said the old lady. "It really is a gorgeous day. I'm taking it all in. Maybe you'll come sit with me later."

"Sure thing, Mom. So, let's fill up the cooler with a mix of beer, cola, juice, and water bottles; all of which are now in the fridge inside. We have three large bags of ice in the freezer. Should be enough. We'll keep it over here where everyone can see it."

"You got it." Michael darted a look at Anna. She knew that he wanted to talk. He couldn't have suffered through that godawful experience with her father earlier and not want to get a thing or two off his chest. It would have to wait, however, until they were by themselves, which might be hours later.

A flurry of activity followed, then everything was set in under ten minutes. Anna placed the last tray on the table and, precisely then, Frank arrived with Sarah. It was 5:29. She waited for them right where she stood.

Frank looked very tense. Conversely, Sarah had the expression of a curious little girl arriving at the county fair. Anna greeted them both warmly before whispering to her brother, "Take a deep breath. We are doing this for Mom. Whatever you do, don't lose your temper. Let's stick to the plan."

"I can't believe I'm here," Frank whispered. "Do you think I might burst into flames the moment I walk in?"

"Very funny. You might, though."

A muted laugh broke from Frank. He kissed her forehead. "It's show time. Let's go."

Sarah observed them with amusement from a few feet away. She had been surveying her surroundings with interest. "That is one big house," she said.

"And it's haunted too," Frank joked as they began their slow approach.

Lydia came out and met them by the picnic table. She hugged and kissed her son effusively, and then Sarah as well. Her eyes were brimming with emotion. "This is such a happy moment for me," she said with her hands on the shoulders of Anna and Frank. "I'm so happy you could come, Sarah. Come on, I'll introduce you to Frank's father, and also my mother and my sister, who came here all the way from Baltimore."

Victor came out of the house and greeted them at the top of the steps. He spoke to his son first. "Hey kid, it's good to see you," he said, and their hands met in a handshake that seemed like they would arm wrestle.

"Hi, Dad," Frank responded coldly, and quickly gestured for Sarah and his mother to come up beside him. Sarah grabbed his hand as Lydia introduced her with a propriety that struck Anna as antiquated and contrived.

"It's lovely to finally meet you, Sarah. I was told you were beautiful, but words couldn't do you justice. Frank, well done, my boy, well done indeed."

Frank's face wouldn't budge.

"Why, thank you, Mr. Goddard," said Sarah bashfully, her cheeks blushing instantly.

"Oh, not Mr. Goddard, please. Just Victor." He smiled like a suave British spy. Frank's face appeared carved in granite. Lydia's reminded Anna of very expensive porcelain.

Victor looked over Frank's shoulder, and his face lit up. Mark Goddard, his favorite nephew, had just arrived with his wife, Jackie, and their twelve-year-old son. "Well, Frank," he said, slowly stepping aside, "after Sarah meets everyone, you should give her a tour of the house. I'll catch up with you later."

Victor went to greet Mark and his family out in the front yard. In the meantime, Frank introduced Sarah to his grandmother and Marlene before going inside the house—for the grand tour, Anna presumed, but surely Frank would not miss the opportunity to examine the views from every window upstairs. No doubt, he would begin considering potential scenarios in his mind. They had agreed that Frank would be in charge of initiating their little operation, but only when they could get Victor and Marlene in a satisfactory position, in full view from his vantage point upstairs.

Anna looked around for Michael and spotted him getting something from the big white cooler. He was alone, which presented a rare opportunity for Anna to go talk to him about what had happened earlier. She dashed over there and kissed him before he could say a word.

"Well, I've missed you too, gorgeous," said Michael when their lips parted.

"I'm so sorry you had to see that awful scene earlier with my father. I didn't think anything like that was in the cards for you today. Perhaps…I don't know. Promise me something—if at any point things get weird or uncomfortable for you, in any way, just take off. Don't even bother to say goodbye. I'll understand."

Michael delicately tugged on her chin and kissed her lovingly. "Nothing is going to scare me away from you. There could be a dragon hidden in this house, and I wouldn't care. You're the most amazing thing that's happened to me, ever."

A warm sensation of pure joy overtook Anna. She threw her arms around him and buried her face between his neck and shoulder, taking in his sweet, musky scent. "I feel the same way about you." She pulled back and looked him in the eyes. "I love you."

He said the words back to her, his voice filled with emotion, eyes wide open, his face tender and shiny like honey-butter biscuits. The kiss that followed transported Anna to a place without troubles, without pain, a place hidden from time itself.

And then that moment ended. "I see your father coming back with a couple and a kid," said Michael.

"That'd be Mark, my cousin, Uncle Rick's son. Trust me: you don't want to be stuck in a chat with him and Dad. Come, walk with me toward Mom."

They stood next to Marlene. In front of them, Grandma Rose was rhythmically rocking back and forth while telling some story from when she was young, a period she referred to as a simpler time. Sitting on the other rocking chair was Lydia, who gazed at them with a tinge of warm suspicion.

Anna's phone vibrated at 5:45. It was a message from Diane: "I'm here. Small blue car. I want to talk to Mom out here before going in there."

Anna relayed the message in a whisper to her aunt. Marlene's face brightened up. "Excuse me. I need to, um…Diane is here," she said in a jittery voice.

"Of course, go, go, sweetheart!" said Grandma Rose.

Lydia became visibly emotional as her sister walked out to see her daughter. She gazed at Anna approvingly. Michael kissed her forehead. One thing was certain—she would end this day either as a heroine or a villain.

In another minute, Victor had come over with Mark, Jackie, and their son. Grandma Rose greeted them with a languid gesture—barely a nod and a half smile. Lydia managed to show a little more enthusiasm, though hardly convincing. Anna herself tried her best to look as though happy to see them, but Mark was everything she hated in a man—he was a backward, narrow-minded jerk. And her dad loved him.

"Michael, this is Mark, my nephew. This is his wife, Jackie, and their son, Richard." From Victor's affected tone, one would have thought that he was introducing the duke of Blake County and his illustrious family.

"It's a pleasure to meet you, Mark," said Michael, and they shook hands.

Did Michael and Mark instinctively know that they'd hate each other's guts? Some ideas have a way of permanently imprinting themselves on a person's face. Michael's reflected intellect and curiosity. Mark's, on the other hand, was engraved with self-righteousness and intolerance. And, as if the guy needed to be framed in a more obvious context, his wife looked like a cartoon stereotype of a trophy wife; and little Ricky's face belonged in a school poster about bullying.

"Darling, did anything happen to Marlene?" Victor asked when conversation ran dry.

"Why do you ask?" asked Lydia.

"Because she dashed past us like she didn't even see us."

"Ah yes, Diane just arrived. She went to see her first."

"Oh, good," Victor said. "I should go say hello."

"No," Anna said, "Please, we should give them space. Let them have this moment to themselves."

"Yes, maybe you're right," her father replied, his gaze set on the spot under a dense sycamore tree where a blue car was partially concealed by his Mercedes. "Can't wait to see them together, mother and daughter reunited at last."

Lydia broke the awkward silence that followed. "Yes, we all do."

Victor looked at Lydia, his head slightly slanted, a barely perceptible smirk on his face, as if he found her curious. Meanwhile, Grandma Rose had stopped rocking her chair, the cadenced creaking sound now absent, like a ticking clock abruptly halted. Mark looked uncomfortable, as did his wife. The kid looked dumb, still, unplugged. Anna felt her hand squeezed a bit tighter by Michael's.

"Well," said Victor, his gaze skipping Grandma Rose altogether and finding Mark, "I'm sure we'll be celebrating shortly. What an occasion." Anna recognized this voice, this facade—it was her father's public persona. Charming, spotless, synthetic.

Before long, Victor took Mark and family inside the house. A few minutes later, they came back out and immediately bumped into Frank and Sarah, who seemingly had been taking a stroll through the grounds. Another set of uncomfortable, stiff greetings—Frank loathed Mark even more intensely than Anna did. His face appeared taut, unyielding, like a stone dam holding back a rising tide of turbulent waters.

Then all were gathered together, at least in the strictly physical sense. On closer inspection, three groups—perhaps Michael would even call them factions—now shared the front porch. The Goddard establishment stood like gatekeepers by the front door. Their corner, defended by Grandma Rose's mere presence—what would Michael call them? Anna looked at him now; leaned in and gave him a peck on the lips. The silent majority? Perhaps. On the far corner stood Frank and Sarah, a balanced equation, staying on the sidelines, avoiding collisions.

That was the state of affairs when Marlene came back with Diane. Their faces reflected that the much-expected reconciliation had been realized. Lydia was the first to reach Diane at the bottom of the steps. Her heartfelt hugs and kisses were followed by a surprisingly warm welcome by Victor. He took her hands and spoke kind words to her—Anna couldn't hear them, but Diane's bashful smile was evidence enough.

After that Diane went straight to Grandma Rose, hugged her long and hard. She then turned to Anna. "Hey, cuz. Michael."

"Hi, Diane," said Michael.

"Hey!" Anna said, hugged her, and added, "I take it all is good with your mom?"

"Everything's good." She smiled, eyes sparkling.

Frank and Sarah came over. More hugs, kisses on cheeks.

Frank stole a glance at Anna—no words needed. Soon, they'd begin. A nagging feeling ate at her, though. Should she ask Frank to stop this thing? Her mother was starting to open up to her, so maybe there was another way. But Frank wouldn't stop now; that much, she knew. And he was right, they had to know the truth. Diane too needed to know.

Eventually, everyone started to collect around the picnic table, which was lined up with the various treats that Lydia had prepared for them. Small groups formed and split up as everyone went around seeking conversation with whoever they had not yet talked to. After a while, everyone had sat down in more permanent groupings around the table.

It was 6:28 when Anna and Diane got the first message from Frank— "Great view from Eagle's Nest. Initiating." They had figured that Frank could be out of sight for, at the most, ten minutes, before Sarah would begin asking about his whereabouts. At the moment, she was at the far end of the table, laughing at something Grandma Rose had said. Nearby, but standing off to the side, were Lydia, Marlene, and Diane.

Anna stole a glance at the windows but couldn't spot Frank. That was good news. She darted a quick look at her cousin, and their keen gazes met fleetingly. Michael had just come back with two beers. They were standing about six feet away from the near end of the table, where her father was dazzling Mark and Jackie with his stories. The kid was nowhere to be seen. He was probably inside the house playing with his video game.

While Michael whispered to her a witty remark about Mark, Anna noticed that Diane had succeeded in getting Marlene and her mother to sit at the table with Grandma Rose and Sarah, who seemed to be getting all of their attention. Now, she needed to get closer to her father, at the right angle, without raising suspicions. Only then could Frank initiate their attempt to steal the pass code to their father's phone.

"Let's get some meatballs," said Anna and dragged Michael toward the table. The cocktail meatballs were just to the left of where her father was seating—his phone rested face up on the table. She smiled politely at him and his audience before grabbing four meatballs stuck on toothpicks. She gave two of them to Michael and stepped away, gesturing Michael to come along.

"Do you want to sit down?" he asked quite naturally and, to her dismay, loud enough that her father might have heard him. She needed to position herself behind her father, at an advantageous angle, far enough to avoid detection but close enough to see his phone screen at the right moment. If her father turned around now and asked her to join them, the plan would be ruined. Sitting beside him, she would be neutralized.

Luckily, that didn't happen. Michael read the angst on Anna's face and quietly backed away. "Sorry, I should have guessed that you didn't want to sit next to your father after what happened earlier," he said.

"It's fine. I can't expect you to read my mind all the time. Great meatballs, huh?" She could breathe easier now, but that had been a close call.

She was in a great spot now. Frank couldn't ask for a better moment, and indeed, right then came a message from him, "Be ready. Incoming message for Dad in next 30 seconds."

"Where's Frank?" Michael asked. He lowered his voice almost to a whisper when he added, "I haven't seen him in a while, and Sarah is here. Was that him texting you just now?"

Anna knew Michael was on to them. He was too smart and perceptive; and she didn't want to lie to him anymore. He deserved better from her.

"Come with me. I need to tell you something." Anna grabbed Michael's hand and started for the bench under the big oak tree, where in her dream she had reunited with Bo. She looked up at the window where she assumed Frank was looking down at her. Seconds later, she texted, "Do not abort. Give me a moment. Diane, keep Sarah talking."

They reached the bench. Nobody around. Anna asked him to sit down next to her. Time to confess.

161

"What I'm going to tell you now may or may not shock you, now that you've met my father. I'm just going to come out with it. Frank and I have come to think that, quite possibly, our father had an affair. And…" Her voice cracked up. The shame was too great.

"And," Michael interrupted her, "you believe that affair was with Lydia's own sister, your aunt Marlene. She was the girl from the picture, wasn't she?"

Anna felt her face flushed. "Goodness, how long have you known?"

"It all came together today, really. When I saw Marlene, I recognized her. Same eyes, same smile."

"I'm embarrassed on so many levels, Michael. I just—"

Michael cupped her cheek gently. "Don't be. You have no reason to be embarrassed."

"I'm sorry I kept you in the dark about all this. It's just such nasty stuff."

"Stop it. I don't care. I'm crazy about you, girl." Michael kissed her before she could answer that, but he already knew she was crazy about him too.

She dizzily pulled back from their kiss. "Listen, I need to go back there. We have a plan to find out the truth, for once and for all, but now is the only chance we'll have. It's all in the text messages between my father and Aunt Marlene."

"Is it worth the risk?" Michael asked with a note of genuine concern. He must have really got to know her father.

"I hope so. If we can prove it, I know it would be the final straw, and Mom would finally leave him. She has to!"

He held her hands. "Well, count me in then. How can I help?"

"Why would you want to get involved in this?"

"Because it's important for you."

"You're something else, you know that?" Anna leaned over and kissed him again. "Now, I don't want you taking any big risks, but perhaps, at the right time, you could create a little distraction for Mark and Jackie. I'm going to need their eyes off of me. Come on, I'll explain while we walk back there." She texted, "We are back on. Michael knows."

A text from Diane warned, "Sarah just asked about Frank."

Frank replied, "I'm texting Sarah. Michael knows? Anyway, let's do this now."

Anna hastened to give Michael a condensed version of their plan and tactics. First, to steal the pass codes, they would put two sets of eyes on each phone. Frank, from his vantage point, assisted by binoculars, would attempt to spot the pass codes. However, Anna and Diane would simultaneously try to do the same at close range to ensure the outcome. The key was to know exactly when Victor and Marlene would pick up their phones and enter their pass codes, which Frank would attempt to trigger by sending precisely coordinated text messages to each of them at specified times.

If successful, then they would need to get either Marlene or Victor, through a diversion, to leave their phone unattended on the table, long enough for one of them to grab it, find and take a snapshot of the text messages—assuming they were there—and return the phone, unseen by anyone.

As soon as Anna and Michael were back in position, about three feet behind Victor, Frank's next message came through. "Here we go. Incoming message for Dad. Eyes on target." The quasi-military language was efficient, but Anna suspected that Frank was having a little too much fun with his role as commander of their make-believe rebel army. About two minutes went by without Victor reaching for his phone, which no longer sat on the table.

"Second attempt. Eyes on target." Shortly after Anna saw Frank's new message, her father reached into his pocket and took out his phone. It was white, like her own. He made four lightning-quick taps on the lock screen, corresponding to the four digits of his pass code. From where she stood, Anna could only see where his finger had last landed, either at four or seven—she couldn't be sure which one.

Her father turned around with a malicious smile on his face. "Hey, Anna, when did your brother get so mushy? He just asked me if he could have his old electronic keyboard. I mean, of course he can take that old piece of crap, but doesn't he have a nice piano now?"

"He does. A very nice one." Anna thought she'd stutter. Her throat felt tight, her mouth dry. She'd better try to relax.

"I guess he's up there in his old bedroom, taking a trip on memory lane, huh?"

"Yes, why wouldn't he? So many lovely memories here, everywhere I look."

Her father's lips twisted into a bizarre smirk. "Yeah, yeah. Maybe he'll try on his old Batman costume too." Mark laughed raucously. No one was laughing at the other end of the table. Sarah seemed puzzled.

Frank's latest message came through, "Only got three of the four digits. 8-6-9, missed the last one."

Anna sent a reply, "Last one was either 4 or 7."

"Are you sure???" Diane replied. Anna darted a glance at her. She seemed anxious.

"4 or 7, I'm sure. Frank, your cover is almost blown. Dad told everyone, Sarah included, that you texted him from your old bedroom."

Another message from Frank, "Incoming message for Aunt Marlene. Diane, eyes on target." Only a few seconds later, Marlene picked up her phone from the table and swiped her thumb across the screen. She looked momentarily confused, or perhaps annoyed, but quickly put the phone back on the table and kept listening to Grandma Rose.

"Can you believe that? No pass code!" texted Frank.

Anna replied, "That was easy. Come down and take Sarah for a walk or something. Dad made things a little weird here. She'll have questions. You better have answers."

"Copy that. Heading down. Buckle up, ladies. Now comes the real challenge."

CHAPTER XIV

Tinges of crimson and orange had begun to color the azure-blue sky by the time Frank and Sarah returned from a long walk. The prolonged hiatus gave Anna plenty of time to brood over how she was now keeping a dangerous secret from Frank. Her mind grew restless.

What if her mother stayed there tonight and he hurt her? What if he—God, no!

Anna winced at the thought, tried to will it away but the shadows wouldn't retreat, her nightmare hiding behind every creaky old tree, ready to jump at her, the premonition she chose to ignore, back for more, back to get her.

Small feet, chasing after Bo. Come, boy! What have you got there? Flowers. A bed of flowers. Mom, dead!

Fuck! She snapped out of her vision, gasping. Did she gasp? Michael stood beside her—Anna pulled him closer and propped her chin on his shoulder.

She could tell Frank everything. The two of them could drag their mother out of the house. But who knew what Frank might do if he learned right then and there that his father had already twice hit his mother? He could do anything, blinded by rage. The risk was too great.

Something was eating at Diane. She'd barely spoken in a while and kept darting uneasy glances at her. It wasn't hard to empathize with her cousin. She had just regained her mother and now, perhaps, stood to lose her again. Could she find it in her heart to forgive her mother's sin against her own blood? Would she deem it frailty and not wickedness? Such somber questions, without a doubt, were enough to cast a shadow on the bravest of faces.

It was 7:35 when Lydia brought over her homemade lasagna. The sight of the glorious blend of cheeses that had so many times before made Anna salivate with anticipation now positively turned her stomach. By design, she'd sat next to her father.

Michael had taken the seat across from her and next to Mark, who had lined up a row of four empty beer bottles and was working on his fifth— the effects of alcohol were starting to show on his face, giving it an even more loathsome appearance. His kid, forced to sit between him and Jackie, had his face buried in a video game and headphones stuck in his ears.

Grandma Rose and the two sisters were sitting as before. Frank and Sarah, being the last to arrive at the table, ended up across from each other, such that Frank sat next to Michael and Sarah between Anna and Diane.

Sarah leaned over and whispered to Anna, "Frank told me about your little operation. For the record, I think you guys are crazy. I like it, though. Way to grab the bull by the horns." Anna smiled naturally and kept her mouth shut. This was no time to be reckless. Could Frank really have told her everything?

A sharp clinking sound startled Anna. She turned to see her father tapping his glass with a knife. "I want to thank each of you for coming here today. This has been a real treat for us," he said affectedly, his piercing blue eyes making a stop at every face around him. "And, of course, I want to thank Lydia for preparing this extraordinary dinner for us— thank you, darling." Victor's expertly delivered words were followed by a cacophony of gratitude and praises for the cook. Anna couldn't remember a single time he thanked her mother for a meal in the privacy of their dinner table.

Four flood lights turned on around 7:45. The sun had just set, and a quarter moon was now visible in a quickly darkening, deep-blue sky. Chatter around the table somewhat died down for the next five or ten minutes, as everyone gobbled up Lydia's acclaimed lasagna. Anna got a small piece, butchered it, and smeared sauce all over her plate, concealing the fact that she had barely tasted it. All she could think about was when and how to get her father's phone, which was now on the table, inches away from her right hand.

Her dad was, at the moment, seemingly engrossed in some dumb story Jackie was telling. If she were to grab his phone and walk away, she might go unnoticed for fifteen or twenty seconds. She could walk the first ten feet and then run away. She could run and search for the messages simultaneously. But what if she tripped and fell? What if the pass code was wrong? Then he'd be alerted, and there wouldn't be a second chance, not to mention that she'd have to explain her strange behavior.

She took out her phone and placed it on the table, a mere six or seven inches away from her father's. It was white like his; not the same phone, but same brand—his was an older, slightly smaller, and bulkier model. An accidental swap—that could work. She glanced over at Frank. They made eye contact, but by that, she probably accomplished nothing more than communicating a vague sense of urgency. She texted him, "Dad's phone looks like mine. Attempt a swap?" He read the message, looked at her, and gave her a barely perceptible nod.

Anna gently nudged her phone another inch closer to her father's. He was laughing. In another moment, Frank whispered something to Michael, who now stood up and winked at her. He walked past Mark and suddenly turned around. "Oh, hey, I'm going to grab a beer. Any of you want me to bring you something?" It was the distraction she needed.

It all seemed to happen in the same single instant. Mark thanked Michael more effusively than warranted. Sure, he'd have another beer. Jackie said something else. It was all a blur. Anna had her hand on her phone now, initiating a circular motion to complete the swap. She felt all tensed up, her heart pounding like the hooves of a racehorse on the final stretch. Victor's phone chimed and down came his hand and grabbed the phone, nearly touching her hand. A scream had wanted to come out of her chest; she barely managed to stop it at the top of her throat. It had been a very close call. And a failure.

Victor appeared to be texting, then stood up. "Excuse me," he said and walked away. Michael crossed paths with him at the steps. He darted confused glances at Frank and Anna. Everything appeared to be coming apart. Now, Marlene also left the table. It appeared as though she'd received a phone call and needed to take it in private. Awfully suspicious, though. She walked in the direction of the big oak tree under which there was a bench, then made a turn, and disappeared behind the house.

They must be meeting in the backyard, Anna swiftly concluded. They had taken separate routes to avoid detection, but it was as clear as day. Her father would go out the back door and wait for her there. Someone had to go and check on them right away.

Frank almost got up. Anna stopped him with a subtle gesture. To avoid alerting their mother, only one of them should go. Frank and Diane were sitting too close to her, so their getting up could've tipped her off that something was awry.

Sarah caught on to their situation and grabbed Diane's wrist under the table to keep her from rising. Anna texted, "I'll go. Stay here and act natural." Frank looked down at his phone and whispered something to Michael, who nodded in silent agreement.

Anna got up and walked slowly first, then faster as she approached the steps. Michael was right behind her. She couldn't be sure that her dad and Marlene wouldn't be inside the house. That was another possibility, she thought suddenly, and gestured Michael to avoid making any noises.

They stopped and listened intently as they reached the dining room. Nothing. They went a little further. Anna peered up the dark stairs. They stayed motionless for a few seconds. Not a sound. They made it all the way back. The door was open. Anna carefully approached a window while Michael crouched by the open door. An aluminum screen door provided him some concealment from anyone looking in from the outside.

Anna couldn't see a thing out there. It was pitch black. Michael motioned her to come over by his side. Anna tiptoed, crouched, and crawled her way to him. He pointed to a spot in the garden where something was moving. She stuck her face to the screen and peered into the darkness. In a few seconds her eyes adjusted, and she could make out two silhouettes under the very dim light of the quarter moon.

The female form that more and more resembled Marlene now gesticulated with her arms, as if quarreling. "It's them, all right," Anna whispered to Michael. "This looks pretty damning." She took a picture with her phone, but the quality of the photograph was very poor. It was too dark, and she couldn't use the flash.

Suddenly, they saw Victor holding Marlene, pulling her closer to him. Any last trace of hope was now gone—the affair was real. Her own shame no longer mattered. The thought of revealing to her mother her sister's betrayal made her heart ache more than anything else. And then there was also Diane—poor Diane.

She tried to record a video, as definitive evidence, but by the time she had them on frame, Marlene had pushed him away and was walking back. Her father stayed behind; he lit up a cigarette.

"We need to get back before Marlene gets there," Anna said. Michael led the way back out of the house. A moment later, they were back at the table. Frank and Diane were trying hard to read their faces. Marlene returned in another minute, giving Anna the impression that she may have stopped along the way, perhaps to compose herself.

Anna texted Frank and Diane, "They met in the garden. He tried to kiss her, but she wouldn't let him. Sorry, too dark out there for pictures or videos." Sarah had been looking over her shoulder as she typed. Fine, she might as well know.

In another minute or two, her father returned and sat next to her, as before; he brought with him the unmistakable stench of cigarette smoke. Anna didn't look at him.

Diane replied, "We are doing this now. One way or another, let's get those messages."

"Dad's phone is on the table. Need a good diversion to stage a swap."

Frank sent instructions, "I'll pull him off to the side. Swap phones when you hear me speaking to him. Wait for him to grab the wrong phone before attempting the pass code. My little drama should buy you a couple of minutes."

In another moment, Frank stood up quietly and walked behind Michael, Mark, the kid, and Jackie. He turned around and approached his father from his right side. Anna locked her phone and carefully placed it on the table next to her father's. As soon as Frank spoke and her dad's gaze turned to him, she switched the position of the phones so that now her phone was the one closest to Victor's left hand.

"Dad, can I talk to you for a minute?" Frank asked in a tone that was somehow entreating and haughty at the same time.

"Sure, go ahead." Victor sounded curious.

"I meant alone. Perhaps, we can sit on the porch?"

"Um, sure, why not?" Victor's tone betrayed surprise. Without looking back, he reached for his phone as he rose from his chair; his hand found Anna's phone where his had been and carried it away.

Time to get the job done, but the kid's dumb empty gaze had fixed on Anna, for whatever reason. What would a smeared piece of lasagna look on that goddamned face?

Right on cue, Michael stood up and clumsily knocked off his half-full beer bottle and an amber river spilled out of it in the direction of Mark. "Oh Jesus, I'm sorry, Mark. I'll clean it up. Hope I didn't get any of it on you." It was a crafty distraction to get all eyes away from her. She took her dad's phone and brought it down to her lap.

Anna darted a look at Diane, and their eyes met. Her cousin's expression revealed not only great anticipation, but also dread. Anna entered the pass code 8-6-9-7. It didn't work. Then it must have been four, she thought, and tried 8-6-9-4. It unlocked.

Holy crap, it unlocked. Her sweaty hands fumbled through screen after screen—heart throbbing, throat knotted, temperature rising—she found the damned messaging application.

Marlene's name at the top of the list; he had texted her only minutes ago, "Meet me in the back." Even that might be evidence enough. She started scrolling up in a rush to find older messages—one month old to be precise. It was then that she was startled by her father's powerful, ominous voice.

"Hey, Anna. Anna! That's my phone." A chill ran through her body, and her hands shook violently as she scrambled to close the messaging application and lock the phone.

Her father stood next to her now. Dead silence, then his voice again, collected, cool. "That's my phone you have there, Anna. Here's yours."

170

"Yes, I just noticed that myself. They're almost identical, aren't they? We must have got them mixed up."

"Evidently," he said, now with a raspy voice, as he unlocked his phone and scrutinized it with glittering, beady eyes. He stood there for a moment before returning to the porch, where Frank awaited him.

A message from her brother asked, "Did you get it?" Michael's inquisitive eyes asked the same question. Sarah whispered to her, "Are you all right?" Diane couldn't wait any longer—she came over and crouched next to Anna. She spoke in an urgent whisper, the way a prisoner of war would speak to another during a fleeting lapse in surveillance.

"What did you see? Tell me, please. Tell me now," she said.

"I could only see one message before Dad came back. It said, 'Meet me in the back.' That's all. I didn't have enough time."

"You did get in, then?"

"Yes, I did."

"The pass code, which one was it?" Diane asked with urgency, as if she needed it to defuse a bomb.

"Why does that matter now?" Anna stole a glance at her mother and Aunt Marlene. Thankfully, they were chatting away, oblivious to the drama unfolding so very close to them.

"Which one was it, Anna? Was it 8-6-9-4?"

"Yes, that was it. What's going on with you?" Anna felt a pang in her heart when she saw Diane's eyes fill up with tears. Something was very wrong.

"August 6, 1994," she said somberly, her lips quivering like tiny leaves trying to survive a blustery fall evening. She put her hand behind Anna's back, pulled her toward her, and whispered to her ear, "It's my fucking birth date, Anna. It's me. I was born that day. Why? Why? You tell me: Why the hell is your father's pass code my birth date, not yours or Frank's?"

Anna felt suddenly cold, as if turning to stone. What Diane was implying was too terrible to imagine, let alone utter. She dared not say it or ask her cousin to spell it out.

"Anna, listen to me," Diane looked her straight in the eyes, and re-markably, there was now resolve in hers—those icy-blue eyes. "Please do as I say. No questions. I'm going to stand up now and I'm going to walk past Mom. At the exact moment when I'm behind her, you're going to call her name. Make it loud. Startle her. I don't care what you say to her afterward—it's not going to matter."

Diane did as she said. At the right moment, Anna called out, "Aunt Marlene!" It was loud enough that not only her aunt, but her mother, Grandma Rose, and even Michael and Sarah, all started in their seats. None of them seemed to notice when Diane snatched her mother's phone and kept walking with her own phone to her ear, simulating being on a call.

"Goodness gracious, Anna," said Lydia. "You're either a little deaf or a little drunk."

"I'm sorry, I…just want to tell Aunt Marlene, and Grandma, that their making the trip to be here with us today, well, it's amazing. I'm really happy you came."

"I think we all agree with that," her mother said. "But maybe also no more beer for you, darling, okay?"

"Aww, aren't you sweet?" said Marlene. "Let her drink all she wants, Lydia. Just don't drive, Anna. You should stay here tonight. Right, Lydia?"

"It sure looks that way." The Wilde sisters shared a good laugh at her expense. It would be their last laugh of the night.

Once under the cover of darkness, Diane ran toward the bench un-der the big oak tree. Soon, all Anna could see of her was a shadowy silhouette dashing though the blackness. It was at least another minute before Marlene noticed that her phone was missing. At first, she re-mained calm, as she rummaged around in her bag. When she didn't find it there, her demeanor began to show some urgency. She looked on the grass around her, got down on one knee to search under her chair and under the table.

When she rose again, she appeared unhinged, darting frantic glances around the table, repeating over and over, "Have you seen my phone?"

Her eyes settled on the empty chair where Diane had been, and terror sprang from her eyes and spread through her face, like it had always been there, waiting for this moment.

Anna heard her father's voice coming from the porch, getting a little closer every moment. "I'm glad we talked, kid" were his dad's last words before he was standing silently next to her. One ominous glance from Marlene had frozen him in place. Then the whole table went quiet. Frank seemed stunned at first, but in another moment, he had understood something, and his eyes gleamed like hellfire. About a hundred yards away loomed, floating in the dark, a light, like a large firefly. Marlene started marching toward it, and instinctively, it would seem, everyone followed her. So did Anna.

The light became Diane's face, illuminated by the bright, white screen of her mother's phone. She was seating on the bench, sheltered by the big oak tree.

"Diane!" Marlene called out. "What are you doing there? You're scaring the heck out of all of us."

"It's you, Mom, who's going to scare them now," Diane said in an eerie monotone voice, as if possessed. She stood up on top of the bench, such that everyone could see her intense countenance floating in midair.

"Whatever this is, Diane, stop it." Marlene's voice faltered. "Please, let's talk inside."

"Oh, no, no. It seems this little chat is more than two decades over-due, and it doesn't concern just us, does it, Mom? Let's stay out here and do a little light reading from your chat with Uncle Victor. Well, you know what? I'll just call him Victor for now."

Victor intervened, "Diane, you're embarrassing yourself with this spectacle. Come down from there this very second." His voice sounded commanding but hollow, like a corrupt general giving out his last orders before being court-martialed.

Frank's voice broke out from the shadows, loud and clear, triumphant even. "Let's hear it, Diane. Let's hear it all."

Anna sought out her mother in the dark. A faint ray of moonlight shone upon Lydia's motionless face; she gave the impression of being made of marble. Anna stood beside her and held her hand; it felt in her grasp like a cold river stone. She braced for impact.

Diane began, "Four weeks ago, on a Sunday, this was Victor's first message of the day to you, Mom. 'I want to see you again. I know you must feel the same. Our attraction is inevitable, a law of nature.'

"And you answered, 'We can't do this anymore. I moved out to Baltimore to get away from you. You made your choice. You have a wife, my sister!'

"He replied, 'I asked you to be my wife. I would have left Lydia. At least, I'm honest about it. Will you deny that you left George because you were still in love with me?'"

Diane glanced at her petrified audience. Her theater mask had worn off, and tears were streaming down her face. Her voice now began to break up. "There's more. Mom answered, 'Don't even mention George. That saintly man was to Diane the father you would have never been.'" Diane paused, wiped her tears. "Oh, dear God. He says, 'But I am her father.'"

Gasps, weeping, and murmuring filled the air. Anna embraced her mother. "I'm sorry, Mom. I'm so sorry." What else could she say to her? "Let me get you the hell away from here."

Her mother said nothing, just hugged her back.

Diane kept on, her face soaked with tears. "My father, Mom? My father? Your sister's husband? Have you no shame? And this…this is how I find out? You'll both burn in hell."

Diane read from Marlene's phone. "Oh, but you knew that already. 'You and I are both to blame for this, and we shall be judged in the end.' Your words. Yes, I do hope you're judged in the end, but I will judge you now. We will all judge you now. You're guilty! You're horrible creatures, both of you—you've caused nothing but pain to those you were supposed to love."

Diane threw the phone at her weeping mother's feet. "I'll say one more thing, and then I'm going to leave. Victor Goddard, you may have impregnated my mother, but you're not my father. I'm the daughter of George Jennings, a great man who I adore, who has shown me unconditional love, and who has always been there for me, no matter what. Nobody will take that away from me. Anna, and Frank, whatever we are to each other, I do want you in my life. Aunt Lydia, I'm so very sorry. You deserved better than this."

With those last words, Diane dashed through the darkness before anyone could react. In another moment, she had made it to her car and was gone. Marlene was on the ground, crying bitterly, holding her head with both hands. A few steps away, Lydia wept in Anna's arms, quietly, in a dignified manner. Frank too came to console his mother, and they melded in one embrace. Michael and Sarah stood around them in stunned silence. Grandma Rose sat on the bench, crying wretchedly for her daughters.

Mark and his family had apparently bolted during the commotion. Off to the side, Victor remained, alone, staring at them like a sinister presence. He finally spoke in a callous voice, without a trace of remorse.

"Here we are, in a way, right where we started—me and the lovely Wilde sisters. I tried to make up my mind—I really did; but you made it so damn hard. Oh, Marlene, the prophecy is now fulfilled. I always thought this day would come. It was naive of you to think that we could live our whole lives hiding this secret. All those years ago, the truth could have liberated us. Now, the truth has come back to exact its vengeance."

Marlene would not speak, or stop crying pitifully, and she would not raise an inch of her body. It seemed like she was begging for the earth to open up and swallow her whole. Lydia pulled back slightly from Anna and darted a glance at her sister. Which emotion it was that flashed on her face at that instant, Anna couldn't say.

When Frank abruptly turned around and dashed toward his father, Anna knew he wasn't about to have a chat with him. She tried to stop him but wasn't quick enough.

Lydia cried, "Frank, don't!"

"Take it easy kid," said Victor. "I'd hate to have to give you another beating."

Frank was not in the mood for talking; he was in the mood for hitting. The first punch he swung just missed Victor's face. His father countered with a short punch to the ribs, which seemed to stop Frank for a second, but he recovered quickly and launched a vicious left hook that landed on Victor's chin. Just then, Michael grabbed Frank and pulled him back, saying, "Come on, man, stop this. Escalating matters won't help anyone. You got him pretty good there. Now, let him go."

"Ugh, you're right, buddy," Frank said to him while stepping back, his eyes never leaving the sight of his father.

Victor stood there nursing his chin. His eyes glimmered menacingly. "I guess we are done talking for now. I'll get out of your way. We'll talk later, Lydia, when cooler heads can prevail," he said.

Lydia finally blew up. "What is there to talk about, you dirty, rotten bastard? You piece of shit! I'm leaving tonight. Tonight! You hear me? Tonight!"

"Are you? Well, I guess it's never too late to start over. Yeah, I'm sure you'll be fine."

"She'll be fine. I promise you that, you monster!" said Anna.

"You better get the fuck out of here already, or I swear I'll rip your head off!" Frank bellowed out, his face contorting with primal rage, his fists clenched and ready to make true on his threat. Sarah put her hand on his chest and looked him in the eye; he took a deep breath, and his fists loosened.

"Like I said, we'll talk later. I'll be in the basement, out of your way." Victor's moonlit small eyes glowed spitefully, chillingly. He turned around and walked away.

CHAPTER XV

Once Victor was gone, a sudden, awful silence engulfed them. Marlene had sat up on the grass, her face still drenched with tears. She looked absolutely shattered, as if she had aged five years in five minutes. She now spoke for the first time since Diane had left. Her voice came out subdued, brittle, and imbued with a sense of hopelessness.

"Lydia, I wish there was something I could say to you that would make things better. I know there isn't. I know I'm dead to you, now. And dead to my daughter, too. I'm as much of a monster as he is. Perhaps, I'm worse. Hell must be full of shameless wretches like me."

Lydia looked at her sideways, saying nothing to her directly. She spoke faintly to Anna, "I want you to make sure that Mom and Marlene are okay. Frank can go inside with me while I pack some things." She was lost in thought for a moment, then took a deep breath and exhaled slowly, while her lips made a cynical smile. "You know what? That rotten bastard has $12,000 of rent money stashed up in the basement, which is exactly why he's there now. He's guarding the goddamned money. He wants to cut me off entirely. He will call the bank first thing tomorrow morning, you'll see."

"Everything's going to be fine. We'll get help. You must have some legal recourse. Not everything could be covered by..." Damn, she'd forgotten Frank was right beside her.

"Covered by what?" he asked.

"A prenup. Dad made her sign a prenup. Please, let's talk about it later."

Salt sprinkled over an open wound, Frank's face contorted into a tortured grimace. "Ah, that fucker. That miserable steaming pile of shit. Oh, Mom…why'd you…ugh!"

Sarah's comforting arms came around Frank; her chin landed softly on his back, just below the base of his neck. He closed his eyes for a second. "But, hey, forget about that now, Mom. Anna is right. It will be fine. You will be fine." He exhaled so hard he might have been expelling a demon from his chest. "Let's go get your stuff and get the hell out of here."

Frank turned to Sarah and kissed her, then put his hand on Michael's shoulder. "Hey, buddy, I need a big favor. Sarah has seen enough of this shit show already. This is a fucking nightmare. Could you take her home for me?" Sarah mounted a weak protest, but she couldn't hide her weariness from all the tension she had experienced.

Anna sent Michael off with a tender, grateful kiss. "Frank and I have this covered here. After you drop Sarah at her place, please just go home and rest."

"Okay, but you call me if—"

"Yes, I'll call you," Anna interrupted. She gave him another peck on the lips, then turned to Sarah, and gave her a heartfelt hug. A moment later, they were gone.

Lydia kissed Frank's forehead and grabbed on to his arm. She was ready. Anna watched apprehensively as they walked away and went inside the house. A part of her wanted to run in at full speed and get them out of there that very instant.

Behind her, poor Grandma Rose had all but cried herself to sleep on the bench. It was a strange sight; so still she was that Anna imagined she had grown roots and turned into wood, forever to be part of that haunted place.

Marlene had just gotten up from the ground. Her expression was numb and dreamy, as if she suspected that it was all a nightmare from which she would soon wake up. As she gazed at Anna, fresh tears came rolling down her cheeks, slowly, as if for dramatic effect.

"I don't even want to imagine what you think of me. I'd rather you didn't tell me. Let me assume the worst because the worst is probably right." Marlene gave a despondent sigh. "God, that was one short-lived reconciliation, wasn't it? I had my daughter back for, what, two hours? And now, I've lost her for good. I hope she's fine. Oh God, the way she drove off...I'm sure she's speeding right now. Where's she going to stay tonight? Some random motel out there?"

Anna had no answers for Marlene. She'd hardly begun to work out her own answers. Did she hate Marlene? She was surprised to find she didn't. Did she think her base? Perhaps. As much of a monster as her father? Not even close. Marlene didn't have a malicious bone in her body. The truth is she'd always been weak. In that, the two sisters were much alike. The Wilde sisters, the dirty son of a bitch had called them suggestively, as if they were a combo deal. They'd been easy targets for the cunning devil they fell in love with when they were just two stupid girls. He was truly an evil creature; making cruelty look easy, as if a dark fairy godmother had released him from the burden of carrying a conscience.

"Would you help me take Mom to the car?" asked Marlene. They held Grandma Rose from both sides and began bringing her to her feet.

"I can walk just fine," she protested, suddenly coming back to life. They walked beside her all the way to the front passenger seat of Marlene's white SUV. She was lying back on the seat, about to doze off again, when she said to Marlene, "I'm fine here. Don't worry about me. Just, please, before this night is over, ask for your sister's forgiveness; get on your knees if you have to. She might be too hurt to forgive you tonight, but she'll remember your gesture."

Marlene kissed her mother's cheek. Soon, she was fast asleep. Marlene and Anna leaned against the side of the vehicle, looking in the direction of the house. Several minutes passed before Marlene spoke again.

"If there's something you want to say, or ask me, this seems like as good a time as any."

"Honestly, I don't think it would do any good," Anna said. "I'm tired of looking back, digging up dirt."

"I think I know what you mean," said Marlene. But she probably didn't.

"You do?" asked Anna, tempted to tell her everything. But what would that accomplish?

"When you dig up the past, all you get is dirty."

"That's from a movie, isn't it?"

"Isn't everything?" Marlene's lips began curving up, quivered, went still—a stillborn smile. "We both fell in love with him in high school. God, he was handsome, your father."

"Really, you don't need to tell me this, and I'm not sure I want to hear it." Not anymore, anyway.

"Don't you want to know why?" asked Marlene, her voice feeble, eyes on the ground.

"I'm a big girl, Aunt Marlene. I think I know why a man and a woman end up in bed." That came out edgier and meaner than she had intended.

"I guess you're right. Everything else is just excuses, lies that I tell myself. He did it. He cornered me, he kissed me, he…but I was there too. I didn't run. I didn't scream to wake up Lydia. Oh, how I wish she had taken it easier with the wine that night. But, no, you're right. I let it happen. Deep inside. I must have wanted it. In her own house, no less. Right fucking there, with you and Frank sleeping upstairs."

Anna felt as nauseated as she knew she would. Marlene must have needed to hear herself say it all out loud. "So that's when you got pregnant with Diane?"

"That's right. I thought of having an abortion, but I just couldn't. I decided that I no longer mattered; my child was innocent, and I was going to make sure that she could have a happy, normal life."

"And you met George." Anna hoped to end this awful chat now.

"I had known George for a while. He'd been in love with me for a very long time. But, yes, George rescued me. He loved me so much that he was willing to raise Diane as his own daughter and keep my ugly secret forever. I was four months pregnant with Diane when we got married." Marlene threw her head back and looked at the stars. "I was never unfaithful to him, you know—not that I deserve a medal for it or anything."

Victor's black Mercedes, barely visible in the dark, reminded Anna of Diane's account. "Were you ever with Dad again after that?" she asked. The question came out as if someone else had taken control of her mouth.

"Ugh, yes, I did. Not long after George and I had separated Victor showed up at my place late one night and…well, you know. That's when I knew I had to get away from him. My parents had returned to Baltimore a couple of years back, so I knew that I could go there and count on their support."

"And was that the last time?"

"You seem to know that it wasn't," Marlene said curiously, her eyes meeting Anna's momentarily.

"The messages between the two of you seem to suggest so."

"Yes, there were other times. Victor would tell Lydia that he was going on some bullshit business trip, and instead came to see me in Baltimore. I had to give myself to him, or he would tell Lydia everything about us, even about Diane. That's how he kept me as his slut on the side." Marlene's head sank on her chest, tears streaming down her cheeks. "I've feared this day for a very long time, Anna. Twenty-four years I've spent trying to spare Diane the pain I saw in her eyes tonight."

A text message rang in on Marlene's phone. She grimaced as she read it but said nothing. Anna wanted to ask her—perhaps the message had been from Diane. But right then, Marlene's phone rang again, this time repeatedly, as it was a call coming through.

"I need to take this call in the car," she said with a note of urgency and went inside her vehicle, turning her face down and away from Anna. Her own car was only a few steps away, and she figured she could call Michael from there, while still keeping an eye on her aunt.

Michael answered quickly, "Anna, hi, how's everything over there? Is your mom with you?" Anna explained to him the current state of affairs, at least what she knew. The thought that she really didn't know what was happening inside the house unnerved her all of a sudden. They had been inside for a while already. "Perhaps, you should text Frank, just to be sure that they haven't run into your dad or anything," Michael suggested. "I just dropped Sarah off at her place. I could go back there now."

"No, it's fine. I'll be sure to call you if anything changes. Otherwise, I'll call you tomorrow morning...I love you."

"I love you too, gorgeous." Second time today, she thought—a rare moment of bliss in this very dark night.

Anna must have taken her eyes off her aunt for only a few seconds, but she wasn't inside the car now. She gazed around and didn't see her. Michael was still on the phone, saying something about having lunch tomorrow. "Michael, I got to go now. I don't see Aunt Marlene. She was in the car and...I'll call you later. Love you. Bye."

Anna got off the car and looked about the house. She barely managed to see the front door closing behind a figure that looked like Marlene. A rush of panic coursed through her body, and she started running to the house. She tried to call Frank while running, but her hands jerking up and down with every stride made it impossible. She ran up the porch steps and into the house. She heard Marlene's voice coming from the basement, her father's man cave.

"You son of a bitch!" Marlene screamed. "I swear to God, you're done ruining my life! You're done ruining all of our lives!"

Anna dashed through to the top of the stairs as fast as she could. Marlene's voice got louder.

"How far should I have moved to escape from you? Alaska? And now, this—are you out of your fucking mind? Do you really think I'm going to keep on being your mistress, your slut? Or that I'm going to replace my sister and be your little wife? Can't you see what a goddamned creep you've become? I should fucking kill you!"

Along with Marlene's last words, Anna heard the sound of a solid wood object tapping on the floor. She ran downstairs in a panic, stumbling and almost falling at the second to last step. When she came out into the basement, she saw Marlene with Victor's baseball bat in her hands. She had taken it off the wall, where it had always been, mounted on a display stand, beneath a baseball signed by Barry Bonds.

"You stupid bitch! How come you let Diane just take off with your phone? And don't you have a pass code on that thing? Jesus! Now put that bat back in its place before I lose my patience with you." Her father's voice rolled like thunder. Anna could hear her mother and Frank rushing downstairs behind her.

"Aunt Marlene, what are you doing? Put that thing down," Anna said in as commanding a voice as she could muster. Her heart was thudding violently, like it might break through her chest at any moment.

"He says I can finally be with him in the open. He just said that to me!" Marlene gripped the bat tightly, ready to swing, her gaze like a crouching panther's. "His wife, my sister, has not even left the house yet. He's not human; he's a reptile!"

The instant Marlene took her eyes off Victor, he snatched the bat from her hands and threw it behind him, almost hitting Anna's legs. He cornered her menacingly. "How dare you come into my house and threaten me like this? You're going to kill me, you said? Is that right, you dumb whore?"

"Dad! Stop this now!" Anna yelled, but her words were drowned out by her mother's furious bellowing.

Lydia emerged from the stairs and dashed fearlessly toward Victor. "You filthy bastard! You had to have us both, didn't you? Because you're so special! Such a remarkable specimen, Victor Goddard—you motherfucker!" Her face had come within inches of Victor's.

"Oh, Lydia, you're such a naive little woman," Victor said disdainfully. "The truth is that you were always second place. Marlene was the prettier, sexier, more interesting sister. It was my great mistake to settle for you. So, when I saw Marlene within my grasp, of course, I had to make a move."

His lips warped into a sickening smile, his eyes glittered with uninhibited malice. "In a different time and place, you could have both been my wives. Anyway, you should be grateful that I stuck with you, Lydia. Look at the life I've given you."

Frank was now standing next to Anna. Their mother had never as much as raised her voice to Victor. Now, the intensity of the moment reached a boiling point when Lydia suddenly slapped Victor hard across the face.

"Yes, I know, the first time feels very strange," she said with spiteful sarcasm. "I think we can all see the life you've given us, Victor. Some fucking life it's been!"

Victor's face transmuted into a hideous, almost unnatural scowl, his little eyes beaming as if containing a bright-blue flame. Lydia stepped back, but Victor closed the distance.

"He's going to hurt her!" cried Frank, and instantly charged at his father. As if the older man had expected his son's move, he clutched him, spun around, and threw him across the room like a sack of potatoes. Frank came crashing down against the wooden arm of a large sofa, grimacing with pain.

Victor kept coming at Lydia like a seething bull. That slap would not be forgiven. Anna grabbed her mother and pulled her back, saying, "Stop, Dad, stop! Don't hurt her!"

Marlene came behind Victor and struck his back with both fists repeatedly, like a girl desperately knocking on a massive door. He turned abruptly toward her. She stepped back horrified and fell to the floor.

"You little bitches!" said Victor, towering over Marlene, helpless at his feet. "I guess it's time I reminded you who's boss, huh?"

"Mom, no!" Frank screamed, still trying to get up.

Anna had lost sight of her mother for a split second. There she was now, stepping forward, the baseball bat in her hands. Anna tried to grab her; she was out of reach. Tried to yell; her throat tangled up.

Victor turned around, his gorilla hand going for Lydia's neck. She closed her eyes and swung the bat, hitting him squarely on the temple.

There was a sharp, cracking sound; and Victor's body fell to the floor with a loud, dull thump.

A stunned silence was followed by Marlene's frightened whimpers. Lydia dropped the bat, covered her face with both hands, and wailed dreadfully. Anna dropped to the floor beside her father's still body and checked his neck for a pulse. There was none. In a daze of shock and disbelief, she looked up at the bewildered faces of her mother, Frank, and Marlene, before uttering those surreal words, "He's dead!"

"Oh God, no!" Marlene cried wretchedly, curled up on the floor with her eyes closed and her face drenched in tears.

Frozen still, Lydia gaped down at her husband's body, horror crystallized on her face, tears streaming down. Her lips quivered now. "I killed him! I killed him! I'm a murderer! What have I done? What have I done?"

Frank embraced Anna. Coming out of shock, tears came rolling down her cheeks. She didn't know what she was feeling, exactly; it was a muddled but intense, harrowing emotion.

Lydia threw her arms around her kids, buried her face on Anna's shoulder and wept quietly. "Call the police. I'll face the consequences of my actions."

"The real criminal is dead," said Marlene with a shattered voice, still hunched over on the floor. "You slaughtered a monster, Lydia. He would have killed you. And maybe me too."

"You don't know that. He wasn't even holding a weapon," Lydia said between sobs.

"He could have easily killed you with his bare hands," said Frank.

Anna was surprised by her own composure all of a sudden. She was now thinking coolly about their situation. "Mom has a good point, though." Their embrace broke off as she spoke. "Look at it from the police's perspective. He didn't have a weapon, and he didn't actually hit Mom or Aunt Marlene. Frank punched him earlier, and that left a mark on his face, separate from the baseball bat injury."

Anna pointed at her father's face. It had a small, red bruise on the side of the chin, along with a cracked lower lip, and a ghastly purple bruise surrounding a gash that marked the baseball bat's exact point of impact. "That's evidence of earlier violence. But most importantly, there is the issue of motive. Both Mom and Aunt Marlene have very strong, obvious motives. Perhaps, Frank too—he did get in a fight with him earlier. Even I could be supposed to have a motive. We all had reasons to, potentially, want him dead. And, of course, he was killed in his basement, with his own baseball bat."

"None of you will be suspected after I confess. It's my fingerprints on the murder weapon, anyway," said her mother.

"You would almost certainly be convicted for manslaughter, if not second-degree murder. I won't let you do that." Anna herself had been the architect of this catastrophe. Her hands had been on the steering wheel from the very instant the train left the station, that fateful Sunday, to the unfortunate moment in which it went tragically off the rails, only minutes ago. She had as much blood on her hands as her mother. Perhaps more.

"There has to be another way," Frank said. "But whatever we are going to do, we have to do it fast. It will be very suspicious if we call this in hours after the estimated time of death, which, from what I've heard, they can calculate rather precisely."

Ideas started to stream into Anna's mind as if an emergency flood-gate of cunning had been opened just in time to avert a disaster. She began thinking aloud as she organized her thoughts, "If all of us had left around eight thirty, and Mom, being very, very tired, had gone upstairs to lie down before nine…and maybe…sleeping pills…yes, sleeping pills…Mom, remember that—you took sleeping pills. I know you have them. When you go upstairs, take two pills out of the package, flush them down the toilet, and leave the package lying on top of your nightstand.

"So, okay, are you following this? With Mom on the top floor, in a state of deep sleep, presumptively, someone could have murdered Dad in the basement without her waking up. Maybe Dad forgot to lock the front door—be sure to leave it unlocked—and a burglar came to rob the house; perhaps a lowlife who knew Dad kept lots of cash in here. The criminal found him in the basement and struck him before running away with the rent money, which is down here somewhere, right, Mom?"

"It's in that cabinet under the TV," said Lydia, pointing to the spot where she would find the money.

"All right, Mom. Here's the rest of your story. Just after midnight, you will wake up and come down to the kitchen for a glass of water. You will hear the TV on in the basement and go downstairs to check if Dad fell asleep watching sports or whatever. And that's when you find him, dead on the floor. Horrified and inconsolable, you'll call 911 and report that your husband has been murdered. Only describe what you're seeing. Remember, you know nothing. You were out cold from around nine until midnight."

"The baseball bat has to disappear," said Frank.

"Yes, there can be no murder weapon here," said Anna. "It has to disappear for good. We cannot risk it being found, ever."

"It's made of wood," said Lydia. "We could burn it, right?"

Her mother was right. "Yes, yes, we'll burn it. Not here, though—out in the woods, somewhere far away from the house. Aunt Marlene, you need to leave now. Go home. Listen, this will all come as tragic news to you tomorrow. Right now, you know nothing about it, because you left here around eight thirty, after the other guests had left—remember that! If you can manage to drive away from here without waking up Grandma, that would be best. Frank, you should also leave. Your story is that you left around eight, right after Mark left with his family. Aunt Marlene and Grandma were the only guests still here. You went straight to your apartment and stayed there."

"Don't you need my help here?" Frank asked. "What are you going to do?"

"I have it all planned out. Mom, I'm going to need a large plastic bag. And the cash, the rent money." Anna went and checked inside the center drawer of the wide cabinet below the wall-mounted TV. She pulled out a bulging yellow envelope, inside of which were twelve stacks of twenty-dollar bills. "Listen up," she said as she walked back to them, avoiding stepping anywhere near her father's corpse. "This money was stolen."

Anna took out one of the stacks and threw it at the bottom of the stairs. "The man dropped one stack of bills as he ran out. Don't touch that stack. It will be evidence. Mom, it's very important that you tell the police about the yellow envelope full of cash that was inside that cabinet drawer, which you found as it is now, open, and empty. The TV needs to stay on, as you found it when you came down here. You would have run back upstairs, horrified, and not come back down again. Okay now, go upstairs, and don't touch anything. I'll be there in a moment. Mom, I'll need that bag I asked for."

They did as Anna asked. No questions. No arguments. Her mother brought her a large black garbage bag, gave her a hug, and went back upstairs, leaving her alone with her father's lifeless body.

Even now he looked intimidating, as if in another instant he might wake up and exact his vengeance upon them all. She imagined his spirit, floating above his body—above her—sullenly asking himself how the hell he ended up dead. "Who fucking killed me?" he would ask. "Really, Lydia? Well, I'll be damned." Such crazy thoughts. Post-traumatic stress disorder, perhaps.

If Frank and Michael were right, her father was just gone, lights out; no more awareness, thoughts, desires; no more anger, disappointment, hatred, fear. Just an easy way out. She found herself wishing that for him. No hellfire, no torments, no judgment. Just lights out. The anger and longing for retribution that had possessed her before was gone. It had been extinguished somehow. She almost felt sorry for him, wondering what might have driven him to become such a contemptible human being.

She knelt down and examined the baseball bat. It was chipped at the top of the barrel, right where a smudge of blood baptized the bat as a murder weapon. She put it inside the bag and brought her gaze down, scanning the floor for the missing piece. Found it! She grabbed the blood-splattered little witness. It would have been an absolute disaster if she had left it there for the police to find. She took one last look at her father. "Well, this is goodbye, Dad. Guess I'll see you at the funeral if I'm not in jail."

When Anna reached the top of the stairs, Marlene and Frank had already left. "I asked them to leave already," said her mother in a numb, distant voice. *That's a good thing*, she thought, and would have uttered the words had she not seen, at that very instant, Michael coming toward them.

"Anna, what's going on? I ran into Frank outside, and he asked to me take off, but I won't. Whatever happened, I'm here for you; I want to help you, and I won't take no for an answer. Just tell me what you need."

Anna grabbed his hands, pulled him closer, looked into his eyes. "Well, Michael, if you must help me, and won't take no for an answer, then go grab a shovel, lighter fluid, and matches. We'll drive two or three miles out of here, find a desolate place deep in the woods, and burn to ashes the baseball bat that killed Victor Goddard."

CHAPTER XVI

The call came in at 12:55 a.m. He had slept less than two hours. Still in a daze, he heard every other word from the patrol officer who had secured the scene of the crime. "Murder…Blake County…just off Twin Oaks Road…victim has been…as Victor Goddard."

Goddard? Detective Andrew Wozniak thought he might know the man. He had known a Goddard once. Was his name Victor? He couldn't remember. That had been many years ago.

He splashed cool water on his face, put on his one good suit; grabbed his keys, badge, and his Glock. In another minute he was inside his unmarked black Dodge Charger. He tossed a handful of mixed nuts in his mouth and drove away. He'd have to make a quick stop at McDonald's for a black coffee, no sugar. Jesus! What a splitting headache he had!

It was just past 1:30 a.m. when he arrived. The first odd thing that he noticed was the picnic table out on the front lawn, which looked as if the guests had left in a hell of a hurry. There were plates full of food and bottles of beer from which no more than a sip had been taken. Moreover, it was evident that no one had attempted to clean up or save any of the leftover food, and there was a whole lot of it. Pity that he couldn't nibble on the evidence. That lasagna looked amazing—sure, it would be cold now, but he'd done much worse, especially during long stakeouts. Of course, eating lasagna right before inspecting a corpse wouldn't be smart.

Officer Gutierrez greeted him at the front door. As he signed the crime-scene logbook, he sensed a faint smell of smoke. Curious. "Do you smell that?" he asked Gutierrez.

"Smell what?" His voice reeked of mediocrity.

"Smoke. Do you smell it?"

"No, not really."

"Hmm, have the rookie do a perimeter search around the house," said Wozniak, looking back and sideways at a young officer standing idly at the bottom of the stairs. "Have him report to me anything that seems out of place, especially any evidence of a burn site." He then saw two ladies, one much younger than the other, sitting together in a corner of the porch, to his right. "Who are the two ladies?" he asked.

"They are the wife and the daughter of the victim. The wife was alone when we got here. Her daughter arrived twenty minutes ago."

"Who called the daughter?"

"Her mother did."

"Has she called anyone else?" asked Wozniak.

"Yes, her son. He should be on his way here as well."

"Nobody enters the house without my express authorization."

"Understood, Sir."

Wozniak took another glance at the ladies. "And their names?"

"The wife is Lydia Goddard, and her daughter, Anna Goddard. The son's name is"—he pulled out a little spiral-bound notebook with a few scribbles on it—"Frank, Frank Goddard."

"I'll want to speak to them after we complete the crime-scene investigation. Officer Mitchell is inside, I presume?"

"Yes, he's down there in the basement," said Gutierrez. "The crime-scene technician and the medical examiner are also there."

"Yes, I saw their names on the logbook just now. Very well, let's see what we've got."

Wozniak hoped no one other than his old pal, Gary Mitchell, the medical examiner, and the technician had been allowed to enter the scene of the crime. The latter two he could trust by virtue of their specialized training. But Mitchell he trusted implicitly. He was an old-school, straight-arrow professional like himself, and smart too. He had met him over two decades ago at the police academy. One of the best cops he'd ever had the pleasure to work with; and yet, somewhere along the way he had managed to piss somebody off, someone high up the chain of command—fucking politics. If he was ever put in a position where he could help Gary make detective, he wouldn't hesitate for a second. As he came out into the basement, careful not to step on any evidence, including a conspicuous stack of twenties at the base of the stairs, he was glad to see only the three people he had hoped to see there.

Then he saw the body. It was him! That was the man he once knew when they were both much younger. He'd been more of an acquaintance than a friend, but they did play basketball together at the YMCA many times. They talked about stuff between games. He couldn't recall much of it, but it stuck with him that the man was in the real estate business, quite successful too, and seemed like a real upstanding citizen. And, boy, the guy could play too. He was a beast. Look at him now. Jesus! What the hell happened here?

No matter how many corpses he'd seen before, being in the presence of death was something he would never fully get used to. Death made the air feel thicker, and silences more unbearable; its unnatural stillness seemed to slow down time. Already he sensed here the scent of death—not putrefaction; that would come hours later. Something else, as if death itself, the moment in which a human being became a big hunk of raw, dead meat, gave off a subtle stench, like walking into a kitchen where a whole raw chicken has been sitting on the countertop. Maybe that's why he hadn't cooked anything other than breakfast since his wife left him five years ago. Thank God for frozen microwave meals, sandwiches, and takeout.

"Hey, Wozniak," said Mitchell, "you all right, man?"

"I'm fine. Good to see you, Mitchell." He acknowledged the other two men with a nod. "Gentlemen." Had he been wearing a hat, he would have tipped it toward them as a gesture. "So, would you like to fill me in?"

The technician spoke first. "The body's core temperature, taken today at 0116 hours, was 92.8 Fahrenheit. Livor mortis has set in. Estimated time of death is between 2130 and 2200 hours. It does not appear the body has been moved since the time of death."

"So, he was killed about four hours ago. Mitchell, who called it in and when?"

"His wife, Lydia Goddard, called it in after midnight, at 0015 hours. I was the first responder at the scene of the crime. When I arrived at 0033 hours, Ms. Goddard was alone, waiting on the front porch. She seemed quite agitated, as one would naturally expect."

Wozniak scanned the floor around the body, then the corpse itself. No gunshot or stab wounds. A damn awful bruise on the head, though. Who could have taken down this Goliath? "What did Ms. Goddard say to the operator, and to you upon arrival?"

"She stated to the operator the same she said to me; that she had taken sleeping pills after their guests left, approximately at 2030 hours. Near midnight, she woke up thirsty and came down to the kitchen for a glass of water; she heard the TV on in the basement, came down, and found her husband dead on the floor."

"How about that stack of twenty-dollar bills over there by the stairs?"

"Yes, there's that," said Mitchell. "Ms. Goddard indicated that there were twelve stacks of a thousand dollars each in a yellow envelope inside that open drawer in the cabinet under the TV, and it's gone now, except for that one stack. On the surface, it would appear that the motive for the murder may have been robbery, and that the attacker dropped one stack as he ran back upstairs to flee the crime scene."

"He?" asked Wozniak.

"Well, in most likelihood…"

"We don't know that. Assume nothing. Assumptions make one eliminate viable explanations. You must avoid them like the plague."

The medical examiner spoke next, his voice imbued with expert certainty, almost boredom. "The body presents a head injury consistent with blunt-force trauma. It appears the victim received a single blow to the temple, with enough strength to cause a severe traumatic brain injury."

"Murder weapon?" asked Wozniak.

"None have been found," said Mitchell.

Wozniak looked about him. One big fat clue stared back at him. "I think we are looking for a baseball bat, gentlemen, a baseball bat that, perhaps, the assailant picked up right off this wall mount. Well, look at that, a baseball signed by Barry Bonds. Oh yes, I bet the murder weapon was sitting right here five hours ago."

"A baseball bat would certainly be capable of producing an injury such as this," said the medical examiner.

"Any signs of forced entry?" asked Wozniak.

"No evidence of forced entry," said Mitchell. "Ms. Goddard said that she found the front door unlocked when she stepped out after midnight."

Already, some things didn't seem to be adding up. Wozniak approached Mitchell. "So, you mean to say that upon discovering her husband brutally murdered by who knows who, this woman's instinct is to go and wait outside alone?"

Mitchell's face lit up, eyebrows shooting up. "Sharp as always, Wozniak."

"You know, nine out of ten times, in a murder case that looks the way this one is starting to look, the murderer ends up being the spouse."

"You're right. I wouldn't be surprised if the little lady did it. And the competing theory here would be that a burglar came in without a weapon of his own—or her own—resorting to use the victim's own baseball bat as the murder weapon. Seems farfetched."

"It does, doesn't it? God damn it, Mitchell, you'd make a fine detective. I want your help cracking this one. I bet we can make an arrest within forty-eight hours."

"I bet we could. It would sure help if we found the murder weapon."

"Yes, that would be splendid." Wozniak turned around and addressed the technician, "Um, Scott, right?"

"Yes, sir, at your service," he said, as though he were a concierge at a luxury hotel, instead of someone who specializes in dissecting murder scenes.

"Please be sure to dust for fingerprints all over this basement, those stairs and the front door. And I'd be very interested to learn if you find any traces of foreign material within the injury site itself, perhaps wood particles from a baseball bat." He turned back to Mitchell. "I assure you, this is, at best, the work of an amateur; but most likely, a crime of passion. Either way, mistakes will have been made, and we just need to find them."

"There's no substitute for experience, right?"

"True enough, though I've met plenty of people whose minds appear to reject the benefit of experience. Say, Mitchell, did you smell smoke outside of the house?"

"Smoke? I can't say I did, no."

"I did smell it, sir," Scott, the technician, interjected. "Right outside of the house, as I was coming in. It was a faint smell, probably carried by the wind from a distance; something like burnt charcoal. I figured someone might be having a bonfire nearby."

"And when did you get here?"

"Not more than fifteen minutes before you did, sir."

"Thank you, Scott. Good insights. Here's what I'm thinking, Mitchell." Wozniak tapped him on the shoulder. "Sure enough, the smell may have come from some neighbors' bonfire, but we aren't going to assume that. Another plausible explanation for the smell is that someone burned a wood baseball bat, our missing murder weapon. That's why I have an officer searching the premises right now. Should we find a charred baseball bat anywhere around the house, even if we couldn't lift fingerprints from it, that would be a major piece of evidence."

"It sure would be. The random burglar theory would go out the window and the wife would become our prime suspect," Mitchell observed.

"Without a doubt. A burglar-turned-murderer would have not lingered around here, but rather taken the weapon and disposed of it far away from this place. Let's go talk to the family."

As they reached the stairs, Wozniak turned around. "Gentlemen, I trust that you will do a thorough examination of the body and sweep this place for evidence. We'll leave you to it. Officer Mitchell and I will be right outside. Please keep me appraised of anything noteworthy."

Coming out into the porch, Wozniak noticed someone new sitting with Lydia Goddard and her daughter. It was a young man about the same age as the daughter; Anna was her name, he recalled. "That must be Frank Goddard, the son," he whispered to Mitchell. "Let's go. Try to get a good read of their body language and micro expressions."

Wozniak approached the table where Lydia Goddard was sitting, flanked by her daughter and son. Her big dreamy eyes had been following him all along.

A cool draft brought again that faint smell of smoke but only fleetingly.

"Ms. Goddard, I am Detective Andrew Wozniak. First and foremost, I am so very sorry about this terrible tragedy that has befallen you and your family. Please accept my sincerest condolences."

"Thank you, Detective, for your kind words," said Ms. Goddard dejectedly. "This really is a devastating tragedy for our family." He couldn't be sure, but perhaps sadness was not the only emotion he detected in her subdued voice. Could it be fear? She didn't hold eye contact for very long. Her eyes were wide open, eyebrows flat and still—her whole face looked too still, like a mask. Her daughter, Anna, did seem quite distraught. The son, Frank, was a puzzle. His face looked hard, impenetrable.

"And these young folks, am I correct to assume they are your son, Frank, and your daughter, Anna?"

"Yes, they are," said the widow, looking at their faces. Anna made a sad attempt at smiling; held her mother's hand. Frank's eyes seemed distant, clouded.

"All right. Again, I am very sorry for your loss. I just have a couple quick questions for you, Lydia. May I call you Lydia?"

"Yes, you may." Lydia darted a fleeting glance at Wozniak—glassy green lanterns, like windows to a rain forest.

"I was told there's a significant amount of money missing. Is that right?"

"Yes, twelve thousand dollars," said Lydia, her gaze now fixed on her daughter's hands.

"That's a big chunk of petty cash, isn't it?" Wozniak asked; at once both Anna and Frank looked up at him like he was getting fresh.

"Some of our tenants prefer to pay cash," Lydia explained. "My husband kept that money in an envelope in the basement."

"Hmm, I see. Sadly, Lydia, Blake County has seen an increase in break-ins in the last few years." That was a lie. Crime in the area had remained steadily low for decades. One thing that he'd learned in this line of work was that the best way to catch criminals is to let them think they are beyond suspicion. When they loosen up, that's when they start making mistakes, saying too much, and contradicting themselves.

"Oh, I didn't know that. It's always been so quiet here," said Lydia. "It wouldn't be the first time we forgot to lock the door. The possibility of being robbed, or attacked in our home, wasn't something we ever thought about."

She seemed too willing to accept the robber-turned-murderer assumption.

Wozniak took out his little notebook and pen; scribbled down the date, time and three names; wringing his face like he had just solved the case. "It's really quite unfortunate that the burglar found your husband down there. These robbers usually just want to get in, get the loot, and get out quickly. Tragedies such as this happen when the criminal miscalculates and comes face to face with a family member. Once he's seen, fear takes over and he attacks in a panic."

"That must have been what happened," Lydia said. Her voice did something there for a fraction of a second. Had that been a trace of relief? And Anna, did she just now steal a glance at her mother? She looks smart. Perhaps, she was trying to tell her to stop jumping at every get-out-of-jail-free card he was throwing at her.

Wozniak brought a hand to his chin, slanting his head. "Lydia, as far as you know, who else knew that Victor kept that much cash inside the house?"

"Um, I can't think of anyone. Only family," she said. That seemed to give Frank a jolt, his eyes suddenly more alert.

"Only family," Wozniak repeated slowly while jotting it down on his tiny black notebook. Then, briskly, "I see that you had visitors earlier."

"We had a family gathering earlier," Anna said with aplomb. The daughter coming to the rescue, perhaps worried that her mother is starting to loosen up.

"Did they not like the food?"

"What do you mean?" The daughter again.

"It would appear most of the food is still there. Seems odd, that's all." Wozniak smiled.

"Oh, that," Lydia cut in, "I guess I served too much food. There were only twelve people here, us included. I must have cooked for twenty-four."

"Better too much food than too little, right? And, Anna, how late did you stay here?"

"It must have been about eight when I left." She didn't need to think much about it.

"How about you, Frank? Can I call you Frank?"

"Yes, just Frank is fine, Detective." He seemed on edge, little wrinkles showing between his eyebrows. "I left a bit later; around eight thirty, I think."

Wozniak jotted it down. "And were you the last to leave?"

"No, our grandmother and our aunt, Mom's sister, were still here when I left."

"Lydia's sister, what's her name?" asked Wozniak.

"Marlene," said Lydia.

Wozniak scribbled down her name. "And she was with your mother, yes?"

Lydia nodded, "Rose Wilde is her name."

"Thank you for all that. Now, I'm sorry to ask this question, but I wouldn't be doing my job if I didn't. Was anyone at the family gathering that you could suspect of being involved in this crime somehow, even indirectly? Perhaps, someone in a dire need for money; someone with an addiction, or a gambling debt, anything like that?"

"God, no! Of course not!" exclaimed Lydia Goddard.

"I'm sorry, but I had to ask. I will need, of course, the full list of guests who came to the family gathering, and their phone numbers. With this family gathering happening here only hours before your husband's murder, it is important that I speak to each of them. Perhaps, one of them knows or saw something that could lead us to the capture of the killer."

"Yes, of course," said Lydia.

"All right, here's a piece of paper and a pen. Could you please write them down for me? Name, phone number, and relationship to you, your husband, son, or daughter. Don't leave out anyone, and please include your names as well."

The rookie officer came over and addressed Wozniak. "Detective," he started, but Wozniak motioned him to walk with him. They stopped right at the front door. "Detective, I conducted a full search around the house and found nothing out of the ordinary."

"Are you sure? No evidence of a burn site, no ashes, or a patch of freshly loosened soil; nothing like that?"

"No, sir. It's very dark out there, but I utilized a thorough search pattern. I'm convinced there's nothing of that sort around the house. No smell of smoke either."

"That's disappointing. We'll need to conduct a search with a wider ratio when the sun comes up."

Lydia had written down the names when Wozniak returned. "I'll be in contact with you shortly," he said. "Again, I just want to reiterate how sorry I am that this happened to you."

Mitchell followed Wozniak to the front yard, away from the Goddard's. The night was getting cooler.

"So, Mitchell, what did you observe?"

"I think the wife could be hiding something. Her grief seemed a little contrived to me. And her son might know something too—he was awfully quiet. And I spotted some odd glances between Anna and her mother. There was a strange vibe. What do you think?"

"Yeah, something was off. There're two things we need to do in the next twelve hours. First, we'll talk to each person on this list and find out if anything out of the ordinary happened during this family gathering."

Mitchell followed Wozniak as he stepped closer to the picnic table. "Take some pictures. Look at this—two full beers side by side, and over there, a perfect square of lasagna, untouched. The way all this food was left on the table out here is suspect. You'd think someone showed up with a chainsaw. I also find it odd that the whole thing was wrapped up by eight thirty."

"Yeah, that's odd, tomorrow being a holiday and all," Mitchell said as he snapped a picture of a tray overflowing with meatballs.

"It's just too much of a coincidence that the man was murdered on this particular day, don't you think?"

"I sure do." Mitchell turned around to look at the swaying tree tops behind him; they seemed to murmur in the wind. "On the other hand, a burglar could have taken advantage of their family dinner to break into the house unnoticed."

"That's true, but then, why wait until everyone was gone? The advantage was lost."

"Maybe someone came back, or never really left the premises. The wife could have left the door unlocked on purpose."

"To steal the money?" asked Wozniak.

"Or to kill her husband."

"It's possible, but we'll need to establish a motive before we go any further. Otherwise, we are just making wild guesses. No offense to you."

"None taken," said Mitchell. "What's the other thing we need to do in the next twelve hours?"

"I'll order an expanded search for the murder weapon, most likely a wood baseball bat. We'll start with a two-mile radius."

"It could have been an aluminum baseball bat too."

"Plausible but unlikely. It wouldn't have looked as good with the baseball signed by Barry Bonds. Think about it. The man was a few years older than me. Look at his house—a big farmhouse out here, not a modern home in town. Look at that black Mercedes. It's maybe twelve years old—the previous chief of police had one of those. Very nice, but this guy could have bought himself a brand-new Mercedes anytime he wanted. Instead, he kept this one, a more classic design. So, what baseball bat would a man like that hang on the wall below his treasured baseball signed by Barry Bonds?"

"A classic wooden one, of course, probably MLB-grade handcrafted maple."

"Very impressive, Mitchell."

"There's a lot of stuff I don't know, but baseball, I know very well. I played two seasons in high school, and I wasn't all that bad either. I got injured at the start of my third season, though. That was the end of my short baseball career."

"That's too bad, but maybe you were needed more as a police officer." Wozniak walked away from the table. He'd seen enough leftovers.

Mitchell caught up with him. "You know, with all the money and properties that Victor Goddard had, maybe that's the motive right there. With him dead, his wife gets everything."

"Perhaps, but that motive would have more likely led to a cold, calculated murder. Instead, this looks messy, like a crime of passion."

The rookie officer came up to them. "Detective," he said, "I found a shed in the backyard. It wasn't locked. There's plenty of gardening tools, a ride-on lawn mower, and a bunch of other stuff, but nothing unusual."

"Excellent, officer. Please show us there." Wozniak turned to Mitchell. "As you've seen already, sometimes, it's not about what's there, but rather about what's missing."

The rookie officer led them to a dark corner of the lot where there was a red barn-style storage shed. He opened it and turned on the light. Right in the middle, there was a large green ride-on lawnmower, and to either side there were a myriad of gardening tools hanging from hooks on the walls. In the back there were pails of paint and bags of gravel, garden stones, and red mulch. There was also a red charcoal grill stuck in a corner.

Wozniak inspected the tools hanging from the walls, but nothing struck him as abnormal. Then he noticed something.

"This is interesting," he said. "See these two shovels over here? This one is tiny, for gardening, and this other one is enormous. Neither one is what you would buy as your everyday shovel—that intermediate size seems to be missing here. And what do we see smack in the middle of the two shovels?"

"An empty hook," said Mitchell, nodding in agreement.

"Exactly. It's quite possible that a shovel is missing. It might have been taken from here and used to dig up a hole and bury the murder weapon somewhere. So, we are now looking not only for a baseball bat, but also for a shovel. Perhaps, we should also be looking for a can of kerosene, lighter fluid, or gasoline, and matches. See, if I had just murdered someone with a wood baseball bat, I would want to burn it, which might explain the faint smell of smoke I keep sensing every now and then. There might be a burn site not too far away from here. They may have covered it with dirt, but the smell carries anyway. If we make haste, we could find it. But first things first—let's go open some car trunks. The murderer might have been stupid enough to drive back here with the shovel, fuel, and matches, everything in their car."

"That would be a hell of a jackpot," said Mitchell.

"It wouldn't be the first time. One time, back when I was a patrol officer in Philadelphia, I caught a notorious gang member drugged out of his mind, in his driveway, with blood stains on his shirt. He'd just slaughtered a rival gang member with a machete. Truly gruesome stuff. That man is now in prison, doing twenty-five to life."

Wozniak dismissed the rookie officer. He was no longer of more use there than patrolling the streets—he might yet save some lives tonight by pulling over some drunk idiot now getting behind the wheel.

Wozniak and Mitchell walked back to the front porch, where the immediate family of the diseased were congregated. The crime scene had not been released yet, proof that the medical examiner and the technician were doing a thorough job down there. The Goddards had been talking as Wozniak approached them, but their discussion was abruptly halted the instant Anna saw him coming.

"Detective," Anna acknowledged him with an elegant, formal demeanor.

"I hate to inconvenience you at a moment like this, I really do, but it's necessary to perform a cursory visual inspection of the vehicles within the property. It is, of course, a mere formality." He'd been careful not to state that he had the authority to search the vehicles. He didn't. This was the moment when one of them could ask if he had a search warrant for the vehicles. But that, of course, would be extremely suspicious and, in itself, clear justification for a warrant. He would simply leave Mitchell stationed at the house while he went to get the search warrant from the judge. "You don't all have to go over there with me. Just one of you will do."

"I'll go with you," said Anna after a brief silence.

"Great, thank you Anna. May I call you Anna?"

"Yes, of course," she said and proceeded to collect keys from her brother.

"The keys to the Mercedes are inside," said Lydia.

"Not in the basement, I hope," said Wozniak.

"They're in the kitchen."

"I'll fetch them," said Anna.

"Officer Mitchell will escort you, as the crime scene has not yet been released."

They went in and out of the house rather quickly. Now in possession of the keys to the three vehicles, her own included, Anna followed Wozniak to the spot where the three cars were lined up next to each other. Anna unlocked the black Mercedes first. "Go ahead," she said.

They conducted a search that was much more than just a cursory one. Anna didn't protest it, though her face showed some edginess. The only thing of interest they found inside the car was a cool five hundred dollars in cash, haphazardly tossed inside the center console. It served perhaps only to establish a pattern; that the victim was in the habit of stashing considerable sums of cash in various places. Wozniak asked Anna to pop open the trunk. She didn't hesitate to do it. No baseball bat there, and no shovel either, nor matches or fuel of any kind. In fact, it was completely empty.

Inspecting Frank's car was a dull affair. There was absolutely nothing there that could be of interest. Hers was the last car left to inspect. It was a nice Volvo sedan. Wozniak's ex-wife used to drive one.

He thought Anna flinched when he asked her to open the trunk. Could he have imagined it the same way he was now imagining that he was about to see in there a freshly muddied, fire-blackened shovel, a red can of kerosene and a box of long matches?

But, no, there would be no shortcuts tonight. No bloody baseball bat with the murderer's fingerprints all over it. No shovel. Nothing there but old psychology magazines and a crumpled-up grocery-store receipt.

"Thank you, Anna. You've been very helpful. That will be all for now," said Wozniak, and at that moment a cool breeze swept through them, ruffling Anna's golden hair and bringing him, once more, that subtle scent of smoke. He had to ask.

"Say, Anna, have you been anywhere near a fire tonight?"

CHAPTER XVII

How stupid! Anna berated herself. It was 5:36 a.m., and she was back home, sitting on her couch, staring at a TV screen that wasn't on, staring at herself.

Her father's body had been released to the morgue at 4:30 a.m. Such a surreal sight, him being carried out in that body bag. They'd been allowed back inside the house a few minutes later. The place felt different, intimidating, like a mausoleum that ought to be sealed, never to be opened again. The air felt heavy, the silence deafening.

Frank stayed there, partly to demonstrate to the cops that their mother was afraid to stay in the house alone, as would be expected of a woman whose husband had just been murdered by an intruder; but also because it really wasn't right to leave her alone in there. Anna felt relieved that she could leave though; she couldn't stand being there another second.

"My father was smoking next to me earlier," the angry blonde on the dark TV screen mocked her. That was the only response she could come up with under pressure. Oh, that was a stupid answer! Everybody knows that cigarette smoke smells very different from the smoke produced by an actual fire, or more precisely, the burning of wood. That detective would surely know the difference, and now, he probably knew that she'd lied.

He terrified her, that man, Detective Wozniak. His eyes possessed an intensity which made her feel like he could read her thoughts, especially the ones she was desperately trying to hide. Every movement of his, every gaze, conveyed to her the inescapability of detection, capture and punishment. He was like a hawk stalking and toying with his prey. Every gracious uttering and every seemingly naive question of his was a trap he was laying, and they would inevitably start stepping on some of those, like clumsy critters driven by treacherous instincts.

The stench of smoke must have stuck to her hair. Why did she not think of washing it? The unsettling fact was that she had not even thought about it. Somehow, she herself had not smelled a thing before Detective Wozniak questioned her about the unmistakable scent. Only then, after taking a long sniff, she sensed it, although she still lied to the detective. "I really can't smell anything," she said to him, hoping that he would doubt his own senses. His partner, whatever his name was—Officer Mitchell, that was his name—didn't smell anything. What a relief. Maybe that had been enough to, literally, throw him off her scent. Maybe, just maybe.

Anna had come home and changed clothes after her clandestine bonfire in the woods with Michael, but only because she had tripped on a raised root and fallen down on her hands and knees, getting her pants dirty. Her face had come close enough to the ground to smell the moist soil, a jagged stone staring at her. Thankfully, she didn't get any cuts or bruises that she'd later have to explain to the police. Oh, Wozniak would've had a field trip with that.

The question in her head now was whether she and Michael had driven far enough from the house before stopping to get rid of the base-ball bat. She reckoned they must have gone out at least two miles down the road. How far out could Wozniak extend his search? How many police officers would they put under his command? Could the county's scanty budget save the day for them sinners?

Anna had not wanted to risk coming back to the farmhouse and finding the police already there, so they drove both cars. Anna followed Michael this time; he found a place which was perfectly secluded, if also very frightening. From the main road they turned right on an unmarked narrow road which went on for about half a mile. The only structures out there were a small, fenced-up electrical substation and an abandoned, torn-down, creepy old house. They pulled over at a small clearing from which a rough trail zigzagged deep into the woods.

Michael's countenance betrayed trepidation, but he wouldn't say a word about it. He must have had questions but stopped her when she tried to explain. She only got out bits and pieces of the story—Marlene going back inside as if possessed, a terrible argument, a slap on her father's face, the fear on her mother's eyes, the baseball bat in her hands. "You can tell me everything later," he said while leading the way with a small flashlight that barely illuminated the next three feet in front of him; that's when Anna took a tumble.

After walking nearly two hundred yards, they veered off the trail and picked a spot to do what they were there to do. The air was cool, and the silence deafening. The first time the shovel hit the ground, it hit a rock and made a piercing sound that, for all she knew, could have traveled for miles. Reason abandoned her for an instant, and she had the distinct feeling of having her father standing behind her. Even now, she shivered at the thought. Michael dug up a hole about two feet deep and long enough to fit the baseball bat. He put it in, doused it in lighter fluid, and lit it up. He kept it burning, periodically pouring in additional lighter fluid, until only a thin charred stick remained.

And so, the murder weapon was all but gone, except for the blood-stained splinter Anna had kept inside a mint tin case in her purse, a decision which she didn't yet fully comprehend. A vague but powerful idea had descended upon her when, alone in the basement with her father's corpse, she first saw the flung-off splinter lying on the floor—if everything else failed, at their most desperate hour, she could still use that tiny piece of damning evidence to save her mother from her father's ultimate vengeance at the hands of Detective Wozniak, though it would require a great sacrifice from her.

Anna kept wrecking her brain, her very tired brain, trying to see all the angles. So many questions flooding her mind. What would Wozniak do next? Who did he suspect? What did he know already? What mistakes had she made? Would her mother break under pressure? Would Aunt Marlene? Did the crime scene really look like a break-in gone bad? Had she made it too obvious? What hadn't she planned for? The storm of thoughts was overwhelming. Her exhausted body could go on no longer.

She slipped in and out of consciousness; she rested her eyes for a minute, but thirty minutes passed. She saw her mother swinging the bat in terror, eyes closed, tears streaming; then her father lying dead on the floor, like a dragon slayed in its own cave. Her saintly mother now a murderer. A dreaded nightmare reimagined, rewritten, but just as ugly as the original. "Guilt is the cruelest of creatures," Frank once declared. What a prophet he had turned out to be. Here it was, indeed, showing its ugly face, sneering, baring its fangs, just like he'd said.

Her eyes were closing again; she could hardly fight it anymore. At the outer rim of consciousness, delirium awaited its turn to whisper some final commentary. Is Dad in hell, Frank, or is he nothing now, molecules being returned to the universe to make other, better things? Hope you're right, Frank. Hope he doesn't know, feel, suffer, want, or hate anymore. These thoughts became more weightless and farther apart with every passing second—or perhaps minutes, hours? She drifted off into a deep, dreamless sleep, like death itself.

She woke up in a panic, a name echoing in her head as if the devil himself had just whispered it to her ear—Mark Goddard. That slimy bastard. He was the unforeseen storm she'd been dreading, wasn't he? How was she only now thinking of him? Mark would spill his guts, without a doubt. Not only would he give Detective Wozniak a full account of the ghastly, scandalous affair that abruptly ended the family gathering shortly before her father had been killed, but he would certainly do anything he could to smear her mother's character and make her the primary suspect for her husband's murder. Victor Goddard had been not only his uncle, but also a revered mentor and an example of strength and success he aspired to emulate. Surely, in his twisted mind, his uncle's exploits with the Wilde sisters had been justified by the man's stature.

To Anna's dismay, her phone confirmed that she'd been out cold for six hours. It was noon now. Surely, Detective Wozniak had not taken the morning off. He must have had a black coffee at 7:30 a.m. and headed out to solve the murder case. He could have already ordered a sweep of all areas surrounding the farmhouse, searching for the murder weapon. There's a lot of woods in a two-mile ratio from the house, though. Also, that charred remain they'd buried, were he to find it, couldn't possibly tell him much, could it?

More crucially, though, by now Wozniak could have already talked to Mark. He could have talked to poor Grandma Rose, too. "How come, Mrs. Wilde, all that food was just left out there to rot—the perfectly good lasagna, the meatballs—all gone to waste, attracting animals and insects; it's just strange, isn't it? Something must have happened. What did happen, Mrs. Rose? Please tell me everything."

Grandma Rose wouldn't lie about it. How could she? She wouldn't even know what to say. Diane, too, if Wozniak interviewed her, could only speak truthfully about it all. Therefore, Anna reckoned, none of them should lie about the scandal. All their stories must line up.

Wozniak would unavoidably come to know everything about her father's affair with Marlene, and about Diane, their long kept unholy secret that just happened to have been revealed in dramatic fashion hours before the murder. No doubt, he'll conclude that her mother could have killed him; Marlene too; but that does not mean any of them did kill him. He could have very well been killed by an intruder. Without the murder weapon or some other hard evidence, the mere existence of a motive would not be enough for a conviction. How long before Wozniak got his hands on some kind of evidence, though? Mistakes are always made, and it was all so fast.

Anna saw now that she'd missed phone calls from Frank and Diane. She'd call Frank first; she was dreading calling Diane. What if no one had told her anything? She could be calling just to talk, maybe even to apologize for the mess last night, not knowing that what they did, and what she did, ended up causing the death of her—well, the death of Victor Goddard.

The moment she made the call, while it was ringing, Anna wondered if it was even safe to be talking on their mobile phones. In movies, cunning gangsters always said it was a bad idea. Wozniak himself, or his people, could be listening in to all their calls. She just couldn't know what was real and what was fiction. True career criminals, cops, and lawyers—only they knew all that stuff. She would have to tread carefully, like the rookie she was.

"Anna," Frank answered at the third ring, "how are you holding up?"

"Um, okay, I guess. Still pretty shaken up, though. Now, I have to call Diane, and I just—"

"Don't need to, not right now. I already talked to her."

"You did? Oh God, thank you. And, how is she?"

"Well, she's devastated, same as us. I told her that the police will likely want to talk to her, because she was at the family reunion." Frank was being careful not to say anything incriminatory. He watched more crime movies than she did and was likely wary of speaking freely on their phones.

"And did you tell her that, if they call her, she should just be calm and tell them what she knows, just the truth?" She changed her intonation slightly at the end, like she did at the dinner table when they were kids—he'd get it. That message was also for him and her mother.

Frank paused for a moment. "Yes, of course, I did. She'll be fine."

"Great. Is Mom resting?"

"She is. Do you want me to get her?"

"No, no, let her rest. Can I ask you to call Aunt Marlene?"

"Yes, I got it," said Frank. "Take it off your mind."

"Thanks Frank. I'll, um…I'll talk to you later."

Anna barely had time to drink a cup of coffee and shower. She was towel drying when her phone rang. It was an unknown number, and she knew it could only be one person. She took a deep breath and answered the call.

"Am I speaking to Anna Goddard?" She recognized Detective Wozniak's rich, polished, assertive voice.

Anna sat down on her bed, shaking all over. "Yes, this is her speaking."

"Good afternoon, Anna. This is Detective Andrew Wozniak. I hope you were able to get some rest," he said in a rather gentlemanly manner. "Are you holding up okay?"

"Thank you, Detective. I'm doing as well as I can, considering the circumstances," Anna said dejectedly, taking care not to overdo it. She figured Wozniak could probably spot cheap acting from a mile away. The thought made her heart race faster.

"Yes, of course. I can only imagine how hard this must be for you. Anyway, I was hoping you could come down to the precinct, just for a moment, this afternoon. I only need to ask you a few questions. It is my experience that the immediate family members of a victim often know details that might seem irrelevant at first, but actually end up being critical in solving the case. Memories, however, aren't impervious to the passing of time—they can be quite fickle, in fact—which is why it is of the essence that we speak today."

Anna remembered a lawyer in some TV series saying that it was never a good idea to talk to the police without a lawyer. She thought of responding, "I'm going to need a lawyer first," or perhaps ask, "Should I get a lawyer?"

But the common belief is that guilty people need lawyers, and if she were to lawyer up already, she would certainly bring suspicion upon herself. So, what she did respond was "Sure, what time would be convenient for you?"

"Um," Wozniak paused casually, as though he had not thought about it in any precise terms until now. "How about around five? I don't want to rush you, and I have plenty of things to do between now and then."

"Five it is then, Detective. Until then."

"Until then, Anna," Wozniak responded with unnerving gracefulness. Somehow, a tough cop act would have been less threatening.

Alone with her thoughts, half naked and cold, an awful sense of impending doom came over Anna. What if Wozniak was already on to them? The forensic investigation may have uncovered some sort of evidence. He may have squeezed something out of Marlene. He may have gotten some dirt from Mark. Wozniak could already have enough on her, or her mother, or both. There was a distinct possibility that she might never come back from that police station. She could be arrested and read her Miranda rights as soon as she walked in there.

And then Anna remembered—she still had the mint tin case in her purse, and her father's rent money under the spare tire in the trunk of her car. She'd already almost been caught last night. Now was the time to smarten up. She couldn't afford any more mistakes.

CHAPTER XVIII

Two hours before her appointment with Detective Wozniak, Anna arrived at the Green Valley Mall, on a mission. Inside her purse, $11,000 in cash and a grisly souvenir—her fingerprint stamped on her father's blood dried upon a wood splinter that was shaped uncannily like a dagger, unceremoniously placed inside a mint tin case. She bought a small plain vanilla ice cream and sat down on a bench near the locker rentals.

Casually observing her surroundings, Anna ate her ice cream mechanically, the way a cow grazes on grass, with no interest in tasting it, let alone enjoying it. It was a mere decoy. A moment later, satisfied that she hadn't been followed, she rented a locker, put the tin case and the money inside, locked it, and got out of there fast. Outside, azure skies without a cloud in sight, and a balmy breeze caressing her face—deceptively glorious, an invitation to recklessness.

Her next stop was Michael's apartment. As she fumbled and dropped her keys, the door opened from the inside and there he was, looking a little tired, but charming as ever. They fused in a tender, loving embrace, and for a moment, Anna felt protected from the ominous shadows lurking inside her own head. If only they could disappear together. Was it horribly selfish of her to even imagine a future with him as fugitives of the law? Would he want to live that kind of life? No, it wouldn't be right. If she truly loved him, she wouldn't let him sacrifice everything for her. He could still do great things—he would do great things. True love demands sacrifice, she reproachfully reminded herself.

But even as the sting of her verdict lingered, a more urgent matter made its way through her crowded mind and insisted to speak with the boss at once. Michael had kept all that stuff in his car! What if the police showed up with a search warrant right this instant?

Anna pushed Michael inside and closed the door behind her.

"Are you okay?" Michael asked, off-balance, with a hand on the wall and another behind her back. She crashed into him, pinning him against the wall. It would have been sexy had she not been so scared. Scratch that—it was sexy anyway. Bad timing, though.

Anna's heart raced as she imagined cops pounding on the door the next second. "Listen, Michael, the shovel, the lighter fuel, the matches; did you—"

"Yes. Yes, I did. I threw the whole box of matches in the fire, and I used up all the lighter fluid. Remember?"

She didn't but still nodded. "And the shovel?" Her voice came out breathy, the question more like a plea. Please tell me you got rid of it.

"I took the shovel and the empty can with me. After we split up, I stopped at the mini mart and bought vinyl gloves, an abrasive sponge, and a bottle of dishwashing liquid. Then I drove fifteen miles just to find an empty, coin-operated car wash. Long story short, by midnight both the shovel and the lighter fluid can were sparkling clean and far away from here. Dropped the can in a dumpster and threw the shovel inside an abandoned work site covered in tall grass. Then I cleaned the interior of my trunk."

"Goodness," Anna said breathing easier now, "I'm very impressed with you." She felt her shoulders and neck relaxing; she closed her eyes, exhaled with relief; their noses touched. They stayed like that for a moment, even as Michael spoke again.

"Well, you know, watching all those gangster movies have been a real education," he said. "Speaking of which, I had just got off the phone with a police detective when you got here."

Anna pulled her face away. "A detective spoke with you? Just now?" Her heart was racing again.

"Um, yes, a Detective…Andrew…Wozniak, yes, Andrew Wozniak, that was his name."

Oh, this wasn't good. But why wouldn't Wozniak question him? She would have if she was him. But why him first? There must be a reason, a logic, a system to how he conducts his investigation. "Wozniak, yes. We've been acquainted, Detective Wozniak and I. Met him last night. What did he want with you? What did he ask you?"

"He asked me some general questions about myself, our relationship, how long we've been dating, if I knew your parents before yesterday, that kind of stuff. He's very polished, this guy, let me tell you. He can talk."

Anna felt like she'd start shaking any moment now. "What else did he ask?"

"He asked what time I got there, when did I leave, oh, and he wanted to know why you and I went there in separate cars."

All good questions. Wozniak was setting up his traps. "And what did you say?"

"I just told him the truth, that you wanted me to be free to leave anytime if I didn't feel comfortable. Of course, he wanted to hear more about that. I didn't tell him much, but I did tell him that your father was hard to get along with, that we didn't exactly hit it off. And then I used that to dodge his most dangerous question."

"What question?" she asked.

"He asked why I left so early, and by myself. I told him that I felt out of place and decided to take off right after dinner."

"So you lied to him then," said Anna, her voice betraying disappointment. She should have thought of preparing Michael for a police interrogation. Just the latest evidence that she wasn't in control; Wozniak was.

Michael opened his eyes wide. "Well, I had to, Anna. The truth would have instantly made your mother the main suspect."

"There were too many witnesses there last night. He'll find out about the whole damn thing anyway." And he'll know that Michael lied, but she could protect him; she could get Wozniak's attention off of him.

Anna wrapped her arms around Michael's neck and gave him a long, tender kiss. She had a feeling it could be the last. She pulled back, looked him in the eyes and spoke earnestly, "Listen Michael, this could end badly for me. If it does, I'll face the consequences with my dignity intact. I've made my decisions, good and bad, knowing there were risks, to stand for something good, to still like tomorrow and every day the person I see in the mirror. If I have to spend the next ten years in prison to give Mom the rest of her life back, it will be well worth it."

"Come here," Michael said while leading her to sit on the couch with him. "Get that out of your mind. You're not going to prison. You can't. It would be too unfair."

"Too unfair; lots of things are too unfair. Justice is in short supply in this wretched world we live in. Bad people win every day; good people suffer every day."

"Wolves and sheep," said Michael.

"What?" Didn't sound like him. Was he citing scripture?

"Your father's words, wolves and sheep. He kept saying he was a wolf amongst sheep."

"We are the sheep," added Anna.

"Is it possible his view of people, and life, rubbed off on you just a little?" His voice swung to a higher pitch toward the end; eyes squinting, leaving a trace of tiny wrinkles.

"Perhaps more than a little," Anna admitted more to herself than to Michael.

"Well, this wolf got killed by his sheep. I'm sorry. That's insensitive. What I mean is he was wrong. Sure, some sheep get slaughtered every day, but many get away; and sometimes, the wolf goes hungry."

"You should write this stuff. Sometimes, the wolf goes hungry…will it go hungry today, or are there sheep to be had? I guess we'll see soon enough. I have to go see Wozniak at the precinct now."

Michael winced briefly before putting on a calm face. "Please call me when you leave the police station. Promise me you will."

Anna felt her face flushing, eyes welling up with tears she'd be embarrassed to shed. She was frightened. "I promise to call you if I get to leave."

Michael wrapped her in his arms and held her tightly. "You will. Of course, you will, Anna. Believe you can get through this. Really believe it."

Anna managed to stave off the tears; now she started getting up. "It's time. I need to go now." Time to get it over with.

"Remember," said Michael, holding her hands, not letting go just yet, "you're not going there as a suspect; don't act like one."

"I wonder, though, Wozniak interviewed you over the phone—why did he ask me to go down to the police station? I don't think I'm just another witness."

"Well, no, you're Victor's daughter; it's different. This detective seems like a proper gentleman; maybe he simply wants to talk to you face to face out of respect."

"I don't know, Michael. He gives me the creeps. I feel like he sees right through me."

"He doesn't. He's just a man trained to seem like he's more than that. It's just mind tricks. Remember this one thing—it will serve you well. Police detectives are legally allowed to deceive you during an interrogation. That's how they get confessions out of people. If you sense that Detective Wozniak takes an accusatory tone with you, stop talking and get a lawyer right away."

"I will. Thank you, Michael." Anna hugged him and kissed him again. When she did let go, she wouldn't dare to look back.

The door closed behind her. A dark, empty hallway; no cops running upstairs, not a sound. A faint smell of moisture reminded her of the woods, of the soil covering the blackened remains of her father's baseball bat. She closed her eyes and took a deep breath. When she opened her eyes again, she was still there, still guilty of accessory to the murder of her father. It was worth a try.

CHAPTER XIX

The thirty minutes that it took Anna to drive down to the precinct served her to settle down and carefully consider Michael's advice. She would pay attention to any changes in Wozniak's demeanor toward her. That seemed quite logical. Thus far he'd been very polite, composed, and even graceful, though somehow, that was precisely what made him so unnerving.

The police station looked rather unremarkable, at least from the outside, just a dull ivory square building. Upon entering the station, Anna found herself in a small lobby facing a reception desk enclosed in thick glass. The small rectangular window on the glass panel, positioned almost at waist level, forced Anna to stoop down to talk to the unenthusiastic short, stocky lady sitting behind it, who advised her that Detective Wozniak would be informed of her arrival and asked her to please take a seat.

Metal chairs were lined up on either side of the room. She sat on a corner, facing a small TV; a local news show was on, though muted, but thankfully nothing about her father's murder at the moment. There, she waited for fifteen minutes before a young officer asked her to accompany him. She had to go through a metal detector; it made an alarming sound which prompted a tank of a policewoman to ask her to spread her arms and legs and inspect her with a metal detector wand. She had forgotten to take off her watch.

Anna followed the young officer through a narrow aisle flanked on either side by ugly metal desks, half of them empty, and then through a hallway leading to various offices and conference rooms. He opened a door and asked her to step inside. "Detective Wozniak will be with you in a few minutes," he said amiably.

This was an awful little room she had just stepped into. It was tiny, with plain white walls and no windows; all that was there was an empty table with two armchairs on one side and a rolling office chair on the other. Certainly, this is not a room where officers gathered around to share a laugh. This wasn't anybody's office either. This was an interrogation room. Anna had never been in one before, but she had seen some in movies.

She sat down and started looking at pictures on her phone—that way her eyes would actually be looking outside of that awful room designed to break her spirit. There were pictures of her with Michael, Frank and Sarah, and Diane too, from their trip to Boston. She found a picture of her mother sitting in the garden on a perfect sunny day; and her mind flew there. She'd taken that picture maybe three years ago. Her father had been on some trip and they had the house to themselves. They made pancakes, watched old sitcoms—*Bewitched*, if she remembered correctly—and soaked up the sun in the garden.

The door opened, and in came Detective Wozniak and Officer Mitchell.

"Good afternoon, Anna," said Wozniak before sitting down. "You did say I could call you Anna, right? Is that okay?"

"Good afternoon, Detective. Yes, of course you may call me Anna. And good afternoon to you as well, Officer Mitchell."

"Good afternoon, Ms. Goddard," Mitchell said deferentially as he sat down next to her.

Wozniak was now seating across from Anna, on the better, bigger chair. The psychology of it all didn't escape her. He could recline and move around, while she was stuck against the wall, surrounded by him and Mitchell. But the real question was, why did she choose to sit where they had expected her to? What would have happened if she had waited for Wozniak sitting down on the chair that she knew was meant for him? That would have been an act of open defiance. A strong move, no doubt, but that was not how she wanted to play this game, at least not yet.

She did need to say something to project confidence; to show that she was not there as a suspect. What would she say right now if she was completely innocent? Well, of course, "Detective, have you been able to make any progress with the investigation? Are you any closer to finding out who killed my father?"

"Rest assured, Anna, that we will bring the killer to justice. The fact is we've done much already, and the pieces of the puzzle are starting to fall into place." This, he said with an earnest expression, and yet there was a glint in his eyes that she didn't trust.

"Of course," Wozniak continued. "I suspect that you will be of great assistance to us in that regard. Like I said earlier, sometimes, we don't know what we know. Often enough it is tiny details that one has not given a second thought that turn out to be definitive evidence. But, before we go any further, may I offer you a cup of coffee? We just got a brand-new espresso machine and it is truly fantastic. I will confess a little peccadillo of mine. I don't like the cheap coffee folks buy here, and I do fancy myself somewhat of a coffee aficionado, so I bring my own organic, top quality coffee. So, would you like a first-class cup of coffee?"

"When you put it that way, Detective, how could I say no? Sure, I'll have it with cream if you have it, and one sugar."

"Excellent. Mitchell, could you ask Katy to make us three coffees? I assume you want one as well. Mine is easy to remember—black, no sugar."

Officer Mitchell stepped out. "I do apologize for the room, Anna," said Wozniak, leaning slightly forward. "It's awful, I am well aware of that, but it does provide privacy."

She understood all too well their need for privacy. "I understand, Detective; don't give it another thought."

"May I ask what you do for a living?" Wozniak's lips curved up into a delightful smile, one that felt jarring in their current setting.

"I'm a school psychologist."

"Ah, that's admirable. If I understand correctly what your profession entails, you help kids deal with difficult situations at home and school. Is that right?"

"Yes, that's actually quite accurate." He probably already knew what she did for a living.

"That must be very rewarding. And what made you choose that line of work?"

"Um, I don't know. Like you said, it's very rewarding work." She wasn't going to open that door to her psyche.

"I think maybe I do know," said Wozniak with an air of mystery. "If I may be so bold, I believe you're one of those people who are born with an instinct to protect others, especially the innocent and vulnerable. It takes one to recognize another. That is what drives me too; it's why I became a cop." There was that smile again.

"Thank you. That's nice of you to say," Anna said as Officer Mitchell returned with her coffee. A moment later, a skinny lady brought the other two cups.

"It's pretty good," Anna said after tasting the coffee, though it really wasn't nearly as good as advertised.

"Anna, I'll ask the obvious question first." Wozniak sipped his black coffee sans sugar. "Are you aware of anyone who may have had any kind of animosity, a recent heated argument, perhaps a dispute over money, anything like that, with your father?"

"No, I can't say I do. He did increase the rent to his tenants every year. He was kind of ruthless in his business dealings, that's true, but I doubt that would drive someone to murder."

"There's all kinds of crazy people out there. Who knows? I've learned not to rule anything out prematurely. I'll always remember a homicide I investigated about eight years ago. A man killed his boss at the company parking lot apparently because of a disciplinary action he had taken against him for absenteeism—it had been just a memo, not even a suspension. Then I found out that the man's wife had cheated on him with his best friend and was about to get their house and custody of the kids in the ensuing divorce proceedings. The man had been in a homicidal state of mind and his boss just happened to press the red button. In his mind, the man was probably murdering his wife, not his boss."

"That was a hell of a thing, Wozniak. What a messed-up world we live in," said Officer Mitchell. Anna had nearly forgotten that he was still there, beside her.

"Yes, that's quite a story," she said. It really had made an impression on her, but why did Wozniak bring it up? What was he driving at? His story involved an affair—coincidence or not.

Looking straight at Anna, Wozniak leisurely rotated his cup of coffee clockwise, then back to its original position before lifting the cup to within an inch of his lips. "So you don't remember your father having any major arguments with anyone recently?" He sipped his coffee now with an odd air of royalty, his eyes never leaving her.

Wozniak could already know all about the disgraceful conclusion of their family gathering. To be caught lying about that now would send her down the route of being read her Miranda rights. She needed to tread carefully here. Still, she couldn't just give it all away at once. That would be too obvious. What would a spotless, proud Anna Goddard have to say about it?

"Well," she said, "nothing outside of the family circle. There were strained relationships in the family, but I hope you will respect my wish to not speak about private family matters."

Wozniak placed his cup back on the table and leaned forward. His voice came out soft and comforting, the way good fathers always spoke to their daughters in movies. "I can understand that. You lost your dad only last night, and here I am asking you to divulge sensitive family matters, perhaps even tarnishing the memory of your loving father. It doesn't seem right, I know."

The detective picked up his coffee and seemed to sink into deep thought for a moment, two dark eyeballs just sitting above the rim of the steaming cup, like moons on the night sky of an alien world. Then an earnest expression returned to his face, the brows shooting up as his voice came out slightly apologetic. "However, it is important that we thoroughly investigate all the leads we get, no matter where they take us, and I'm afraid they might take us to uncomfortable places."

The scent of coffee saturated the air; it was a smell she associated with happy times, and friendship—to smell it now as she felt the walls closing in on her was jarring. Was this the time to ask for her lawyer?

Anna tried to regulate her breathing, keep a straight face, and play the part of Charles Goddard's granddaughter, above suspicion and proud, speaking to the help. "What exactly do you mean by that, Detective? What are these leads you're referring to?"

Might have overdone it too, but she'd rather sound arrogant than guilty. Anna looked to her right and found Mitchell's face only inches away from hers, lips pursed, eyes squinted, scanning her deceitful face. Her body instinctively recoiled away from him.

Now, Wozniak spoke with a hint of compassion, likely feigned—a warm blanket he threw over his callousness. "Anna, I'm sorry to have to tell you this, but we cannot discount the possibility that this may have been some kind of domestic incident. We cannot at this point in time rule out any family members as potential suspects."

"What are you saying here, Detective?" The words barely came out. Anna's heartbeat sped out of control; she focused all her strength on keeping a calm demeanor.

"Look, Anna, I'm not going to ask you to tell me anything you don't want to talk about. You're here as our guest, cooperating with our investigation voluntarily. The last thing I want to do is upset you. That said, I am going to tell you some things I have come to know in the last few hours, and all I ask is that you confirm if these things did happen."

"All right, please go ahead," Anna said. She could feel her hands beginning to shake.

"Thank you, Anna. I meant to tell you earlier, but I must have been distracted, that between the time we spoke on the phone and now, we've been able to speak to some of your relatives who attended the family reunion. Your grandmother, Rose—who is such a lovely lady—and your cousin, Mark, were the first we spoke to. Their recollection of the events last evening at your parents' house match quite closely. So let's begin there."

It was all as Anna had feared, and it was happening so quickly, too. "All right, please continue," Anna said.

What else could she have said? She could have stopped talking and demanded her right to legal representation, but that would have seemed grotesque given the amiability with which the conversation had been proceeding. She had not been accused of anything, at least not yet, and was being treated as a collaborator and interested party, being the daughter of the victim. She tried to remain calm, and reminded herself that she had foreseen this moment; that it was, in fact, inevitable that Wozniak found out about the affair, the scandal, about everything up to a mere hour before the murder, and yet, not about the murder itself.

Wozniak straightened up in his chair. "It appears the evening went quite as expected until around eight, or eight fifteen by your grandmother's recollection. Slight variations like that between witness accounts are normal and more often than not inconsequential. In fact, I get much more suspicious when witnesses give the exact same version of events, with exact times and exact words. Well, you're a psychologist, so I don't need to bore you with my rudimentary understanding of the human mind. You're well aware that not two people remember events exactly the same way."

What was Wozniak driving at? "Yes, I'd agree with that, generally speaking." It would be best to keep her answers short.

Anna stole a glance at Wozniak's silent partner. Mitchell had eyes only for her, it seemed. He'd also been scribbling something down. What could he have jotted down? Not Wozniak's words, of course. Maybe just words—scared, nervous, shaking, lying; maybe those. Would they replay this later? She hadn't seen any cameras in the room, but there could be one behind her.

Wozniak continued. "Right, generally speaking. So it appears that sometime after eight, an incident completely unexpected, and shocking, took place. A terrible revelation. Truly, something no one would forget. Do you recall what that was?"

"Yes, it involved my cousin, Diane."

"It did. It most certainly did." Wozniak sat back straight in his chair, eyes narrowed, lips arching up lopsidedly, revealing the hawk Anna knew him to be. "Tell us, Anna, what do you recall, exactly? What happened?"

Where to start? What to say? What to hide? The silence was unbearable. Wozniak glanced at Mitchell, so she did too. The officer had a reception desk smile plastered on his face, and that little notebook in his hand.

"Well, Detective, it must have been around that time, eight o'clock. I couldn't say exactly. Diane took her mother's phone—"

"Your aunt, Marlene Wilde," interrupted Mitchell, jotting down his notes.

"Yes," Anna continued. "Diane took off with her mother's phone and read her messages…including some that she had exchanged with my father. They were, um, inappropriate…and revealing. She and my father had had an affair." The memory of her mom humiliated made Anna's voice falter. That was real pain, and she could use it too.

Anna sipped her coffee. "I'm sure you can appreciate that talking about such an embarrassing, scandalous situation is extremely painful for me right now. If you don't mind, I'd much rather stick to confirming the facts as you heard them from Mark and Grandma Rose."

"Certainly," said Wozniak. "Believe me: I understand. I really do. Would you like some water before we continue?"

"I'm fine, thank you." She wasn't. Her hands were under the table, shaking. She needed to get a hold of herself.

"Let's continue, then. It shouldn't be much longer." Wozniak bent forward with his hands clasped together on the table. His gaze moved from her to Mitchell, then back to her. "Apparently, last night, your cousin, Diane, proceeded to read the messages aloud for everyone at the family gathering to hear. All about your father's affair with your aunt, Marlene, was revealed in very dramatic fashion. Is that how it happened?"

Anna lowered her gaze and spoke weakly, "Yes, it happened just like that. It was terrible."

"Jesus, I can only imagine," said Officer Mitchell. "He had an affair with your mother's own sister. I mean, that's unforgivable, isn't it?" Wozniak gave him a quick stern look, and Mitchell didn't utter another word.

Unforgivable, he'd said, as in bad enough to kill him. It had all been leading up to this. Anna knew just the thing to say. "Well, it was an awful, awful thing; but who's to say what's unforgivable? Only God, right?"

"Only God," said Wozniak. "We don't get to decide. You're quite right there, Anna."

"That's right. We don't," said Anna, looking him straight in the eyes.

Wozniak brought a hand to his chin and rubbed it. "There's one more thing, isn't there, Anna? There was another revelation last night, before the tragedy."

This could only be one thing. "Yes, Diane—she's my half-sister."

"Yes, these are all very much established facts now," Wozniak said, shifting his gaze between her and Mitchell. "We actually spoke to Diane as well just before you got here."

"Oh, and how is she?" Honest question, she didn't know.

"Well, she's pretty shaken up by the whole thing, of course. It's a lot to take in." Wozniak slowly rotated in his chair, a quarter of a circle to his left, then back facing Anna, a sly smirk sprouting up on his face. "I asked Diane why she took her mother's phone."

Anna's heart skipped a beat; her spine froze solid. Her throat was knotted; her mouth wouldn't open.

Wozniak kept on, "Imagine my surprise when she told me that you made her suspect her mother. You knew something, didn't you?"

"I...yes, I suspected something was going on between my father and Aunt Marlene."

"Because you saw that message on your father's phone. Diane told us. Everything." Wozniak looked triumphant. He was enjoying this moment.

But so what? Wozniak had nothing. "Fine, we suspected them, and sadly, we were right. But, Detective, why are we talking about this? We aren't investigating my father now—that case is closed. We are investigating his murder."

Wozniak's voice grew more intense, his eyes narrowed, focused. "You're quite right. We are investigating a murder, a murder for which there is a clear motive. Your father, Anna, was not a good man, was he?"

"No, he wasn't. He was a shitty husband. So what?" Calm down, Anna. You're the psychologist here. Don't let him work you up.

"He was a horrible father. I know about that too. Your grandmother made that very clear. I even see it in your eyes." Wozniak paused, then continued in a softer, composed voice. "I have been where you are, Anna, sort of. My dad was a piece of crap, a deadbeat, and a drunk, and he beat my mother. He deserved to die. A hundred times, I wished he died, and then one day, he did. Liver cancer—his drinking finally caught up with him. Honestly, I didn't know what to feel, but I couldn't get myself to shed one tear for him."

"I'm sorry to hear that, Detective, but that is not how I feel. I loved my father, even with all his terrible faults. We all did. Now please tell me exactly what you're suggesting with all this, because it sounds like you're spinning theories and making wild accusations."

"I'll get to that soon. Let's not get ahead of ourselves." Wozniak sat back and propped one leg on top of the other. "I haven't really asked you, how did you feel last night when Diane exposed this whole thing about your father's affair with your aunt?"

Anna took a deep breath. "Of course, my heart broke for my mother. She was not only betrayed by her husband and her own sister, but also humiliated in that public spectacle."

"And your mother, how did she take all this?" Wozniak asked.

"She was devastated, obviously, but she demonstrated great character. She actually asked me to make sure that my aunt was okay. Can you believe that?"

"That is remarkable. Your mother seems to be an exceptional woman."

"Yes, she is," Anna said. Where was he going with this? What was his game plan?

"How unfortunate it is when good women fall in love with bad men. It happened to my mom, and it happened to yours. I know he was your father, and you loved him unconditionally, but you deserved better—you must know that. Even your cousin, Mark, who apparently worshiped your father for all the wrong reasons, unwittingly confirmed a pattern of neglect and cruelty. Accepting these things is healthy, Anna. It's not your fault that you had a lousy dad."

He was more of a psychologist than he gave himself credit for, but that was his game. "He could have been a better father. He wasn't the most loving, but like you said, he was my father still, and a daughter can forgive."

"Well, then you must be a better person than I am." Wozniak rolled his chair closer and put his arms flat on the table. "Now, Anna, here's what troubles me. We lifted fingerprints at the scene of the crime and ran them through the system. We had no matches with any previous offenders. Either the intruder wore gloves, or this was done by a first-time offender, someone without a record."

"And why does that trouble you? What does it mean?" Anna asked as naively as she could.

"It doesn't mean much by itself, but it does eliminate possible paths for the investigation, while also heightening the likelihood of alternate explanations."

"I'm still a little confused," she said. But she wasn't.

"I understand, of course. You haven't spent decades investigating homicides, like I have. There are patterns that emerge. I dare say that there are no unique crimes. There are no real surprises for an experienced detective. Every type of crime has been committed before. Here, there were two main possibilities. The first was that a known career criminal had targeted your father, knowing that he kept cash in the house. That seems less likely now, so we must focus our efforts on investigating a second theory."

"Which is what?" Still playing innocent.

Wozniak's countenance hardened into a grim monolith. "Anna, I know you don't want to hear this, but your father may have been killed by someone close to him. There are some elements in this case that cannot be explained away by other potential scenarios."

Impeccable Anna Goddard would be impatient, not alarmed. "I wish you would get to the point, Detective."

Wozniak didn't react but carried on. "Let's begin with your mother's story. There's something there that doesn't quite check out, but maybe you can help us with it. Your mother said that, right after everyone left, around eight thirty, she took sleeping pills and was probably asleep by nine. Now, that she would be distraught enough to want to force herself to fall asleep immediately and not even attempt to save any of the food left outside, is odd, but not entirely irrational. After all, she did have plenty of reasons to be upset. What is much more difficult to understand is why, if she was that upset, she decided to stay in the house with Victor. She could have left with Frank, or with you. I bet you offered to take her with you, didn't you?"

"I did. In fact, I insisted that she came with me, but she wouldn't have it. She said that it was him who should leave." Dodged that one. Breathe, Anna, breathe.

"Well, I would have to agree with your mother—he should have left. So that would make sense, but it makes it all the more strange that we found, in the guest room next to the master bedroom, a large suitcase half packed with her things, like she had been getting ready to leave."

"Huh, that is strange," she said. A problem is what it was, something she couldn't easily explain. Keep calm and think fast, Anna repeated in her mind like a mantra. "Perhaps," she finally said, "Mom did decide to leave in the morning and started packing before the pills took full effect. I'm just guessing here, of course."

"Perhaps. Let's put that aside for now." Wozniak looked at Mitchell. "I'll have the opportunity to ask her myself tomorrow morning."

"Oh, right. She's coming here then?" Anna asked.

"She is, yes. Officer Mitchell scheduled the appointment before you came in."

"You've been busy these last few hours." She sounded edgy; shouldn't have said that.

"Yes, we've been busy," said Officer Mitchell. "The first twenty-four hours are critical in solving a murder case."

"So I've heard," Anna said to Mitchell before returning to Wozniak. "Well, good, no one better to ask than mom herself." Anna couldn't be sure how adeptly she was hiding her true feelings on the matter. Her mother might crumble under the kind of pressure Wozniak could exert on her. Clearly, he had her pinned down as the main suspect, which made perfect sense—she had had plenty of reasons to want to kill the man. She just hadn't killed him for any of those reasons.

"Anna," Wozniak's voice deepened, "did you know that your mother signed a prenup agreement when she married your father?"

How the hell did he know that? "Did she tell you that herself, Detective?"

"Your cousin, Mark, told me about it. His father told him years ago. God, I hope you're not finding out from me just now."

"No, I did know about it," Anna confessed.

Wozniak's dark moons eclipsed everything else; it was all she could see. "How long have you known?"

"Not very long. My mother told me just recently."

"Recently, huh? That's a long time to keep a secret like that. How did you feel about it?"

"Well, I hated it, of course." Keep a lid on it, Anna—he's trying to rile you up.

"Naturally. How could you not hate it? I bet your mother feels quite raw about it too." Wozniak tapped his fingers on the table—a tell that he needed something from her: a mistake, that she spilled her guts.

"My mother is the most forgiving human being I know. You and I would be demons by comparison." Whoa, that might have been a notch too much.

Wozniak laughed, with Mitchell as his echo. "I'm flattered that you even put me in the same category as you, even if it's demon. You're probably being too harsh on yourself, but I get what you're saying. Your mother does strike me as some kind of saint."

Anna smiled as genuinely as she could muster. Said nothing.

Wozniak erased any semblance of a smile from his face. A nearly unendurable silence followed, his gaze keen on her. Now, he spoke deliberately, enunciating every word, "Anna, the forensic evidence from the crime scene suggests that your father knew the killer and was attacked by surprise. The evidence also strongly suggests that whoever committed the crime didn't plan the murder. This is made obvious by the fact that the person didn't bring a weapon, but rather improvised, grabbing a baseball bat that your father kept on a wall display; you must have seen it a hundred times."

"Yes, I follow your logic," Anna said, immediately realizing she had spoken too fast.

"So, you do remember seeing your father's baseball bat on the wall?" Wozniak asked, a thinly veiled smile flashing on his face.

"Yeah, sure. In the basement. Dad was a huge baseball fan," she said as ingenuously as possible.

Officer Mitchell found this to be a topic he should comment on. "He had a baseball signed by Barry Bonds. A cherished possession of his, I'd bet."

"Quite so," Anna responded.

Wozniak downed the last bit of coffee left in his cup, wincing slightly as it was probably already cold. "And what sort of baseball bat deserved to accompany that prized possession on the wall? Could you describe it for us?"

"I can't remember a lot of details." Yes, she did. It had a black handle, unpainted wood the rest of the way, shiny from top to bottom; and it burned really, really slowly. "It was just a regular wood bat. I believe the handle was painted black."

"Thank you, Anna, that is useful information." Wozniak clasped his hands, elbows on the table, eyes on Anna. "So, you see, this looks too much like a crime of passion. Yes, there's money missing, but that could have been staged by the killer, hoping that the police would attribute the homicide to a burglary gone awry. In fact, the one stack of cash that was found by the stairs was in too obvious a place. It did look staged." Wozniak sat back in a laidback demeanor, the left side of his lips twitching as if being deterred from smirking.

"I understand what you're saying, Detective, but these are only theories." No, they weren't. He had it all figured out. The only thing missing was hard evidence—that he didn't have. Not yet anyway.

Wozniak allowed his lips to curve upward ever so slightly. "Right, it would have been a lot simpler to find the murder weapon with fingerprints of the murderer. It really would have, right Mitchell?"

"Ah, that would have been a walk in the park, but not as interesting," said the officer.

"Well said, Mitchell. It's the challenging cases that sharpen our skills and instincts." Wozniak tapped on the table three times with his empty coffee cup, making a hollow sound that reverberated throughout the tiny room. "But you're quite right, Anna. None of this is conclusive evidence. Lucky for us, we did find something within the crime scene that should give us the conclusive evidence we are looking for. In fact, this evidence we found on the body itself, your father's body."

Wozniak darted a look at Mitchell, then back to Anna, a sly glint in his eyes. "You might find this astounding—I know I do. Recent technology developments now allow forensic investigators, in certain cases, and under the right conditions, to lift fingerprints from a victim's body." Anna felt a shiver down her spine. She tried to keep her composure and even appear glad. Wozniak continued, his voice suddenly lively, enthusiastic.

"This tends to work only in controlled, indoor environments and within a tight window of time. Fortunately for the three of us, our crime scene technician got there only about three hours after the estimated time of death, and the basement was nicely air conditioned; a little chilly, in fact. Here comes the best part—he found two very interesting sets of fingerprints. Two fingers"—Wozniak demonstrated, putting together his index and middle fingers—"on his neck, right on the carotid artery. Not his own fingerprints, but someone else's. Clearly, these are the fingerprints of someone who checked if Victor was dead, after he was struck down. The other set of prints corresponds to four fingers, put together"—he demonstrated again—"as in a slap, on his left cheek. The fact that the fingerprints are exceptionally conserved is a clear indication that they were imprinted on the victim right before or after he was killed."

"That's...great news, Detective. You should have started with that." Anna felt like fainting, her legs like plastic straws—had she tried to stand up she would have fallen on her knees. She focused all her willpower on not blushing. *Do not blush, Anna. Breathe, Anna.*

Wozniak's face glowed with satisfaction. "Oh, it wouldn't have been the same. Deliverance can only be experienced after you've come to think that you're lost. Earlier we thought that we were taking shots in the dark; and now, we feel victory is at hand—truth and justice are within reach." He grabbed Anna's hand on the table and held it gently, while a half-smile curved up on his face. She felt the same paralyzing fright that must feel a mouse caught outside in a moonless night upon hearing the screech of an owl coming from somewhere, from nowhere, from everywhere.

"Of course," the detective carried on, "I'm sure you understand that this means we need to collect fingerprints from anyone who was at the house yesterday, yourself included. Let's go collect yours. It will take just a moment. And don't worry: I have a special hand cleaner that will get that ink right off your fingers."

There will be no fingerprinting, and I want to call my lawyer is what a voice in her head yelled, but what she said was nothing. She went along with them and Officer Mitchell took her fingerprints. Tomorrow perhaps, she would be in police custody; a warrant for her arrest issued as soon as they identified her fingerprints on her father's neck. "Sometimes, it's the tiny details," Wozniak had said. Her mother's fingerprints were all over her father's face—that hard slap he had earned years ago and many times over since then.

She knew in that instant that this was that most desperate hour she had foreseen, and she knew what she must do. Real love requires sacrifice, and she understood now that sacrifice ran deep in the Wilde bloodline; and she was a Wilde, not a Goddard, that much she knew. Her mother had sacrificed her happiness to protect her and Frank. Now, it was her turn to save her.

"Detective, I can help you with one of your mysteries. The fingerprints. The four fingers on my father's face. I was the last of the guests to leave the house yesterday, and therefore, the only one to witness that slap, which my father more than deserved, I'm sure you must agree. We were in the kitchen. My father came and made an insincere mock of an apology; I don't remember the exact words. My mother cursed him like she never had in her life and slapped him really hard. She had needed to do that. Only then, she regained her self-respect. Even my father understood this. He said, 'I'll let you get away with this one, this one time.' Then he went downstairs, and they didn't speak again."

"I do thank you for sharing that, Anna. What a night you had, huh? What a night!" Wozniak looked back and forth between her and Officer Mitchell, who was seemingly scribbling down every word she'd said.

"It's a hell of a thing, hell of a thing," said Officer Mitchell.

"I can't help you with the other fingerprints, but I reckon whoever's fingerprints are on my father's neck will have a lot of explaining to do."

"And a lot of time to serve, probably," said Wozniak, suddenly looking weary. "Go home now, Anna. You could use some rest."

"Yes, you're right. Good night, gentlemen."

As she got in her car, Anna knew exactly what would happen now. She'd seen it in their faces. Letting her walk out of there was just another part of their plan.

CHAPTER XX

Anna had only driven one or two miles when she first noticed the gray Crown Victoria; she made a right turn, then a left turn, and the Crown Victoria was still there, staying behind about a hundred meters. She couldn't identify the driver from that distance, but she had a pretty good idea of who it would be. She purposefully slowed down at a yellow light, enough to get stuck with the red light, with the Crown Victoria approaching slowly until it stopped two or three car lengths behind her. Yes, it was Officer Mitchell.

Anna took him for a ride to Green Valley Mall. Surely, they would be intercepting and listening to any calls she made from her phone. But that was something she could use—she called a hair salon at the mall and asked if she could come as a walk-in. The snappy lady on the other end of the call told her that she'd have to get there by 6:30, and Anna confirmed that she could make it. Hopefully, if Officer Mitchell was listening in to her call, he'd believe that's what she was planning to do for the next hour or so. He'd be wrong.

She parked on the north side parking lot and saw the Crown Victoria about ten parking spots away on the opposite row. She stepped out of her car and walked briskly toward the elevator; it was 6:27. While waiting for the elevator, she casually looked back and saw that no one was coming. Officer Mitchell, she reckoned, would wait for her to return from the hair salon. Just what she had wanted.

Her plan was fast and furious. They had her fingerprints already, so there might not be a second chance. Making sure she wasn't being followed, she went and got her stuff from the locker she had rented earlier; made it to the bank just before closing time and bought four cashier's checks of $2,500 each. She wouldn't walk around with the $11,000 missing from her parent's basement; instead, she kept just under a thousand dollars cash. Next, she bought a prepaid cell phone and called Michael.

"Hello, this is Michael," he answered guardedly.

"Michael, it's me, Anna."

"Hey, beautiful! What phone is this? How did it go at the police station?"

Anna looked from side to side, then behind her. Her heart was racing. "Not that great. They got my fingerprints. Now, I'm being tailed by Wozniak's bloodhound, Officer Mitchell. This phone is a prepaid."

"Oh, that sounds bad. What can I do?"

"I don't have a lot of time. If you come pick me up at the south side of Green Valley Mall in twenty minutes, I'll tell you everything about it on a long, long drive…to Canada."

"Canada? What are you…never mind, you can tell me later. I'll be there. I'm leaving right now." His voice was amped up; he sounded alarmed but also thrilled. Maybe he'd been waiting his whole life for a moment like this.

Anna walked into a Macy's, and within the next fifteen minutes, she bought a carry-on suitcase and enough clothes for the next five days. She felt like a crazy person stuffing her suitcase with clothes her size—no time to try anything on. She paid cash and nearly ran out of there, always looking around, expecting to see Officer Mitchell at every turn. "Hey, doll, where are you going in such a hurry?" He looked like someone who might say something like that. "It's a hell of a thing, Wozniak, I had to tackle her and everything."

Michael showed up right on time at the south side entrance. Nobody seemed to be following her, but just to be sure she went into a restaurant from inside the mall and left through the outside door facing the parking garage. She got in the car, kissed Michael, and they were off. She looked back repeatedly—no tail.

In the next two hours, Anna gave Michael every detail about her interview with Wozniak. She explained her intentions to him the only way she could, "I have to let the dogs chase me so that they will leave

Mom alone. She deserves a new chance. She still has a life to live, even if she doesn't know it yet."

"You have a life to live too," said Michael.

"And I plan to live it."

"Will we see each other again somehow?"

Anna nuzzled his neck and whispered in his ear, "Somehow, yes. Somewhere. Sometime, soon. I promise you."

"Then I know we will. I trust you blindly. Don't ask why—I just do."

They were halfway to the crossing at Niagara Falls when Anna's phone started to ring. The name on screen—Detective Andrew Wozniak. She let it go to voice mail three, four, five times; she didn't dare listening to the—she imagined—increasingly threatening messages. By now he would know that she abandoned her car at the mall and became a fugitive, in a mad dash somewhere. Canada, of course he would figure that out.

"Should we listen to the voice mails?" she asked Michael nervously.

"I think we should. It could give us an idea of what he's thinking, what he'll try to do."

"You're right. Let's start playing them."

The first message was a Wozniak classic—polished, polite, deceivingly charming. The second message urged her to call him, but it didn't say why. The third message started with a breathing sound, then went on, "Anna, I know you got scared. Something scared you, but I don't know what. I certainly didn't mean to scare you. Was it the fingerprinting? That is just standard procedure; it means nothing. We can't pick and choose whose fingerprints we take, and you were at the house, same as the other guests. That's all there is to it. Please call me; don't do anything rash."

The fourth message began with four seconds of heavy breathing, then only, "Anna, please call me. I'll be expecting your call."

Finally, on the fifth message, the gloves came off, "Anna, for God's sake, what are you doing? Where are you? If we have to chase you, it won't be pretty. You're making a big mistake. If you don't call me back immediately, I'll have to get a warrant for your arrest. I swear, I can get it in under one hour, and then cops will be looking for you everywhere, and at the border crossings too. Don't try that, Anna. Don't put me to the test. You will be very sorry you did. Ten minutes, Anna, you have ten minutes to call me."

"What was the time of that last call?" asked Michael.

Anna felt panic creeping in under her skin. "Michael, are you sure you want to do this? If they catch you with me…"

"I'm in this with you now. We've come too far to give up. When did he last call you?"

"It says nine fifty-eight."

"It's eight after ten. If he's not bluffing, you have to call him right now, or he'll go get a warrant for your arrest. It will be another fifty minutes to an hour before we get to the border crossing. If there's a warrant for you in the system when we get there, it's all over."

Anna had Wozniak's contact on screen. "Okay, I'll call him."

"You need to stall, keep him from pursuing the warrant. What will you say to him?"

"No time to explain. I'm calling him now." Her heart felt like it might explode; she had trouble breathing.

Calm down, Anna. Breathe, Anna. She placed the call. Wozniak picked up at the first ring and spoke with a tone not unlike that of a father whose fifteen-year-old daughter just came back through the window at 3:00 a.m. "Anna, where the hell are you? I was just heading out to get that arrest warrant. What's got into you?"

"I'm so sorry, Detective. You're right. I panicked. I saw a Crown Victoria following me everywhere, and I decided to ditch my car at the mall."

"I see. And where are you now?" He lowered his voice considerably, but he was not quite his usual suave self.

"Frank picked me up. I'm at my townhouse. I went to bed early, and my phone was in silent mode. I'm so sorry I worried you like that."

"All right…Anna, I'm going to have Mitchell drive by your place. He should be there in ten minutes. Just open the door for a second and say hello to him, okay? That's all. Good night."

Now, she had lied to the police; there was no turning back. This would be the beginning of the rest of her life, whether as a prisoner or as an exile in parts unknown.

She warned Michael, "In ten minutes, Wozniak is going to find out that I just lied to him. He'll try to get that arrest warrant immediately. I just hope time is on our side this one time."

"Is it ever?" Michael winked at her. "Well, I better step on it," said Michael, and he did. He'd never been more handsome than tonight. There was something wild and unleashed about him—he looked like a wolf. Made her wonder, though, should she be wary of this instinct? No, all those stupid notions be damned! She felt more alive than ever.

Twelve minutes later her phone was ringing non-stop. The sound of new voice mails became deafening. She turned off the damned thing. If they didn't hit any slow traffic, they would make it to the border crossing around 10:45. The race against Wozniak was on. Whatever happened, happened. She had put in a great fight.

They were at the border crossing at 10:43. "Oh God, I didn't ask you to bring your passport," she fretted.

"I got it, relax. You did say Canada." He smiled and held her hand, squeezing it gently.

There were three cars in front of them. The first one went through almost immediately. Next, a group of college age girls were having a party inside their fancy SUV up to the instant in which they came up to the inspection point. They breezed through like they were Canadian diplomats returning from a hard day's work negotiating a brand-new NAFTA agreement with their American allies. It was 10:47.

One more car to go. It was a couple, probably about their same ages. Several minutes passed. The border security officer inspected their passports carefully, looking at their faces, then their passport pictures and back again. They looked stiff. Anna imagined their tensed-up faces. Perhaps, they had a forbidden article in the glove compartment. They probably looked guilty. Looking guilty was half the problem.

Anna surprised Michael with a deep, passionate kiss. Halfway through he had figured out what she was doing. He whispered to her ear, "Good thinking," and proceeded to hungrily kiss her neck, playing his part perfectly, as she pretended to be ashamed that the young border security officer was looking right at them. "It's our turn, Michael. Here goes nothing!"

"Young lady, see you on the other side," Michael said like a goddamned rock star.

They drove up to the inspection point. "Hello, there. Having some fun tonight eh?" asked the cheery young officer.

"It's a fine night, and it's getting better," said Michael, brimming with panache.

"It's mighty fine, indeed. All right, then. Let's see your passports. Thank you, Michael, Ms. Goddard. Please open the trunk." He went behind the car, took a quick look, and closed the trunk, then came back around with their passports in one hand. Any moment now, he could hand them back and wave them through.

An older officer beckoned from within the booth. "Excuse me for a moment," said the young officer and went inside the booth. The older officer showed him something on a computer screen. The younger officer looked hard at the screen, scrunching his face like he didn't like what he was seeing.

"Don't show any concern," said Anna. "Stay loose. Look at me, not them."

The young officer came back. "My apologies. My supervisor just indicated to me that an incident has been reported. A semi-truck rolled over on Queen Elizabeth Way. It's a mess. If you were heading to Toronto, you might want to consider staying for a night here in Niagara Falls."

"Oh, we were planning to do that anyway. It's terrible about the accident, though. Hope nobody was seriously injured."

"Yeah, you and me both, bud. Michael, Anna," he said as he handed back their passports, "enjoy your stay in Canada."

They were through. Whether they had outmaneuvered Wozniak, or the sly detective had bluffed about the arrest warrant, she would never know.

Anna spent one last night with Michael, a night she would remember for quite some time. In the morning, he drove her to the Toronto International Airport, not knowing where she would be going. The real question was, where would she go first? Even she didn't know that. Only one thing she knew for sure—she could never return home.

While on route to the airport, Anna called her mother from the prepaid cell phone and gave her clear instructions. "Mom, please listen carefully and do as I say. Cancel your meeting with Detective Wozniak immediately. Don't talk to him at all. If he tries to force you to talk, get a lawyer and stall for a few days. That's all I need."

Anna could hear her mother trying to stifle her crying. She felt Michael's hand taking hers in, holding it—somehow, he'd known she needed it right then. "Tell Frank and Aunt Marlene to do the same, Mom, even if you're not yet on speaking terms. I'll call Diane from the airport. Do not talk on the phone among yourselves about any of what happened. Not once, not ever. Bury it all down."

A single tear ran down her cheek. "Though I'm an exile now, I'll reach out to you. I'll always be near, one way or another. You should know that I'm living my life as I choose, and that is what happiness means to me. Be happy for me, as I'll be happy for you. Become Lydia Wilde again, don't look back, only forward, and live freely. Bye Mom. I love you."

Under the first colors of a new sunrise, Anna and Michael hugged and kissed goodbye. The sound of airplanes taking off served as ambiance music for their tender scene. Her eyes welled up with tears, but she held them at bay until she turned around. As she walked through the glass doors leading to her future, they soaked her face.

CHAPTER XXI

Detective Andrew Wozniak stared at the padded envelope left on his desk for a whole minute. The return address—Anna Goddard, Somewhere in the World. The package had been postmarked in Toronto, but he knew damn well that she would by now be thousands of miles away. It had been three days since her escape.

He finally opened it. Inside there was a letter envelope and—a mint tin case? His curiosity made him open the tin case first. As soon as he looked inside, he knew what he was looking at. He closed his eyes and pressed his lips, then put it back, and picked up the letter envelope. He opened it and sat down at his old metal desk to read the letter.

Dear Detective Wozniak,

By now, you must have figured out that I killed my father, Victor Goddard. This letter should serve as my formal confession. I hereby declare, in no uncertain terms, that I killed my father.

I apologize for lying in my interview with you and Officer Mitchell. I want you to know that I have great appreciation for the work you do and never intended to disrespect you in any way. I simply had no other choice, other than going to prison, which wasn't to my liking. I'm sure you understand.

Without a doubt, you must have already matched my fingerprints to the ones found on my father's neck, the ones I left when I knelt beside him and, to my horror, found no pulse. I now want to tell you the entire true story of how it happened.

My mom was going to leave my father. She was coming home with me in the morning, and I was helping her pack her suitcase, the one you found. When she fell asleep, I went to the basement to talk to Dad. There were some things I wanted to ask him. I needed to know there was a part of him that was decent, that regretted hurting Mom, and all of us. I didn't find a regretful man in there; I found a vengeful, hateful man; a man that would hurt Mom. He asked, "What is that whore of your mother doing up there?" He walked past me, saying, "The only way she'll leave me is in a body bag." He meant it. I knew he meant it. So, I grabbed the baseball bat from the wall and called his name. He turned to me, menacingly, and that's when I took a wild swing at him. I only intended to knock him out and get Mom out of there, but as fate would have it, he was dead before he hit the ground.

I am ready to give you the evidence you need to have closure on the case. I knew that finding the murder weapon would be your main objective, so I burnt it far away from the house. Remember that smell of smoke that you sensed that night? You asked me if I had been near a fire. By God, I thought you had me. You will find the buried charred remains of that baseball bat about two miles away from the house, in the woods near an old electrical substation and a torn-down creepy house. But more importantly, open the tin can I have sent you. I saved you a piece of the murder weapon. Yes, that's a piece of my father's baseball bat. Yes, that's his blood. And, yes, that's my fingerprint.

What I did, I did it to protect my mother. Now, you know everything. I know I can never return home. Think of that as my punishment for slaying the beast.

Sincerely yours,

Anna Goddard

Wozniak carefully put the letter back in its envelope. A forlorn little smile crept up on his face. It was late. Nobody but him was there. Slackers, all of them. He opened his bottom drawer, took out a metal flask and a glass, and poured himself some whiskey.

CHAPTER XXII

Two months had passed since Michael left Anna at the airport in Toronto. Outside, the yellow maples and the red oaks were still wearing some of their best fall colors, but winter had already claimed its first night. That morning he had woken up to find his little world covered in an inch of snow. The first snow of the season, and he didn't have Anna to enjoy it with. He could see himself with her in a coffee shop downtown, flurries falling outside, the smell of pumpkin spice and nutmeg, and her smell—oh, her smell! How he longed to bury his face in that piece of heaven between her neck and shoulders. And kissing her; how he wished he could kiss her right now.

He had kept in touch with Frank, and through Frank, Michael had come to know how it all panned out for everybody else. Though Detective Wozniak continued to harass each and every one of them for the two days that followed Anna's escape, they put up a wall of silence, and Wozniak didn't seem to have enough evidence to put any of them under arrest. It all died down after that. Life went on just fine without Victor Goddard. Nobody felt the need to mention his name anymore.

By virtue of the prenup that Lydia had signed when she married Victor, none of his properties, including the house, went to her directly. Ironically, the mighty wolf had never bothered to consider his own demise and therefore had left no will. State law determined that Frank and Anna were the rightful heirs, but with Anna being a wanted fugitive who had fled who knows where, the entire Goddard estate went to Frank. He wanted none of it, though, not a penny from his father, and therefore transferred all assets to his mother. Lydia, in turn, had been busy selling everything off, turning it to cash. She had already found a buyer for the big house and had moved to one of them colorful houses in the town center. A locally famous painter had lived there. It suited her perfectly. As a matter of fact, she had taken up painting again, a hobby she had long forsaken.

Frank himself was doing quite well. He had, after much insistence from his mother, accepted a modest contribution from her to expand his music school, which was already attracting customers from neighboring counties.

About Marlene and Diane, he didn't know much, only that Lydia had talked to her sister briefly once or twice in the last few weeks. It was a start. Frank remained optimistic that as their new lives took shape, the old scars could begin to heal. Recently Michael had given some thought to the possibility of calling Diane, just to check on her. Perhaps, he would.

Michael had not remained stagnant either. He felt like Anna was somehow always in a corner of his mind, egging him on to be daring. His article had just been accepted to be published in a reputable history journal, and that had only inspired him to start writing another. He had been casually researching graduate programs, and he had drafted his resignation letter to the Blake County Historical Society—three weeks ago. If Anna was here, he thought, she would probably push him to do it. "Today, do it today. You know you want to," he imagined she would say.

He went downstairs to get a cup of coffee. It was starting to look like another long day of doing nothing. Well, he had his books. "Hey, Michael," said a museum employee as he dashed through artifacts and pictures of slave owners. "This came for you. It's a package...from Russia! How very strange. Did you order some kind of rare item online?"

His heart skipped a beat. He felt a jolt of excitement that no cup of coffee could have given him. Everything seemed brighter all of a sudden. Trying to conceal his emotions, he casually went and took the package. It really was from Russia! The return address was from a café in Sadovaya Street. The postage stamps had Moscow's Red Square on it. It was surreal.

He wanted to run upstairs, but walking would have to do. Once in his lonely realm, he used his car keys as a serrated knife to cut through the tape and open the box. Inside, he found a gorgeous ceramic rendition of St. Petersburg's instantly recognizable Church of the Savior on Spilled Blood. "St. Petersburg," he muttered to himself. He admired it and inspected it from every angle, and then he turned it over. There was an inscription under the base, and it read, "Is the professor craving some adventure?"

Without a thread of doubt in his heart, Michael corrected the date on his resignation letter, printed it, signed it, and left it on his desk. He didn't explain himself to anyone; he didn't say goodbye. He walked out the door for the last time, jumped in his car, and let the wind ruffle his hair a little.

THE END